<u>Miralee</u>

A Shadow Knights Tale

By Erik C. Martin

Published by In a Bind Books
Printed in the United States
E-book First Edition published 2013
First Print Edition 2016
ISBN: Softcover: 978-0-9981182-0-8
Library of Congress Control Number: 2016915495

Dedicated to my wife, Toni.

Chapter One

The gray wolf was a big one, hungry after a long winter. The girl, Miralee, was alone in the chilly darkness of predawn. As she left the barn carrying her sack, there was the wolf less than ten feet away.

"Hello, Snowy," said Miralee, holding out her hand for the wolf to sniff, then scratching the animal behind the ears and under the chin.

Miralee had known that the wolf had been there all along, just as she knew that nearby her family was stirring.

"You must be hungry. Well I've got something here for you," she said, reaching into the bag.

Miralee removed a large piece of beef, more than five pounds, and a smaller offering of mutton. The wolf took the mutton from her hand and began to devour it. The beef, the girl threw on the moist ground beside her.

A year ago, several farmers lost animals to wolves when a fierce winter had brought a small pack closer to the village of Brown's Ford than they might have come otherwise. Then the attacks had suddenly stopped. No one in Brown's Ford knew that Miralee had put a stop to the attacks by befriending the wolves.

It had been a simple matter. Miralee had gone into the forest and called the pack by playing her *duduk*, a straight, double-reeded instrument that had been given to her by Olahan, an old man who lived in Brown's Ford and Miralee's only friend. The wolves had come, and then she had talked to them.

For as long as Miralee could remember, she had understood the communications of animals, and they had understood her. When she had been eight, rats threatened to destroy her father's store of grain. Miralee had asked them nicely to find their meals elsewhere, and they had done so. It was the same with the wolves. But the pack had been starving, so Miralee had agreed to provide them with meat to help them through the winter. It hadn't been easy to sneak enough to keep them fed without it being noticed, but she had managed.

When spring had come the pack had moved to a less inhabited region.

Except for Snowy. She had stayed and often kept Miralee company when the girl walked in the forest. Somehow, the wolf had gotten pregnant and littered recently, though Miralee had never seen the father.

All of the queer things she did—talking to animals, sensing and seeing things that no one else could, and influencing the world around her in small ways, especially when she played music—Miralee was careful to keep hidden. But children often make mistakes, and Miralee, though at fifteen was quickly approaching adulthood, was still a child.

She felt her father's surprise and anger just a second before she heard him.

"By Pargestia!"

She turned and saw her father, Wolen, rushing forward with a pitchfork in hand.

"Run!" Miralee yelled at Snowy.

The wolf picked up the beef from the ground and ran toward the tree line. Wolen cursed again and threw his pitch fork at the fleeing animal, missing by a good ten feet. He stopped and watched the wolf disappear.

When Wolen turned to his daughter, his jaw was set and his eyes were narrowed. One person whom Miralee had never fooled was her father; he knew she was odd.

"Miralee, I've spoken to you about...the things you do. But this, giving our food to a *wolf*. You're lucky it didn't want you."

"She won't hurt me."

"It is unacceptable. You leave me no choice but to punish you for it. Get inside the barn and over the rail. I'll strap the strange out of you."

"Father, no. It isn't—"

"Now!"

Miralee started to speak. Wolen ignored her. He grabbed for her and she tried to duck away. She tripped and sprawled forward on the muddy ground. Wolen grabbed a handful of his daughter's hair

2

and pulled her up. She struggled and tried to break his grip, but his strength was tremendous.

From the shadows came a low growl. Wolen stopped and looked for the source. The menace behind the growl was unmistakable. One shadow detached from the rest as Snowy drew closer. The wolf's teeth were bare; her ears were pulled back. Wolen let go of Miralee's hair and backed up, inching his way toward the barn door.

Snowy was not going to let him get there.

As the wolf lunged forward, Miralee jumped toward her shouting, "No!" Wolen stumbled and fell back hitting the back of his head against the faded red barn wall, hard enough to form a knot but no more.

Even though her prey was down, the wolf heeded Miralee's wish and veered away.

Miralee could only think of flight now.

"Come on," she said to her wolf friend. Heedless of anything else, she bounded across an empty field toward the trees and the river.

Wolen was already trying to stand. He had no chance of catching her. Miralee was as tall as her father, who stood six feet, and she was all legs and arms. Besides, there was the wolf and he was unarmed.

Miralee ran half a mile before she slowed. Snowy was gone, probably back to tend her pups. Miralee understood that the wolf thought of her as one of her pack and had been trying to protect her. But the wolf's actions had complicated things. If Snowy hadn't interfered, Wolen would have tired eventually, and her ordeal would have ended. Now, who knew? She might never be able to go back home.

She wandered with no destination in mind.

As she neared the river, a sensation of cold malevolence struck her like a blow.

What in Golgotha is that?

Clutching her stomach, she fought down nausea. She realized that she was on her knees and didn't remember how she got there. Gulping air, she forced herself to relax and extend her senses.

Whatever she sensed was alive. It had emotions, hunger being the overriding one. And it was moving, from the woods to the river.

Whatever it is, I do not want to meet it.

Miralee picked herself up and was ready to move in the opposite direction. Before she did, she closed her eyes and reached out a little further along the cold thing's path.

Damn.

Down at the river she felt people. The thing apparently could sense them too—it was going right toward them. Dawn had broken, so she was probably feeling fishermen from Brown's Ford.

Miralee broke into a run. She prayed that she could warn them in time to get everyone back to the village. But she feared that the village would be no protection from whatever this was.

The demon emerged from the trees just ahead of Miralee.

She knew what it was as soon as she saw it—stories about demons were told to every Istean child starting at a young age.

It stopped less than fifty feet from a group of three older boys and one youngster still in diapers. Fifty feet or so along the river bank, an older man named Medril, and his son, Ederin, stood in thigh deep water casting nets. None of them reacted to the sight of this foul thing slavering over them. Only the toddler appeared to see it. The small boy, Bunx, stared at the demon and began to cry. The boys paid him no attention.

Miralee moved. The demon, attracted by the young child's fear, began to move toward him. Miralee interposed herself between the boy and the fiend, facing it. The older boys saw her and looked at her curiously. Her posture told them something was amiss, but they could see nothing.

The demon paused, as curious about Miralee as the boys were. It could shroud itself from most humans but this girl could obviously see it. And she was not behaving like it expected most people to in this situation.

Miralee found the demon hard to focus on. It had a black aura that wrapped it like a cloak made of deep shadows that made the eyes want to slip away. It was eight feet tall and sinewy. Its head was that of a massive, misshapen dog and it had boar-like tusks. The demon had four arms. Two were man-like, muscular and tipped with filthy, long claws. The other two could not rightly be called arms, but were more like grayish purple tentacles that ended with sharp-looking ridges. The torso was dark purple, almost black, and was covered with bristly hair.

Pargestia, help me. What do I do now?

She could think of only one thing.

Miralee's music calmed wild animals—perhaps a demon? Her hands instinctively fell onto her *duduk*. She raised it and began to play.

The demon was perplexed. It fed on pain, fear, and death. Miralee radiated none of those. Her presence and her song evoked the opposite. The child stopped crying. The sunlight seemed to search Miralee out and coalesced around her until she fairly glowed. It was painful to the demon, enough to confuse it and make it hesitate. Worse for the fiend, the gathering light enveloped it as well. The light ate away at the demon's darkness and it was suddenly visible to the boys and the curious fishermen who had stopped casting their nets to see what Miralee was up to.

The sudden appearance of the demon froze the boys. Medril fell back, splashing into the river as he uttered an oath. Ederin was the only one to take immediate action, though his father recovered quickly and was only a few steps behind. The two men ran over to the boys. Ederin scooped up the still silent Bunx, and his father began to pull the boys toward the village until their legs took over, and they began to run like only panicked boys can.

The demon saw its prey fleeing. It was a lower order fiend, more instinctive than thoughtful. Their fear strengthened it. It tried to move after them and found itself blocked. Miralee was still between it and them and she had filled the area with a golden radiance that acted like a shield against the fiend.

But it was an imperfect shield. The demon pushed forward. Miralee was also operating on instinct and had no idea how to stop it. The demon took a step toward her, then another. It knew that she was the source of its frustration. It would kill her first and then nothing would hinder its feast on the villagers.

Miralee tried harder to focus and to hold the demon back. It was a mistake. Her playing was always an effortless thing and her manipulations subtle. She did not know how to channel her gifts. The demon pushed again and she faltered. The light faded.

The spear-tipped tentacles shot forward.

She hoped that she had managed to save Bunx and the others.

Two shining blades, one silver and one gold, suddenly sprouted from the monster's chest. It shuddered, and the tentacles fell short. As one, the blades withdrew. The golden sword raised high and cut the demon's head from its body. The demon did not die right away. The body fell to the ground, legs and arms flailing. The head, several feet away, was cursing in a guttural language and gnashing its teeth. The eyes still moved about and were full of hatred.

Miralee was amazed that she was still alive.

She saw that the swords belonged to two warriors. Just as she had known the demon on sight, she knew instantly from the U-shaped crescent moon on their black tunics that these were Shadow Knights. She had never seen one before, but she had heard all of the tales—even though her father disapproved. One of the warriors was a young man in his mid-twenties with light brown hair and handsome, boyish features, though they were grim now. The other Shadow Knight, to her surprise, was a woman. She was pale with rich, red hair and green eyes. Miralee had only ever heard of one woman among the Shadow Knights; the tale had been her favorite. This had to be Janessa.

The man lifted his sword again and skewered the biting head. The head and body both shuddered then finally stopped moving. Fascinated, Miralee watched the demon's body begin to melt. Within a minute it had been reduced to nothing but smoking, gooey ichor.

"Are you hurt?" the man asked.

"I'm all right, though another minute and I think I would have been dead," said Miralee, feeling slightly faint but not wanting to embarrass herself in front of the knights, especially not in front of the handsome, young man.

Janessa was cleaning something that looked like black tar off of her sword in the grass. It was hard to get off. She looked at it with disgust.

"The stuff is corrosive. It will eat a regular sword to a nub in a day. It won't hurt this blade, but I can't stand the smell of it," she said. The Shadow Knight turned and looked at Miralee. "We saw what you did. It was admirable. The demon would have slain the children at the very least, before we would have been able to reach them. You didn't act scared, even when the *nalfrezu* was upon you."

"I was terrified," Miralee said. "But I couldn't let that demon kill those children without trying to help them."

"You hardly look like more than a child yourself," said Janessa. "How did you do it? Playing that pipe?"

"Umm, I don't know. I play pretty well. I must have distracted it."

The man smiled at her. The grimness was out of his face now. Miralee noticed that his eyes sparkled when he smiled. She could see the auras of the Shadow Knights now. While they wore all black, except for the crescent moon emblems on their breasts, their auras were anything but dark. Joran's was golden, very much like Miralee's own, and Janessa's was silver tinged with sparkles of pink and purple.

"What's your name?" the man asked.

"Miralee."

"I'm very pleased to meet you Miralee. I'm Joran. This is Janessa. How long have you been able to manipulate *jhi* energies?"

"I don't know what that is."

"It's what you did today. You created what we call an aural shield by manipulating *jhi*. *Jhi* is a word for the energy that runs through and binds together all things. Can you do anything else?"

Panic welled up, but she fought it down. *They know. They'll think I'm a demon or a witch and kill me. That's what Shadow Knights do.*

"No."

"It was no little thing what you did today," Joran said. "Do you live in Brown's Ford?"

She nodded.

"What is your father's name?"

"My father? His name is Wolen Verity. But you can't tell him; he doesn't understand. He'd just think that I was bad, a witch. He's very suspicious of anything unusual. He doesn't like Shadow Knights at all."

Joran laughed. "Miralee, I'm sorry, but I think your father is going to learn that something unusual happened here today. Not from us though—from them."

He pointed toward the village. A group of approximately thirty men approached.

There were few real weapons in Brown's Ford, but many of the men carried hunting bows, some had scythes, and pitch forks. There were many axes, but only two old swords, carried by Dorn and Sulloe, older men who had once been soldiers. These two led the rest, followed closely by Medril, Ederin, and Wolen. Miralee felt a dread now that she had not felt when she had confronted the demon.

The mob spotted the Shadow Knights flanking Miralee and hung back. Most of the people in her village feared Shadow Knights almost as much as the idea of demons and sorcery. Because the knights interacted closely with things no decent person liked to think about, the Shadow Knights were tainted by association. They were necessary, but trusted and liked by few.

Wolen took the lead and came forward, bow in hand but no arrow on the string. The old soldiers were at his sides and Ederin and Medril followed. No one else felt it was wise to come any closer. They had come expecting some sort of beast, not this.

"Miralee," said her father, "what is going on? These two came running back to the village shouting about monsters. Ederin claims a bear attacked. Medril came back shouting to all that would listen that you conjured a demon before his own eyes."

"No," Ederin said. "I told you, I'm sure that Miralee did not bring it here, bear, demon, boogeyman, whatever it was. It almost looked like she was keeping it at bay, distracting it with her music."

"Don't contradict your father," said Medril. "With my own eyes I saw her run out and start playing. Then that thing appeared out of nowhere and attacked the children! If I hadn't reacted as quickly as I had, poor Bunx would have been eaten. I'm sorry Wolen, but that's the truth."

The crowd was shifting and murmuring to one another. Miralee heard snatches like, "she's always been a queer child," "witch," and "black magic." Miralee could sense that they were confused but frightened more than anything. Even her father was frightened—frightened of her, she realized with surprise. She was canny enough to understand the danger of that. Her father was resolute and firm in his convictions.

"Miralee, tell me what's going on," Wolen demanded.

"Father, I…"

Joran cut her off. "Sir, what went on here is this—there was indeed a demon here. And it would have undoubtedly killed the children and probably these two good men." He gestured at Medril and Ederin. "It would have killed them before we could have stopped it, if not for your daughter."

Wolen was puzzled. "My daughter, Sir…?"

"Joran. And this is Lady Janessa. We are of the Order of the Shadow Knights. We tracked this particular fiend all night, fifteen leagues through the rain. It killed an entire family before we could locate it. Miralee saw the demon, saw it going for the children and fearlessly put herself between it and them. It probably would have killed her straight away, but for the fact that in the face of death she began to play music." He laughed. "The demon didn't know what to think. It paused long enough to give us a chance to reach it."

"That's not true!" said Medril. "I saw the girl play and then the demon showed up. Not the other way around."

Janessa advanced two steps toward the older man. "Are you questioning the word of a Shadow Knight?"

"No—of course not, Milady. It's just that… I guess… I'm not sure what I saw," Medril said unhappily.

"No, you saw rightly," Joran said. "That particular variety of demon can go among humans invisibly until they are ready to be seen. However, innocents can often see through the magic that they use to conceal themselves. The youngest boy saw it. Miralee saw it. Her actions saved your life, your son's life, and the lives of those children."

There were no hails. The crowd was divided. Miralee could sense the change. Most of the fear was gone. Some were actually looking at her with admiration. But most didn't know what to think. In her father, she felt relief. He mistrusted the Shadow Knights, but was respectful at the same time. He had been worried about his daughter, what she might be and what he would have to do. But now, for the time being, things could go back to being as they had been. He was even willing to let the incident with the wolf rest—for now.

"Sir Joran, Lady Janessa," Wolen said, "thank you for clearing up our misconceptions. And thank you for your protection. Will you accept the hospitality of our village?"

Joran bowed slightly. "Thank you, sir, but Lady Janessa and I have to return to Magh Moru immediately."

The collective relief of the villagers was palpable.

"I understand. Again, thank you."

Joran and Janessa mounted their horses. Without another word they disappeared into the forest.

"Miralee, it's time to come home now," Wolen told her. He put his hand on her shoulder, squeezing just a little too hard.

She winced, but was hopeful. *Maybe*, she thought, *everything will be all right.*

Chapter Two

Miralee, the demon, and the Shadow Knights were the main topics of conversation in the village. She was unused to celebrity and found it uncomfortable. The tale was told over and over by Medril, Ederin, and the three boys who had witnessed the event. It became embellished and, in the telling, they were all there for the defeat of the demon. The fact that none of them had witnessed this part did not matter. They had seen the demon, they rationalized, and so were qualified to relate the rest of the story as they imagined that it must have happened.

Miralee was reluctant to speak of the demon and her part. She tried to answer questions about the knights as best she could but never volunteered any information. Her father did not speak to her about it and her mother, Myra, was also silent. There had been a whispered argument, but Wolen had put down his foot and declared that they would not talk about the incident in the house. Myra complied.

For the time being, Wolen had also stopped questioning Miralee about marriage. Though she would be sixteen in the winter, she had never been courted by any of the young men of the village. In turn, she had no real interest in any of them. Some of her peers, those who had already turned sixteen, were married. Most of the girls her age at least had prospects. Miralee had none. She intimidated young men. Perhaps it was her height, her comely features, or—most likely—her reputation. She even lacked any real friends among the girls—they were either frightened of her or made fun of her. Her father had constantly urged her to behave as a proper young woman should in order that she might attract a mate and marry. Once married, he would be free of responsibility for her.

But in the two days that had elapsed since the demon had attacked, he had left her alone. He hadn't even mentioned Snowy, though he still wore a bandage on his arm.

Not that she was giving her father any reason to criticize. Miralee was uncomfortable being the center of attention and tried to go about her duties unassumingly. She did chores without prompting. She avoided going off to the woods or river. She volunteered for tasks that others found tedious and undesirable, such as mending nets and cleaning the animal pens.

One thing that Miralee could not avoid was her music. Over the last two days, her playing had been in constant demand. She loved to play and so it was a pleasure for the most part, and she felt an obligation to honor the requests. However, playing took Miralee to that relaxed place where…things happened. The last thing she wanted was to create a light show or summon a horde of squirrels in front of an audience.

Any strangeness would turn whatever goodwill she might have garnered to fear, and fear could quickly become hostility. Even when she held back, her fellow villagers responded enthusiastically. Even Wolen seemed to approve.

Many respectable women were knowledgeable in music, he said. He disapproved of women as musicians—there were no women among the ranks of the Bard's Guild—but he did not disapprove of the acquisition of the skill as a secondary interest. According to Wolen, the highest duty of a woman was to be a good wife and mother, *all* other interests were secondary.

Two days after the demon attack, Miralee was cleaning ashes out of the hearth when there came a knock on the door. Her father was milking the cows; her mother had gone to mill flour. She had no idea where her younger sister and brothers were. Miralee put down her tools and clapped the ashes from her hands. Fearing that she looked a mess, she crossed to the door and answered it anyway. Standing there was a short, dark woman and a tall, thin man. They were Aeilla and Brex, the parents of young Bunx. Aeilla carried a basket.

"Good morning, Miralee," Brex greeted her. His hat was off and he seemed nervous. Aeilla, four years older than Miralee, looked down deferentially. "We just came by to… well from what everyone is saying, that demon… It sounds like that demon would have done in our little boy if you hadn't risked your own life and saved him the other day."

Aeilla, silent while Brex stumbled over his words, shuddered. "It was my fault!" She began to cry. "I let the older boys take him while they played. I should have kept him with me. I was doing laundry and he kept getting in the way, then he would wander off. I thought it would be better if the boys looked after him. I should have kept him with me."

Brex turned to her. "I already told you, it ain't your fault. You couldn't have known nothing like that demon was around. Now settle down.

"Miralee, we just came by because we wanted to thank you. Because of you, Bunx is alive. We owe you everything. We don't have lots, but we brought something here to show our appreciation."

Aeilla uncovered the basket. Miralee, given a year, would not have guessed what was in the basket. It was a small guitar. It appeared old, but was beautifully oiled and polished with lovely, dark brown wood inlays and small opals inset into the reddish wood of the body. Miralee's eyes widened and she drew in a sharp breath.

"This was my grandfather's guitar. I never could play it; neither could my dad at that, no ear for music. Anyway, since it was your music that saved our boy, we thought that you should have it. I know you play that pipe, but I thought that maybe you could learn to play this too. It's too pretty to just sit and gather dust. It was meant to be played."

Brex handed Miralee the guitar. She looked at it in wonder. It never occurred to her to refuse the gift. In Istey, one did not refuse a gift unless they intended to insult the giver.

"Thank you, Brex, Aeilla. This is wonderful".

They thanked her again and left, leaving Miralee staring at the old guitar.

As soon as she had finished her chores, Miralee took the guitar to Olahan's house, which sat on the northern edge of the village. She knocked. When he yelled, "Who is it?" she opened the rough door to his modest dwelling.

"Olahan? It's Miralee."

"Ah, Miralee. Come in."

She did and Olahan came out of the bedroom. His house consisted of only two rooms, the one that they were in and the bedroom. The main room was filled to capacity with a variety of drums, stringed instruments, a flute, various pipes, piles of hand scribed sheet music, and a clutter of knick knacks acquired during the old man's long life.

"It isn't often that I have a hero as company," he said.

"Stop it," she laughed. "It's bad enough from all of them. Don't you tease me too."

"Heaven forbid. I'm just glad to see you putting your music to good use. Though when I taught you, I never envisioned you battling demons with it." He saw the bundle under her arm. "And what is that you've got there?"

"It's what I came to show you. Look!"

She unwrapped the guitar and handed it to him. Olahan's eyes twinkled as he turned it this way and that.

"Oh, I never thought that I would see this again."

"You know it?"

"Hmm? Of course. It used to belong to Pennix Lorexson. He was almost as fine of a musician as I am. We played together once or twice, years ago. I figured that moronic son or grandson of his had long since lost, broke or sold this."

"No. Brex kept it. He gave it to me as a gift for saving his son. Can you teach me to play it?"

"Of course I can." He examined it, tapping the body gently and eyeing it closely. "It's even been kept up well. The strings are in bad shape, but I believe I have some replacements around here someplace."

Olahan dug through an old chest and produced several guitar strings. He showed Miralee how to string the guitar and tune it. Olahan demonstrated basic chords on a guitar of his own. Miralee followed along, quickly picking up what he was showing her. They began to work on a song, "Gaella Marie," and were soon playing it full speed. Before she knew it, several hours had gone by. She finally noticed that the sun had gotten significantly lower.

"I have to get home. I didn't mean to be gone for so long. Can I come back tomorrow?"

"I would be happy to have you. It is a joy to have you in my house. You always seem to set it aglow."

14

"What do you mean?"

"Just that you are so full of life. Besides you are the only real student of music I have here in Brown's Ford."

"You consider me your student? But I just fool around with the *duduk* you gave me."

"And you do it quite well. Now you are learning the guitar. Your love of playing is genuine. Or is it simply a lure to attract a husband?"

Miralee blushed. "Olahan, you know that it isn't."

"Then you must be a student of music real and true. Let's see— is there is a test I can give? A student of music must know all of the ballads and instructionals. Play 'Chora and the Rainbow.'"

Miralee took her pipes and played it flawlessly.

"Now play 'Hunt of the Stag.' Good. 'The Golden Fish.' Yes, that's it. 'The Ballad of Magh Moru.'"

"I don't know that one," she told him.

"Don't know the ballad of how the Shadow Knights came to be? Well, that will give us something to do tomorrow. Now that you have the guitar, you can put words to your songs. You have a fair contralto voice, but can never use it playing a woodwind."

Miralee thanked Olahan and ran home. Myra had dinner ready when she arrived, but she did not seem to be late. Miralee helped her little sister, Anomie, to set the table. Wolen came in, dirty from his day's work, and greeted both of them. Anomie ran over and hugged him and he returned it happily.

"Hello, father," Miralee said, smiling, hoping their unspoken truce held.

"Miralee. Did you have a good day? Did you get all of your chores done?"

"Of course I did," she told him. He was being polite, but something in his tone caused her guard to come up.

He has something on his mind," she thought, *"something about me.*

Her two brothers came in a few minutes later. Like Anomie, who was only eleven, they were both younger than Miralee. Dalton was fourteen, skinny and considerably shorter than his older sister. Laiton was twelve and stocky.

15

After dinner, she showed her family the guitar. The other children were excited and made Miralee play. She improvised a song based on the few chords she had learned that afternoon.

"That was lovely," her mother told her.

Even her father seemed to think the gift was a nice gesture.

That night, after Miralee had prepared for bed, Wolen came into her room while she was sitting and strumming her guitar. Her little sister was sleeping soundly in the bed in the corner.

"That sounds nice," he said.

He sat in the rocker opposite her bed. He said nothing for a moment. Finally, he leaned forward.

"Miralee. You're my oldest child. I've always had hopes of a good life for you. It's why I am strict with you."

"I know, father."

"Your behavior has concerned me in the past. You're different from those around you. I think you scare off the boys and the women too. You don't have any close friends, do you?" He seemed to really want to know.

"No father."

"Unfortunate. You work hard. You're well-mannered, apart from your…incidents. This last thing with the demon will set you apart even more, if that is possible. I'm certain that I don't know the whole story of what happened. I've always had a knack for knowing the truth. I don't think you or those Shadow Knights lied, but I could tell I wasn't hearing the whole truth. Others feel similarly. Many still believe that it was you that brought the demon. There is talk."

She said nothing. She was afraid to. Wolen had never spoken to her so frankly before. He continued.

"I've been thinking a lot these last few days. I think it will be too hard for you to find a suitable husband here in Brown's Ford. There doesn't seem to be anyone here you fancy and, after this last incident, I don't believe any of the men would be brave enough to approach you. That's why, for your own good, I have decided to send you away."

"Away?"

16

"To Conn's Crossing down the Tandy or Gray's Harbor on the coast. We have kin in both of them and there would be fresh faces, new men for you to get to know. One of them should be suitable for you. And no one would have to know about the demon thing. If you went and did your best to act like a proper young woman, demur and accommodating, then I'm certain that you could attract a husband. Think about it. Decide which one you would prefer."

"Father, I don't want to leave Brown's Ford. I'm happy here. Olahan is teaching me to play the guitar."

But am I really happy? A few days ago, I thought I was going to have to leave for good. Father is right, whether they think I'm a hero or a witch, no one will let me have a normal life here. A normal life...I don't even know what that is. Still...

"And that's fine. I don't mind if you pick up what you can, as long as you still get your chores done. It will be three or four weeks before arrangements can be made, maybe a little longer. But I will need an answer from you soon. I can tell you what I know about each village if that will help."

"No father, thank you. I just need to think now."

"Of course."

Wolen left.

Miralee put down her guitar and lay back upon her bed. That he would send her away was unexpected but not surprising.

At least I'm not being chased out by a mob.

She never envisioned herself remaining in Brown's Ford forever, but this was too sudden. While she had vague images of a future in some exciting, new place, Brown's Ford was home. In addition to the attendant comforts of familiarity, there was Olahan and her music. He was teaching her new songs every day. He had just recently taught her to read sheet music. And now they were going to start with the guitar. She couldn't leave.

Besides, Wolen was only sending her away in hopes that she would get married off. Conn's Crossing, like Brown's Ford, was a small village on the Tandy River, laying about sixty miles to the east. Gray's Harbor was a small fishing village along the southern coast at the mouth the Black River, a tributary of the Tandy. Neither

17

option sounded very appealing, more of the same she reckoned, though it might be nice to see the ocean.

The house was quiet, but as children so often can, Miralee could tell that her parents were having a hushed conversation in their own bedroom. She closed her eyes and focused on the murmured voices. Miralee stuffed down a flash of voyeuristic guilt and made herself relax. Her awareness opened up. Anomie was breathing soft, deep breaths just a few feet away. The wind softly rattled her bedroom windows. Opening further, Miralee isolated the vibrations of her parents' voices. Everything else she ignored. The voices clarified as if Miralee was standing next to the bed.

"Please, Wolen. Don't send her away. She's just a child," her mother was saying.

"Do you think I want to? This is the only way that she will find a husband."

"But not now. It's too soon. She's young; she could still find someone here."

"She will be sixteen at the end of the year and she doesn't have any prospects. And she never will, not in Brown's Ford. Myra, she intimidates the men; she scares them."

"But she's so pretty, and she's diligent…"

"Too pretty maybe, and too smart by half. And—different. This incident with the demon, it's the last. I know that some people have talked about her privately before, but now it's in the open. Maybe somewhere else…"

"Do you believe it? Do you think that your daughter is a witch?"

"What? No. I don't know. But—I just wish that I knew what she was. She *is* different. I wish that we knew more about who she is, where she came from."

"Does it matter?" her mother asked. "Miralee is our daughter. It doesn't matter who she was actually born to. No one in the village even knows that she was adopted; she never has to find out. And she was our luck. Remember, I couldn't get pregnant until we adopted Miralee. Now we have four beautiful children, three who were born to us and one that I love as much as if she was!"

Miralee sat up and hugged herself tightly. *I'm not their child! I was adopted!* That night, Miralee cried herself to sleep.

18

Sir Mordis Silverhand, twenty-seventh Grandmaster of the Order of the Shadow Knights, entered the small conference hall. Joran paced back and forth while Janessa had shed her armor and was reclined with her feet up on a chair.

"Joran, sit down. You're making me nervous." Mordis said, taking a seat across from Janessa.

"Sorry. We've been on the move pretty steadily for the last few weeks. I'm not used to being still."

"You'll outgrow that in a few years. It's good to have both of you back at Magh Moru. Now for your report. I understand that there was some trouble."

Joran nodded. "Yes sir. A *nalfrezu* demon manifested and killed a family at a lone farmhouse. It headed for the nearest village, Brown's Ford…"

"Brown's Ford? The name is familiar for some reason. Southern valley country, in Grenfitch, correct?"

"Graelly," Janessa said, "but close enough. Joran and I weren't far off when we felt it, but it had a lead on us still."

"Casualties?"

"In the village, there were none," Joran said.

Mordis looked surprised.

"We made good time and arrived at the village shortly after the demon. Still, it would likely have killed some children and probably two fishermen before we could have stopped it."

"What happened?"

"One of the villagers stopped it."

Joran paused, waiting for Sir Mordis to interrupt. The Grandmaster looked at him expectantly, so he continued. "Umm, it was a fifteen year old girl. She held the demon off with music."

Mordis grinned. "She did? Good for her."

Joran kept going. "Sir, she used the music as a channel to create an aural shield. It was crude, but strong enough to keep the demon at bay until we arrived."

"Where did she learn to do that?" Mordis asked.

19

"I don't think she ever learned. She appeared to be… improvising."

"How did she know you were coming?"

"She did not. We were masked. From what we saw, she fully expected to die. She didn't know we were there until we were right on top of them. Even so, there was no hesitation in her. Sir, I think we should bring her in."

"What? A village girl? No. Women don't become knights."

"*Ahem.*"

"Janessa, you're an exception, and you're also not Istean. If you haven't noticed, the people here can be rather provincial, especially in a small village like Brown's Ford. People expect certain things of men and certain things of women."

"And never the two shall meet, is that it?" Janessa said, "Mordis, Joran is right. The girl, Miralee is her name, has tremendous natural talent. I think that she would be a great addition to the Order. Besides, because of her talent, she doesn't fit in among her people. It's only a matter of time until quaint Istean provincial attitudes get her hurt. She tries to hide her ability, but with her power she won't be able to forever. In her case, it could be her own father who leads the persecution."

"He's not a fan of the extraordinary I take it," said Mordis.

"Not in the least. I read him as a good man, or he thinks he is. He is very stringent about adhering to his particular set of morals, very rigid. He knows what's right and nothing will ever change his mind. I think he cares about his daughter, but he would burn her to death as a witch and say it was for her own good."

"I see. You think she's that strong?"

"Yes, her potential is huge. But she needs to be somewhere where she can learn. She needs to be here."

Mordis leaned forward and smoothed his beard. "Very well, bring her to me."

"We can leave at once," Joran said.

"No. It can wait a few days. You have both been in the field for too long. I want you to take some rest before you go back out."

"But Sir Mordis…"

"Quiet, youngster," Janessa said. "Mordis is right. A few days rest will be beneficial. I feel like I can sleep two days through."

Joran and Janessa left. Mordis was curious about this girl that had so impressed his knights, but that was all. Candidates to his order were located at the rate of several a year; all were unique in some way. What *was* nagging at him was the village, Brown's Ford. From where did he know that name?

"*Sir Mordis*," said a voice in his head, interrupting the Grandmaster's thoughts. "*Would you come to my house please?*"

"*Of course, Ganda Nery*," Mordis thought back. "*I will be there in ten minutes.*"

"*Please, take your time.*"

Even though Mordis Silverhand was the Grandmaster of the Order of Shadow Knights, he jumped when Ganda Nery summoned him. Mentor and mystic, Ganda Nery was not a member of the Order, but the Order owed him a great deal. Sir Osterdan, one of the first five Shadow Knights, had brought the fighting style called *jhiato* from Marya to Istey three hundred years ago. Osterdan had been a competent practitioner. Ganda Nery was a master.

He not only understood the mechanics of *jhiato*, which involved the harnessing of an opponent's energy and strength and using it against them, but the holistic discipline that underlay the art. All of the mental disciplines practiced by the Shadows Knights, Ganda Nery had mastered and passed his mastery onto the Order.

He had been doing it for a long time. *The Grandmaster's Annals*, stated that Ganda Nery had arrived at Magh Moru nearly two hundred and fifty years ago—already old. He had taken the practices of the Shadow Knights to levels never before attained. It was rumored that Ganda Nery had gained his knowledge directly from the gods. Mordis didn't know if this was true, but neither could he refute it.

So it was unsurprising that when Ganda Nery requested one's presence, even Sir Mordis hastened to accommodate him.

It took Mordis a little over fifteen minutes to reach Ganda Nery's home.

The grounds of Magh Moru were large and contained a great deal more than just the castle. The castle was the largest structure by far. Delwyn College was the next largest: the finest school in Istey, it was the place where the offspring of the greatest nobles were educated. The bard's guildhall was actually a complex of two large and four smaller buildings. There were temples, barracks, an open air market, a public house, an ampitheater, gardens, craftsmen, and even an apiary, all within Magh Moru's walls. The conference room, which was adjacent to Mordis' office, was in the western half of the castle. Mordis had to get to the eastern doors, go past the rose gardens—not yet in bloom—and around the large main building of Delwyn College to reach Ganda Nery's little house.

The old, brown skinned man met the Grandmaster at the door and ushered him inside.

"Tea?" Ganda Nery asked.

"Please."

The day was chilly and gray, so they decided not to take their tea in Ganda Nery's garden, but knelt beside the low table in his sparsely furnished dwelling. Mordis sipped his tea in silence, knowing better than to rush the old master. After a few minutes, Ganda Nery spoke.

"Forgive me, Sir Mordis, but I was eavesdropping on the report brought by Janessa and Joran. I believe that this girl will be important."

"Did you have a vision?"

"Not as such, more of a feeling—but a strong one. I think that we should do all that we can to convince her to join us."

"I have ordered Janessa and Joran to go back to Brown's Ford for her. I trust them to be sufficiently persuasive, but we can't force the girl."

Ganda Nery took a sip from his tea cup.

"I don't see persuading her to be a problem. But there will be a problem."

"What? Her father? They said he was rather inflexible."

"I am uncertain. As I said, this is just a feeling. However, I think time is an issue. They should not wait."

"I will have them leave in the morning then. And I will send Artegan as well. Sir Darden can cover his classes."

Ganda Nery said nothing, but a slight inclining of his head marked his approval.

"Joran will be happy at least. He was anxious to go," Mordis said. "Though I daresay that Janessa will be less enthusiastic. She looked a little stiff in the conference."

"And you? Are you less than happy to be sending her off again so soon?" Ganda Nery asked smiling.

"Master Ganda, what are you implying?"

"Me? Nothing. Though you were projecting your feelings rather strongly a moment ago."

"Well, perhaps. But I would never do so elsewhere. She is a Shadow Knight as am I. And she is much younger than me. It is best that our relationship remain professional."

There was a long silence. Then to break it and change the subject, Mordis said, "Master Ganda, the name of the village where this girl, Miralee, lives is called Brown's Ford. I seem to recall the name from somewhere but can't place it."

"It is Master Olahan's home village."

"Of course! I wonder if Master Olahan still lives. It's been over ten years since he left the guildhall."

"He lives still."

"I would very much like to see Olahan again. I'm tempted to go to Brown's Ford myself."

"Perhaps you should."

"Leave with no notice? Thomas Daldum would have an attack. But still, I have been stuck in the castle for over a year. Very well, I *will* go. It will only be for ten days or so. Daldum can manage."

"The company should be tolerable at least," Ganda Nery said.

Chapter Three

Feeling like an imposter, Miralee went through the routines of her chores in a numbed fog. Always different, she had never before felt like an outcast. While helping with breakfast, she scrutinized every line and crease of her mother's (*not my real mother*) face like she was a stranger. Surrounded by her family during the meal, Miralee felt like an unwanted guest. When Anomie told a joke and everyone laughed, Miralee forced a smile, then looked down so no one would see the tears in her eyes.

The meal ended and Miralee quickly ran to the stables to tend to the horses and to be away from the people who weren't *really* her family. The company of the horses was comforting. Animals were always genuine.

When she completed her chores, Miralee took her *duduk* and guitar and went to Olahan's. Her friend greeted her warmly, but immediately realized that something was wrong. Miralee was not ready to reveal what she had learned, even to Olahan. Just the thought of talking about it made a lump rise up in her throat.

Instead, she said, "Olahan, my…father wants to send me away. He's going to send me to Conn's Crossing or Gray's Harbor."

"What? When?"

"He gave me four days to decide where I want to go and said that I will leave three weeks after that."

"And you don't want to go, I assume."

"Of course not! I want to stay here and study with you."

Olahan gestured to a chair and invited her to sit.

"Miralee, I am flattered and I shall miss you, but maybe you should look at this as an opportunity. Can you honestly say that you are happy here?"

"Sometimes. When I'm here with you, or when I walk in the woods."

"So basically, you are only happy with me, an old, old man, or by yourself. We are much alike really, despite our age difference.

Neither one of us really fits in here. Now you are getting a chance to leave and do something different."

"I'll be leaving, but I won't be doing anything different. Wolen just wants me to get married so he can forget about me. And if you don't fit in here, why are you here? You chose to come here. I was only six, but I remember your arrival."

"I've told you already, I was born here and for some reason I thought it would be fitting if I died here," he said.

"You sound like you think you might have made a mistake. Why don't you leave? You're an adult and a man. You can go wherever you want."

He nodded. "Yes, I could. But as I said, I am old—too old for traveling. Whether or not my homecoming was what I had envisioned is not the point. It did give me the opportunity to meet you."

"Yes, and now I am going," Miralee said glumly.

"Yes. So I see no point in wasting any more of our time together. Have you come to play? There is a lot I can teach you still in three weeks."

They played together and Miralee did feel better. Music was her only salve. And she was a quick study. Olahan had only to demonstrate the chording of a song once and she remembered it. With one or two practice runs, she could play most songs perfectly.

But eventually, their time ended and Miralee had to go home. Walking past the public house, she overheard Medril drunkenly retelling the story of the demon.

"I don't care what any Shadow Knight says; the girl summoned that demon. I wouldn't be surprised if the Shadow Knights were in on it. Keep an eye on her. There'll be trouble..."

She quickened her pace and wished it was darker.

He's right, she thought. *There will be trouble.* But it would be the backward attitudes of her neighbors that caused it, not her. Wolen was right too; she couldn't stay. *But not Gray's Harbor or Conn's Crossing. There's only one thing I can do—I'll have to run away.*

It was simple, elegant, and would make everyone happy, she thought. Her mother and father (*not my real ones*) would be rid of her. Medril could quit trying to convince people that she was a demon-worshipper. And Miralee could actually go somewhere where she might really find her destiny. But where to go?

It had to be one of the big cities. She had heard things were different in the cities; people were different. Maybe she could work and then find some way to study music.

Three options came to mind. There was Gedorix, the capitol of Istey and the largest city in the country. But it was a ten day trip on horseback and she had no horse. It occurred to her that she could take one of Wolen's horses, but she dismissed the idea. She would not take what wasn't hers, not big things anyway. She supposed that she would have to take some food, but that was different. Anyway, she didn't really know how to get to Gedorix.

She thought of Magh Moru next. The home of the Shadow Knights, it was also where the Bard's Guildhall was. She imagined that it would be an enchanting place, always full of music. *Women can't be bards.* She rejected Magh Moru—it was almost as far away as Gedorix and the disappointment of being near the Bard's Guildhall and not being allowed to be part of it would be too much to bear. Besides, she was still afraid that the Shadow Knights, if they discovered all that she could do, would decide she was a witch or worse and take action.

That left her with only one viable option—Edain. Edain was in Graelly, where the Tandy met the sea, and was close enough to walk to in a fortnight. And it was the second largest city in Istey. Surely, she could make a life for herself in Edain.

She decided that she would leave in exactly one week. That would give her enough time to gather and hide supplies, but wouldn't be cutting it too close. She would hate to still be in Brown's Ford if Wolen decided to send her early.

Resolve erased her burden. She gave no thought to hardships or the dangers that a pretty fifteen year old girl might encoounter alone in the wilderness. The forests had always been her place of refuge.

Her heart was light when she came into the house. Dinner was not yet ready and Miralee joked with her sister and helped her mother so enthusiastically that Myra remarked about it.

26

"I don't know what's put you in this good mood, daughter, but I like it. You've been so sullen lately," Myra said.

"I've decided that getting out of Brown's Ford will be best for me," Miralee told her mother, truthfully. "I'm going to tell Pa that I'll go to Gray's Harbor—I'd like to see the ocean."

"You haven't called your father, "Pa" for years. You must be in a good mood." Myra's expression grew more serious. "Miralee, I'm glad you're happy. I must say, I was not convinced when Wolen discussed this with me. We will miss you terribly here."

"It isn't far. I can visit," Miralee said quietly, knowing that when she ran away there would be no coming back.

She saw the problem with her plan now. Even though she might not be related by blood to her family—they *were* her family. She loved them, even stern Wolen. *It doesn't matter, I can't stay here.* When she left, they would be gone from her life.

"Miralee's leaving?" asked Anomie.

"Yes, darling," said Myra. "She is getting older and your father thinks it would do her good to go and live with our cousins in Gray's Harbor."

"Live with? Forever? I don't want Miralee to go," Anomie said, starting to cry.

"Stop it. You're too old for that," Myra said, trying to hide the fact that her own eyes were beginning to glisten.

"It'll be alright," Miralee told her sister. "Think about it; you'll have the bedroom all to yourself."

"I don't want the bedroom!"

Wolen and the boys came in.

"Why are you making that demonic racket?!" asked Wolen.

Anomie ignored him and said to her brothers, "Pa's making Miralee move away!"

The next few minutes were chaotic. Wolen was yelling at Anomie, who ran off to her room crying. Miralee told Wolen that she had chosen Gray's Harbor. Her brothers were jealous and wanted to know if they could go too and pouted when Wolen firmly told them, "No!"

Myra had fried a chicken. No one had much of an appetite.

27

The week passed quickly. The day was chilly and wet so Olahan had a small fire built in his hearth.

"You seem melancholy," he noted as they finished a rendition of "Frayley's Jig."

"The weather perhaps."

"You're worried about leaving."

"Yes."

"I was sent away from home when I was ten and I was never more terrified. We had a young, journeyman bard assigned to Brown's Ford by the guild who saw some potential in me. He spoke to my father and a week later I was on my way to Magh Moru."

"Magh Moru, what was that like?" she asked, momentarily forgetting her worries.

"Magh Moru is an…interesting place. Did you know that it is a sovereign state separate from Istey? Yes, as part of the original charter of the Order of the Shadow Knights, Magh Moru proper is subject only to the grandmaster. However, Magh Moru is only the castle and its immediate environs. The nearby town of Moru is part of Telner province."

"I don't care about that," Miralee said impatiently. "Just tell me what it was like at the guildhall. Was it magical?"

"Magical?" He laughed. "No. It was not magical. The guildhall, like any craft hall, is a place of much hard work. Hard work, sweat, study, dedication, and of course, tradition. It is an incredibly busy place, in the midst of an even busier one."

"I didn't mean *magic* magic. I meant that it must have been wonderful to be there, studying music with so many others."

"Yes, it was in many ways, and it was home for many years, but the people were only people."

"What does that mean?"

"Just that bards are only human and subject to the same downfalls—pride, stupidity, stubbornness, jealousy. A few were wonderful to be around and some became close friends of mine. Others…not so much."

"Olahan, why don't they let girls join the bard's guild?"

The old man's mouth formed a slight grimace as he framed his response.

"People give many reasons. They say that women don't have the discipline, talent, and intelligence. Others say women lack creativity. Some argue that the bard's lifestyle is unhealthy for women. You and I both know that none of that is true."

"Then why?"

"Really the only reason that women can't be bards is because none ever have been. Tradition has been an effective barrier for centuries—but I think if the tradition could be broken once, perhaps it might stay broken forever," he said.

Olahan stood up and walked slowly to a head high shelf. He removed a small, cedar box. With deft fingers he unlatched the lid, opened the box, and removed a medallion on a thick, silver chain. He handed it to Miralee.

The medallion had a round silver back and a front of highly polished, inlaid wood that depicted an upside down, green triangle on a black background.

"Why don't we break tradition? That is the emblem of the Bard's Guild. When I became an apprentice, I was given something similar to signify my membership. Now, I give this to you, my apprentice."

"Oh, Olahan," Miralee said, tears welling up.

"I am still a master bard in good standing and as such I can take any apprentice I see fit. So wherever you go, you can take that medallion as a token of your service as my apprentice."

Miralee reached out and embraced Olahan tightly. The old man held back for a moment, then returned the hug. A full minute later Miralee let go.

"I should go," she said keeping her head down so that her hair hid her face.

"Of course, dear. I will see you tomorrow?"

She started to reply, but her words lodged in her throat. A sob almost shook through her. She turned and ran from the house before it could escape.

Miralee feigned illness and went to bed early. When she awoke, it was chilly and her bed had never felt so warm. She slipped out from beneath her quilt and quietly dressed. Everyone else was asleep and Miralee wanted to keep it that way.

Dawn was several hours away. The rain had stopped but thick fog now covered the village. Donning a wool travel cloak, Miralee slipped out of the house, her guitar strapped to her back. In the barn she had hidden a bag in the loft that she had packed with a blanket, a change of clothes, cheese, bread, smoked meat, a water skin, a small pan, a knife, and a few other odds and ends. She balanced the bag over the shoulder opposite her guitar.

Outside of the barn, the early morning was very quiet. Miralee took one last look at her house. Then she turned and began cutting across the northeast pasture, out of Brown's Ford.

The simplest way to Edain was to follow the Tandy. But Miralee would be too easy to find if she stayed near the river. The edge of the Tauton Woods was five miles from the village. By dawn she was well within the woods.

She guessed that it would be hours yet before she was missed, and several more before anyone *really* began to wonder about her.

If Miralee had known how to write, she would have left a note. Still, she thought that by dinner her parents would begin to suspect what had happened.

Despite the fact that she expected no pursuit, especially not into the Tauton Woods, Miralee frequently turned and examined her back trail. She kept getting a nagging feeling, like an itch between her shoulder blades, that someone was there. But she never saw or heard anything suspicious. Once, she stopped, sat on a fallen maple trunk, and centered herself. She reached out with her senses to their limit, which was nearly a mile. Other than the expected animals of the forest, she felt nothing. Surely no people were nearby.

Still, the feeling continued.

Just being in the Tauton Woods did not make her uneasy. She was, perhaps foolishly, not at all deterred by the reputation of the place.

The Tauton Woods, named after an early Istean prince, were older and larger than the little patches of woods that grew up around

30

her village. The Tauton Woods were thought to have once been part of the massive Gorewood Forest, and as such, were reputed to house things that were not quite natural. However, Miralee, during her first day in the woods, neither saw nor felt anything unnatural.

Her biggest problem was trying to maintain an easterly course. She accomplished this by picking a tree that was basically east of her and watching it until she reached it. Then she picked another and did it again.

She figured it should take her two, maybe three days to get to the other side of the woods. The only problem she foresaw was that a river, an offshoot of the Tandy, ran through the center of the woods. Miralee knew about the river from the bargemen who traveled the Tandy, but had no idea how she would cross it.

When the going was easy, Miralee brought out her *duduk* and played as she walked. It made her feel better and she thought the forest appreciated it.

When the going became more difficult, Miralee took her knife from her bag and fashioned a walking stick from a freshly fallen limb. It helped a great deal to navigate the uneven patches and to push through the dense overgrowth.

By dusk of the first night, she had not reached the river, but thought that it could not be too far off.

Tomorrow, she thought.

Miralee stopped before it was dark and gathered sticks. She built a fire using dried leaves as tinder and getting a spark from her knife and the piece of flint that she had packed. It took patience, but after some effort, she had a small, warm fire going.

After she ate some of her meat and cheese, Miralee wrapped herself in her blanket and softly played her guitar. She heard the rustle of movement nearby. It was Snowy. Miralee threw the wolf a strip of jerky, which Snowy snapped out of the air.

"I'm sorry that I don't have more to give, but I'll need my food," she told the wolf, knowing it would understand. "Snowy, I'm leaving the village; stay away from there from now on, and leave the livestock alone. It will just bring you trouble."

Miralee yawned and her eyes drooped. The wolf stayed until the girl was asleep. In the morning, it was gone.

The next day was clear and crisp. She set out before dawn and by the time the long light of the morning began to filter through the trees, Miralee could hear the rushing water of the river. She picked up her pace and soon came within sight of it.

The winter melt off had caused the river to become swift and swollen. The water spilled out over the bank on either side. Crossing it here would be impossible. She could swim reasonably well, but even if Miralee had been a strong swimmer there would have been no way to safely swim across. And she had her belongings with her; she had no desire to see her guitar immersed.

To the south was the Tandy, and she did not wish to go that way. Her only option was to follow the river north and hope something presented itself.

The sun was nearly at its zenith and Miralee was about to stop for lunch when she saw something across the river. It appeared to be a ramshackle house hidden among the trees. Furthermore, affixed to the far shore was a thick rope that stretched all of the way across the river. She could not see where the rope terminated on her side, but she hurried forward to get a better vantage point. Yes, there was a raft tied to the shore near where the rope was secured.

No one appeared to be nearby so she moved closer. She still could not see anyone. Miralee closed her eyes and tried to still her mind and open up her senses. But it didn't take special senses to hear the loud crack of a branch behind her. Miralee spun about.

Her eyes widened as she took in the sight of the troll staring down at her.

Chapter Four

The troll was eight feet tall and half as broad. Its skin was the color and consistency of tree bark with patches of mottled, mossy green, so it very much resembled a small tree. Even its filthy clothes, rough and earthen, could have been part of the landscape. In its long arms was a stack of split logs.

"Boo," it said. "What do you want?"

To be far away from here, thought Miralee. "I need to cross the river." *Do trolls really eat people?* The ones in her mother's stories always did.

"Mmm hmm. I have been known to ferry folks across on occasion. Just the one of you then?"

"Yes, I'm off to meet a friend on the other side of the woods. He's one of the Shadow Knights," Miralee lied.

"Of course. Well, it doesn't matter to me. I'll take you across for one par."

A par was the name of an Istean silver coin. One par for passage was not exorbitant, but Miralee had no money at all.

"I don't have any money. Maybe I could trade a song?" she said, pointing to her guitar.

The troll, who was going across anyway, shrugged.

"Fine. Two songs though."

Miralee agreed. She climbed onto the raft after the troll. It was large and sturdy. The troll guided it across the river by holding onto the rope and pulling them hand over hand to the other side. As he worked, Miralee took her guitar and began to play "Three Mugs," a drinking song that was popular in her village. As he pulled them steadily across, the troll nodded appreciatively.

"Not bad."

They reached the other just as the song finished.

"I have to put this firewood up," he said, picking up the logs that he had been carrying. "You can play me your second song ashore."

The troll walked toward his house. Miralee was relieved to see pens with animals in them. A few boars and several fat turkeys. Her fear of being eaten lessened slightly.

There was a wood pile along the side of the disheveled house. The troll added the wood he carried to the pile and then looked at Miralee expectantly. Instead of her guitar, she brought out her *duduk* and played the upbeat, "Frayley's Jig." The troll seemed to enjoy it, smiling to reveal a mouthful of jagged, black teeth.

"That was very nice," he said when she had finished. "You'll have to stay for lunch. You'll play another afterwards."

"No. I really must be meeting my friend. Thank you for the ride."

"You misunderstood," the troll said, still smiling. "I meant that you *will* stay for lunch. And you *will* play when I tell you to. Or instead of pig stew, I'll be having you for lunch."

He took a step toward her, reaching, and Miralee ran. She was swift enough, but carrying her sack and her guitar she got only ten feet before the troll's longer legs allowed it to catch up and grab her. Massively strong fingers wrapped around her waist. She pulled at the gnarled hands but there was no give in them. Picking Miralee up, the troll took her inside of his home.

The interior was worse than the outside, which had merely been run down. The inside smelled of rotten garbage, and the walls and furniture were soiled with black stains of unknown origins. It was dark, but when her eyes adjusted Miralee saw that one corner was barred to create a small cage. Inside of the cage was a stool, a bucket, and some moldy straw. The troll had apparently kept humans here before.

He took her bag, but let her keep her guitar and her *duduk*. The door closed, and Miralee was locked inside.

"So, what are you called?" the troll asked, placing a dirty, wooden cup of water on the floor through the bars.

"Miralee. Look, you had better let me go. If I'm late, my friend is going to come looking for me."

"The Shadow Knight? No, I don't think so. I don't think you've ever seen a Shadow Knight in your life. Play something for me and maybe I'll let you eat today."

34

She thought about refusing, but decided that such a move would be unwise. Miralee began to play her guitar, not really feeling the music, but the troll didn't know the difference. While she played she thought furiously, hoping to come up with a plan of escape. She was too nervous though and kept hitting dead ends. Two hours later, her fingers were sore and her throat was parched. The troll did not object to her taking a short break. He slopped some foul smelling stew into a bowl, retrieved a key from the far wall, opened the cage with it and put the bowl inside.

"Eat, drink some water. I have to feed the animals. When I return, I'll expect more music."

Miralee watched as he returned the key to its nail, and then he left her alone.

First, she pushed on the bars, but they were unyielding. The walls of the house, despite their rundown outward appearance, were solid and there were no windows where she was being held. She had nothing that might help her pick the lock to her prison. Somehow Miralee had to get that key. It was too far to reach, at least twenty feet away and seven feet up.

A slight scraping sound distracted her. She looked and saw a rat, gnawing on the edge of the troll's table. She saw another rat climb onto the table and eat a crust of stale bread. After a minute or two there were at least a dozen rats visible. Apparently, they avoided the troll but had no fear of Miralee.

She heard the troll returning. The rats scattered and disappeared as he entered. Miralee knew that he would expect her to play so she overcame her revulsion and drank some water from the dirty cup but could not bring herself to eat any of the greenish stew.

"Play for me," the troll said.

Miralee nodded and began. She played her *duduk* this time. She realized that she had to relax if she was going to have any chance of escape. She willed the tension out of her body and soon her mind followed. As she played, the room seemed to dim and became warmer. She felt diffuse as her awareness expanded. The troll's breathing became deep and regular, his muscles slackened. Miralee played the hypnotic, "Eyes of Cassan," and felt the troll respond. His eyes closed. She played a lullaby next, and he began to snore.

35

She stopped playing. The troll continued to snore and she could tell he was in a deep sleep. Outside, it had grown dark, but Miralee was seeing with more than her eyes and could discern everything in the house. She felt the small, curious minds of the rats. They too had felt her music, and their attention was focused on her.

Silently, she called to them. At first nothing happened, but she continued to encourage them and they began to emerge from their hiding places. One rat in particular, chestnut brown and larger than the others seemed drawn to her, coming right up to the edge of the cage. Miralee held out her hand and it sniffed her fingers then let her touch the top of its head.

"I'm trapped in here," she whispered. "Will you help me?"

She didn't know if it would or not, but she knew that it understood her. Animals always did. But was it smart enough to do what she needed?

Miralee pictured the key hanging from the wall and visualized the rat bringing it to her. It continued to sit there looking up at her.

"Go on. Get the key."

She directed her thoughts at the rat and repeated the image of the rat fetching the key. It squeaked and ran across the floor.

"That's it," she encouraged as it reached the wall underneath where the key hung. "Go up, hurry."

The rat climbed the wall easily. The key was fairly large and on a ring. It gave the rat some trouble as he tried to lift it from the nail. He managed to free it, but dropped it to the floor. It made a soft *clang* when it struck and Miralee held her breath waiting for the troll to come awake, but he continued to snore.

She sighed and stretched her arm out through the bars.

"Come on, bring it to me."

The rat started to run back without it. She repeated the image of the key. It stopped near the table where the troll was sleeping and started back. It sniffed the key briefly then grasped the ring in its mouth. The key dragged on the floor but the rat managed to carry it across the room, stopping once to re-adjust its burden.

Finally, it reached the cage and let go of the key where Miralee could grab it. She picked it up as the rat came into the cage and sat next to her.

36

"Good job." She scratched the rat behind the ears and felt its pleasure as she did so.

Miralee stood up and quietly worked the key into the lock. The rat climbed up one of the bars. Miralee was a little surprised but did not flinch as it jumped from the bar, caught onto her blouse and found a perch on her shoulder. It sat there content and watched as she managed to open the door. Ever so carefully, Miralee eased the door open and stepped out. The floor creaked slightly. The troll snorted then resumed its snoring.

"I'm leaving," she mouthed to the rat. "Do you want to come with me or stay with your friends?"

It made no attempt to move, so she picked up her guitar and carefully lifted her bag from where it sat. She tiptoed to the door. The wooden bar was heavy, but she was used to farm work and managed to lift it and get the door open. It was cold and breezy outside. A gust of wind blew into the house, and the door creaked on its hinges.

"Huh, whazzat?"

She ran away from the house, away from the river, not daring to look back. Branches whipped across Miralee's face and thorns tore at her legs, but she did not slow down. She heard the troll shouting and then heavy crashing from somewhere behind her. It was yelling threats of what it was going to do to her when it caught her. Then there was one, short surprised yell, a loud *thud*, then nothing.

Miralee ran. She ran until she felt like her heart would explode and finally came to a stop more than two miles away from the troll's house. Bent over, she gasped for air.

When she was able, she listened for pursuit. She closed her eyes and stretched her senses again. The woods were full of animal life, all aware of her headlong, blundering flight, but nothing that felt dangerous. She could not sense the troll. The rat was still with her, having taken refuge in the hood of her cloak. Now that she was stopped, the rat came out and resumed sitting on her shoulder.

Miralee was suddenly very hungry. Realizing that she had eaten nothing since the early morning, she sat and cut a piece of cheese and tore off a hunk of bread. She offered some of both to the rat who accepted happily. She washed the food down with a mouthful of water from her skin.

For the first time in a long while, Miralee had no desire for music. The day-long, forced concert had taken it out of her. But she was free. However, she no longer saw the forest as a sanctuary. She knew now that it contained malevolent things against which she would have to remain on guard.

The troll came awake suddenly but took a moment to realize what had happened. He saw the open door of the cage and felt the draft coming in.

"Huh, whazzat?"

All at once he realized that his prisoner had escaped. The troll came to his feet and stormed to the door. His keen eyes picked up Miralee fleeing into the woods, and he began to run after her. She had a fair lead and was quick for a human girl, but he was confident that he would catch her.

"Trying to run away are you? When I catch you, I'll break both of your legs if you're lucky. Maybe, I'll just cut off your feet! I'll leave your hands alone though, so you can play for me," he yelled as he closed the distance.

The troll followed her into the trees. Miralee was no longer visible, but he could hear her not far ahead, breaking branches and crunching leaves. In moments he would have her.

A black clad figure rose up right in front of the troll. The troll let out a startled shout. It was all he had time to do before the figure drew a sword and with a quick motion removed the troll's head from his shoulders. The troll's body continued to run for about ten feet, while the head sailed through the air, momentarily silhouetted against the moonlight before it landed not far from where the body fell.

The figure wiped off his blade in the leaves and listened to the ever more distant sounds of Miralee's flight. Not rushing, he set off to follow her.

38

Two days after her escape from the troll, Miralee emerged from the Tauton Woods. The days had been uneventful, but she still could not shake the feeling of being watched.

Two or three times a day, she stopped and practiced stillness. It was becoming easier. She could reach out a little further each time, but never did she feel anything unusual. Once, she sensed a small band of goblins, but they didn't seem to be aware of her and soon moved out of the range of her senses.

On her fifth day since leaving Brown's Ford, Miralee arrived at the village of Briggen. It was a small, isolated place on the bank of a narrow, deep river called the Boddenberry.

The people of Briggen seemed sallow and not particularly bright, even compared to the people in her home village. But they were friendly enough. They lodged and fed her, and asked nothing in return. Miralee was glad to sleep indoors for the last few nights had been cold. But in the morning she was ready to get on with her trip.

On the eastern bank of the Boddenberry, the landscape became more pastoral; fertile fields and lonely farmhouses with small stands of tame woods interspersed here and there. From the Boddenberry was a road, no more than a muddy trail really, that led to the village of Sperry's Knoll, just a long day's walk from Briggen.

Miralee arrived in the village at dusk. She had her rat, who she was calling Orrie after a similarly colored mare back on her farm, hidden in the pocket of her cloak. Normal people did not keep rodents as pets, and she had no wish to attract undue attention.

Sperry's Knoll had a feature Miralee had never before encountered—the presence of nobility. This was Sperry County and at the top of a low hill was Sperry Manor, which to Miralee seemed like the grandest house in the country, or at least in Graelly; though the reality was the house was somewhat mundane as noble residences went.

The house was only three floors with eighteen rooms and it was constructed of planks, not stone. The manor did have a wall around it, but it wasn't a proper wall—stone yes, but barely chest high. The home was residence to the Earl en'Sperry, his wife, and four children, as well as approximately twenty servants who lived in small cottages to the rear of the manor.

The village was at the foot of the knoll. It was larger than Brown's Ford by at least two hundred people. On the outskirts, Miralee had passed some large farms boasting equally large farmhouses. The houses in the village proper were more modest and she guessed that many of these people labored on the farms she had passed.

It was dinner time when she arrived in Sperry's Knoll and so few people saw her arrive. One two-story building had a weathered sign with a picture of a mug on it—a tavern. The smell of roasting meat hung in the air and made her mouth water. From inside, she could hear the sounds of laughter and music. Miralee pushed open the heavy door and went inside.

She didn't notice when, a few moments later, a hooded figure followed her into the tavern.

Chapter Five

The tavern was rustic but clean. Miralee went and stood near the end of the bar in the corner. Her entrance drew attention both because she was a stranger and a female. Like in Brown's Ford, the tavern in Sperry's Knoll seemed to be a place for men. A few women were evident, three serving girls and a few adventurous ladies on the arms of their husbands. There were about fifty people in the large common room total, but space for three times that number.

The musicians were near the far wall, standing on a low stage. One looked to be in his late twenties, a dark-haired, hook-nosed man strumming a guitar larger and deeper than Miralee's. Around his neck hung a necklace very similar to the one Miralee wore—a bard's necklace. He shared the stage with a young man or older boy—he couldn't have been more than sixteen or seventeen—who was playing a drum. She recognized 'Far Green Hills,' a ballad from northern Istey, but popular all over for its upbeat refrain. The older bard had a powerful voice that pierced through the tavern noise. Miralee had no doubt that his voice could be heard even when the tavern was full.

"Can I get you something, miss?"

She turned and saw a middle-aged man. He had no beard, but possessed the longest, bushiest moustache that Miralee had ever seen. He was also slightly stooped, probably from the weight of the moustache.

"Can I have some water? I've been walking all day and I'm parched."

He nodded and moved off to fetch it. Returning a moment later, the bartender set a mug in front of Miralee.

"Sit. If you've been walking all day, I'd feel guilty if you came into my place and stood."

"This is your tavern?"

"Indeed it is. My name is Marlon Mack and I've owned this tavern for close to twenty years now."

"I'm Miralee. Thank you for the water."

He moved down the bar a bit and made a show of polishing its shiny wood, all the while studying her. He only looked away when the door opened and a hooded stranger came in and sat down in the farthest corner. Miralee did not take note of the man; all of her senses were fixed on the two bards.

"So where you coming from, miss?" Mack asked a few minutes later.

"Hmm? I left Briggen this morning."

"Twenty-five miles if it's one." He whistled appreciatively. "You must have a bit of an appetite…unless you ate already, with your family perhaps?"

"No, I haven't eaten. I'm not really hungry." *No, I'm famished! I still have some cheese and stale bread, but that roast smells delicious.*

"Traveling alone, miss?" he asked in a low tone.

Miralee looked at him, reading him and trying to ascertain his motive for asking. She didn't sense any malice in him, just concern.

"You look to be about my daughter's age," Marlon Mack continued. "I'd hate to see her out in the world alone and hungry. From the look of you, you've been traveling longer than a day."

Do I look that bad?

"You just sit there. I'm going to go get you some supper. On the house."

Grateful, Miralee waited. She saw a mirror behind the bar and looked at herself. *I don't look too bad,* she decided. *Just my cloak. I could use a bath though. I feel a little overripe.*

Marlon Mack came and set a plate spilling over with food down in front of Miralee. She dug in.

"This is delicious!"

"Thank you very much. I do all of the cooking myself."

When she had taken the sharpest edge from her hunger she slowed down a bit and began to look around. Most of the patrons were watching the musicians or talking to each other. Then her eyes fell on the hooded man who had come in after her. His hood was still in place and his face was in shadow. He was speaking to no one

42

and when she looked at him, Miralee got the feeling that he was looking back.

"Mr. Mack, do you know that man in the corner?"

"No. Everyone here is from the village barring you and him. Why?" He studied the hooded man more closely. Now the man seemed to be watching the musicians on stage.

My imagination perhaps.

"No reason, I thought he looked familiar was all. Mr. Mack…"

"Call me Marlon."

"Marlon, coming in here I had hoped to trade some songs for a meal and lodging. But I see you have a bard performing."

"Aye, Shondor. Tok on the drum there is his apprentice. I noted your guitar there. You any good?"

"I'm still learning, but the people at home like to listen to me play."

"Well, those two should finish up soon. They often play during dinner then take a break and start up again later when it gets busy. Maybe you could have a try when they get through."

"Thank you. Does Shondar work for you?"

"What? No. Bards work for themselves, or the guild I suppose. I mean, I do pay him for his services, as do the patrons. But I'm not his boss as such. He plays here because this is where the people come. If there is a dance or something, he goes there. Sometimes he goes to the manor and plays for the earl. He also teaches and people consult with him about the law. Bards do more than play music you know. They are historians and keepers of the law as well."

"I didn't know. I have a lot to learn." *And how am I supposed to learn if Olahan can no longer teach me anything. Why didn't he? I can't even read. I never saw any books in the cottage, just sheet music. He* did *tell me stories though. Oh, there is so much I don't know!*

"Oh, it looks like Shondar and Tok are finishing up. You should meet Shondar."

Marlon waved to the bard as he was leaving the stage. He came over and accepted two mugs, handing one to his apprentice. He glanced at Miralee then stared. For a moment, she was self-

43

conscious. Then she realized that he was looking at the guitar slung over her back.

"That is a beautiful instrument," the bard said.

"Would you like to see it?" she asked, taking the guitar from her shoulder.

"Shondar Skale, this is my new friend, Miralee," Marlon said. "She just arrived in Sperry's Knoll. Plays a bit, she said. I was going to let her play a little between your sets, if that's all right with you."

"Hmm? It's your establishment. You can allow anyone to perform here that you wish," Shondar said, turning the guitar over appreciatively in his hands. "This was made by a master. Do you know its origin?"

"Just that it used to belong to a man named Pennix Lorexson."

"I'm not familiar with the name. I'm eager to hear how it sounds though."

"May I?" Miralee asked Marlon Mack, gesturing to the stage.

"I'll take you up."

Miralee followed the tavern keeper through the crowd to the stage. The room quieted a bit.

"Listen up! This here is Miralee. She's going to entertain us tonight."

"She could entertain me all night," a young man near the stage yelled. Someone whistled.

And I look a mess.

"Shut up, Karl. Miralee's a good girl. Okay, they're all yours."

She took off her cloak and hoisted her guitar. She strummed a major chord and began to play "Barley Mash," a regional drinking song. The audience nodded in approval as soon as they recognized it and began to clap and sing along. When she finished she got more than polite applause. Several people in the room, including her admirer, Karl, stood and clapped enthusiastically.

"Thank you," she said.

She was relaxed now and her senses were opening. She played "Hagenstone Reel," which got more people up, stomping and dancing. She could feel the emotions of the crowd now and they

44

buoyed her. She did a ballad next, settling the crowd some but losing none of their attention.

Miralee looked toward the bar. Shondar was still there, watching her, his food barely touched. She looked the other way. The hooded man was watching her as well. From this angle she could see that he was clean shaven, giving the impression of youth, but she still could not see his eyes. She tried to see his aura, but for some reason she could see nothing.

That's strange.

Miralee played her guitar for forty-five minutes before she put it down and took out her *duduk.*

"I'm going to change things up a bit," she said.

She played an instrumental version of "Eyes of Cassan."

Miralee slowed down the tempo and it became very ethereal. To the audience, it seemed as if the lamps and candles in the tavern dimmed while Miralee became brighter, almost like she was sitting in sunlight.

Unbidden, Shondar came onto the stage and sat down at the drum. He accompanied her, very lightly at first. She glanced back at him and smiled. With an exaggerated nod she told him to increase the tempo and volume as they came into the final verse. It lent a sense of hope to the otherwise somber song. When they finished, nearly every eye in the room was shining.

"You are very good for someone so young," Shondar said once they had left the stage. "I've never seen a pipe like that. It has an interesting sound."

"It's called a *duduk.* My friend, Olahan, gave it to me. He told me that they're played in Zahdi and Buladon mostly. This one came from Zahdi."

"Excuse me, did you say Olahan? Master Olahan?"

"Yes, I suppose so. When he retired, he moved to my village."

"And Master Olahan taught you to play?"

"Yes, he made me his apprentice."

Surprise and disbelief were clearly evident on the bard's face. He plopped onto a stool, looking closely at Miralee as if he had never seen her before.

"It's true," Miralee said, before he could tell her that she was mistaken. "He gave me this."

She pulled her medallion out of her shirt and showed it to the bard. Shondar took it in hand and looked at it closely.

"And he said that you were his apprentice? Not just his student?"

"That's what I said, wasn't it?" She was irritated.

"I know, I mean…did he give you apprenticeship papers?"

"Papers? No. He didn't give me papers. He just said that he was making me an apprentice of the guild and gave me this necklace. Maybe he would have given me papers if…"

"If? Did something happen to Master Olahan?" he asked.

"No. He's well. It's just that he thought that he would have a few more weeks with me. You see, my father was going to send me away and I…well I…"

"You ran away, didn't you?"

She lowered her eyes and nodded slightly.

"Miralee, that was wonderful," Marlon Mack interrupted. "Only you didn't check the bucket."

"The bucket?"

"Tips from the audience. They put them in the bucket at the side of the stage," he explained.

"Oh, that's what they were doing."

"Yes," said Shondar. "I'm sorry, I should have told you."

"It looks like you did quite well. Here, count it."

Miralee scooped a handful of coins from the bucket. She counted it out on the bar—twenty-three copper pennies, sixteen tin rounds, five silver pars, and—she gasped—one gold kel. She felt a surge of altruistic happiness from Mack.

"Marlon, you shouldn't have. You've been very kind already."

"Nonsense. I thought you were great. I tipped what I thought the performance was worth."

"Then you at least have to let me pay for my dinner and a room!"

"I told you that the meal was on the house. I'll rent you a room. I've got six, only two are taken—a tinker is in one and that fellow with the hood rented the other. The going rate is one penny."

"One penny won't buy a night's lodging on the floor of a common room, let alone a private one," Miralee protested.

"I'm running a special." He leaned closer. "Miralee. I do pretty well here. It's nothing for me and it makes me feel good to help. As I said, you remind me of my daughter."

Miralee felt sadness come off of the tavern keeper.

"Thank you, Marlon. You're very sweet." She leaned forward and kissed his cheek. The older man flushed.

"It's nothing. I don't suppose that you're staying in Sperry's Knoll for any length of time?"

"I'm going to Edain. Why?"

"Well, I wouldn't object to hearing you play again is all."

"Marlon," Shondar said, "hopefully you'll get your wish tonight. I was about to ask Miralee to play with Tok and I during our evening set. Well?"

"I would love to play with you tonight, but I'd like a chance to wash up first."

"There's water in the basin in your room and I'll have one of the girls heat some bathwater. Let me get your key," Mack said.

When the tavern keeper had gone to the end of the bar, Miralee asked Shondar, "Is Marlon's daughter dead?"

"Yes. Very perceptive. She died three years ago while riding with one of the earl's sons, an accident they said. She was sixteen, which I'm guessing is about your age."

"Nearly, I'm fifteen."

"Gods. Anyway, Mr. Mack was deeply affected. His wife died of fever about ten years ago, well before I came here. So, besides this tavern, his daughter was all he had. It was a terrible tragedy. You favor her quite a bit, though I dare say you would have towered over her. But your hair, your eyes—I'm sure that he's seeing her in you."

But I'm not her. Poor man.

Marlon came back with the key.

As she started to leave, Shondar said, "The evening set usually starts in about an hour, but take your time. I know you had a long day."

"No, I'll be down in an hour."

"Good. Maybe later we can continue our discussion about your apprenticeship."

"Okay." She tried to read him, to get some idea of where the bard fell on the topic of Miralee as a bard's apprentice, but either she was too tired right then or he was good at being inscrutable.

Hefting her bag, she climbed the stairs to her room.

The common room was three-quarters full when Miralee, Shondar, and Tok began to play. Miralee's guitar, with its higher pitch, was a nice compliment to Shondar's. She knew most of the songs that Shondar suggested, and those she didn't know she picked up quickly enough. They sang a few duets and found their voices blended pleasantly. Miralee had a rich contralto voice, while Shondar sang with a deep baritone.

They had just started a duet of "Gaella Marie" when there was some commotion near the door. A group of six men came in, all armed with swords. A short, but powerful-looking man in their center yelled something to Marlon Mack, who hurried to clear a table in the front. There were some grumbles, not too loud, from the men who had been seated at the table, Karl among them, but they hastened to get up and move. When Mack came close, she could feel his displeasure, a combination of anger and apprehension.

When the song finished, Shondar whispered to Miralee, "That's Rupert en'Sperry, the earl's second son."

She didn't know what to make of that and so just filed it away. Shondar took the time to offer a greeting to young Lord Rupert, who inclined his head slightly in acknowledgement. Miralee thought he had eyes like a weasel's. His whole party radiated feelings of superiority.

The three on stage took a few moments to re-tune their instruments and sip some water. Not that they really needed it, but to give the room a chance to settle. Marlon had drinks sent over to the earl's son's table and one of the girls brought food.

"He likes to make bit of an entrance when he decides to slum with the common folk," said Shondar quietly. "'The Golden Fish?'"

"It was the first song I learned."

48

They played, and the room got back to normal. Periodically, one of Lord Rupert's men loudly demanded something, but generally they behaved. Rupert en'Sperry kept his attention wholly on the stage. Between each song, he stood and clapped heartily. Miralee looked at him with her other senses and saw that he had an aura that was barely visible.

It's almost like a few wisps of fog hanging onto him, a chilly mist.

They played until after ten. By that time Miralee was tired, but the excitement of playing before an audience dulled her fatigue. She wanted to keep the excitement going, though she knew that she should really go to bed.

The bucket was heavy with coins. Rupert en'Sperry made a show of getting up and tipping the musicians personally.

"Spectacular," he said turning to the audience as he approached the stage. "Simply spectacular. Journeyman Shondar, thank you for the entertainment tonight, delivered so ably as always. A little something for you." en'Sperry turned and held up a gold kel so the audience could see. "And Tok, keep trying lad, you'll get there." He handed the apprentice something; Miralee thought she saw a glint of silver. "And who are you, my dear?"

"Miralee, sir," she said, curtseying awkwardly.

I'm glad I put on my clean dress. And I'm pretty sure I should call him "My Lord" or something. "Sir" is what I called farmers in Brown's Ford.

"Miralee. A lovely name. I must say, you are quite talented, a welcome addition to our group of musicians. Here this is for you." He handed her not one, but two gold coins. Miralee thought it was inappropriate to give her, an apprentice, two when he had only given Shondar, a journeyman, one—but she said nothing.

"Thank you, Milord."

Rupert en'Sperry offered his hand and helped Miralee down from the stage. She accepted as she thought that the prudent thing would be to accept the young noble's show of graciousness. Once off the stage, he took her arm and began to walk her toward his table.

"I would be honored if you would share my table."

"I guess so," she said, not at all certain that she wanted to.

She looked over her shoulder and was glad to see that Shondar was following them, though he had not been invited. When they reached the table, Rupert en'Sperry noticed the journeyman and didn't look happy for his company, but glossed over it with a smile and gestured to an empty chair across the table.

"So Miralee, where did Shondar find you?"

"He didn't, My Lord. I came here on my own. I'm just passing through on my way to Edain," she said.

"Miralee is an apprentice of the guild," said Shondar. "I'll be escorting her to Edain in the morning. She'll be at the conservatory."

What?

"I didn't know women were being admitted to the guild," Rupert en'Sperry said.

"Times change. Miralee is Master Olahan's apprentice. He is rather elderly and asked me to see her there safely."

He did? No, Shondar is nervous—for me. Rupert is hard to read; he gives little away, but he's irritated.

Marlon Mack came over and brought more food and drink. He kept his head down, but Miralee caught him glance at Rupert en'Sperry and felt a flash of venom.

"If Miralee's safety is a concern, I will have some of my men take her," en'Sperry said. "She would be safer in the company of my soldiers than with a bard and a boy. Besides, your music would be missed too much here. I will happily see your apprentice to Edain."

"My Lord, while I am grateful for your generous offer, I have accepted this task and must see it through," Shondar said. "Besides, no one in Istey would molest a journeyman bard of the guild."

Shondar and the young noble locked eyes for a moment. Rupert en'Sperry broke away first, smiling.

"Very well. Of course, yours is a respected profession. Well, my offer stands. I could even have a few soldiers and one of my knights accompany all three of you. Let me know."

"Of course."

"Well Miralee, it's a pity that we will have so little time to get acquainted. I am great lover of music and wish we had more like you. Would you at least do me the honor of walking with me? The night is lovely and the moon is just risen."

"Thank you, My Lord, but I must decline. I had a very long day and must get some rest. But you are very generous to show me such courtesy."

"I insist."

"No."

I don't know what Rupert en'Sperry wants with me, but he puts Marlon and Shondar on edge. That's reason enough for me to stay clear.

Lord Rupert stood abruptly. His men followed. Shondar and Miralee remained seated. Shondar took a sip from his glass of ale.

"It is late. I must get home. Miralee, it was a pleasure to meet you. Have a safe journey. Shondar, let me know if you require an escort. I've heard reports of bandits lately," said the noble.

"Thank you, My Lord. We will be careful."

When Lord Rupert and his men had left, Shondar let out a deep breath and sank down in his chair. Marlon Mack came out and sat at the table carrying three ales.

"I don't drink ale," said Miralee.

"Have a little tonight. It won't harm you none," said Mack.

She took a sip, finding it a little bitter. It wasn't the first time that she'd had ale, but she had never cared much for the taste.

"Which one of you wants to tell me what just happened?" she asked the two men.

They looked to one another. Then Shondar spoke.

"Rupert en'Sperry took a fancy to Marlon's daughter. He took her riding. She was with him when the accident happened."

"He killed her," said Mack.

"Marlon, you don't know that for sure."

"I know. A father knows. I saw it in his eyes. He ravaged my Alissa and he killed her."

"I'm afraid that Marlon's daughter is not the only one. Over the last six years, there have been no fewer than five women who have been killed or disappeared. Two were from Sperry's Knoll, three were traveling with parties. Each woman was young, pretty, and fair."

"The bastard picked you out right away," Marlon Mack said.

"Hasn't anyone been able to do anything?" Miralee asked.

"No. The earl won't hear a word said against his son. And there is no real evidence against him. But he was seen in contact with each of the women and showed interest in several. In a few cases, bandits were blamed. The parties with whom the women traveled were set upon within ten miles of the village. The girls were taken and the others killed. The girl's mutilated bodies were found a few days after the attack, not far from the manor. And there has been talk from some of the women who work at the manor about Rupert's sadistic side. It seems that he enjoys physically punishing women."

"Most of the bodies were found," Shondar said. "The heads were missing from each victim."

Miralee drank some more ale. Suddenly it didn't taste so bad.

"Okay, Rupert en'Sperry is not a nice man. What about the things you told him? He'll know that you lied when you are still here and I'm gone."

"But I am going. I have no intention of letting you traipse off to Edain now that Rupert has seen you," Shondar said.

"What about you telling him that I'm an apprentice to the guild? And what's the conservatory?"

"I was only an apprentice at Magh Moru for a few years while Master Olahan was guildmaster, but I thought very highly of him and he was always very kind to me. It is obvious that you have great skill and have been taught by a master. Though, truth be told, I would rather take you home than to Edain."

Olahan was guildmaster? I knew that he was a master bard, but he never told me that he actually ran the whole guild.

"I can't go home. I told you, my father wants to send me away to some tiny village to get married."

"Well, maybe you should," Mack said. "Pretty young girl like you alone in the world, too much can happen to you."

"I can't. It's…complicated."

"If Master Olahan were to go to your father and explain that he had taken you as his apprentice, then maybe…"

"No, Shondar. My father would never accept that and Olahan knew it. I'm going to Edain."

"Very well. As to what the conservatory is, the Edain Conservatory is a school of the arts. Music, dance, and theater are all studied there. The guild runs it, though it is not exclusive to the guild. Apprentices also study history and law."

"And you think I could go there?"

"It is my hope. Magh Moru is out of the question. The current guildmaster, Master Berint, is very conservative. But the conservatory? I don't know. I know the headmaster there. He is old, but not as conservative as Master Berint. In fact, he and Master Olahan were friends at one time."

Shondar stood and stretched.

"You were right. It is late and we will leave early," he said. Then he took his leave.

Marlon Mack looked tired as well, and older than he had when Miralee had first met him just a few hours before. She rose and placed her hand on his shoulder. He reached up and patted it appreciatively.

"Goodnight," she said, kissing the top of his head.

"Goodnight, Alissa."

Chapter Six

Tok knocked on Miralee's door around dawn. She was already awake and set to go.

"Shondar is downstairs with the horses."

"Horses?"

"Of course. You didn't think we were going to walk to Edain did you?"

"Oh, no."

At the stable, she found Shondar and Marlon. Like Tok said, Shondar had acquired horses, four in total.

"They're mine," Mack said. "I own several and swap out with travelers needing fresh mounts. These four are my best. Take them. Shondar will return them later—or just let them go. They'll find their way home."

Miralee inspected the animals. They were indeed fine. There was a tall, brown stallion, proud but cooperative; a dun gelding with an even temper; and a black mare with a star and a white stocking that seemed to be the most intelligent of the three riding animals. The fourth was a sturdy pack horse. Miralee went to each animal and quietly introduced herself getting a feel for their personalities.

"I'll ride the mare, if that's all right," she said, liking the black horse best.

"Certainly," Shondar said. "Here, this is yours also."

He handed her a small, but heavy sack. It was full of money.

"That is your share from last night. The audience was particularly generous."

They fit most of their belongings onto the pack horse. Miralee just had her one bag, but Tok and Shondar were bringing quite a few things it seemed. The only thing she kept with her was her instruments and, on impulse, she took the knife from her bag and slipped it into her pocket. She also took some of the coins from her new money sack and put them into a pocket, while tucking the rest into the bag the pack horse carried.

Marlon Mack gave each of them a slicker to wear large enough to fit over their instruments in case it should rain, which it did almost daily this time of year. Miralee accepted it, though her travel cloak had served to keep her guitar dry so far.

She hugged Marlon, thanking him and wishing him well.

"Come back and see me when you're famous," he said. "Or just come back and see me."

"I will."

The morning was chilly and gray. A light drizzle was falling, but it wasn't enough to dampen Miralee's spirits.

Yesterday I was alone, on foot, without money or prospects. Today I have friends, a horse to ride, coins in my pocket, and I'm on my way the Edain conservatory. Things are looking up.

The muddy road took them through fields barely sprouted and wild meadows with high grass and the flowers of early spring: crocuses, hyacinth, and dewberries covered with white flowers, the berries themselves not yet apparent. Here and there were patches of woods, none terribly large, but some were dense.

It was near one of the dense stands that the trouble began.

The three musicians were not quite ten miles from the village when Miralee felt her horse stiffen with sudden nervousness.

"What is it?" she said quietly, stroking the horse's neck.

The horse's muscles tensed, and her ears twitched. Miralee closed her eyes and relaxed, reached out with her senses.

"There are several men and horses ahead," she said after a few moments.

"Where?" Shondar asked.

"The stand of trees just ahead by the bend."

"How do you know that?" asked Tok.

"I saw them for a second before they were hidden," she lied. That begged further questions, but neither man asked them.

It was a great place for an ambush. The dense, concealing woods were on one side, on the other, a stream—possibly not a barrier in the summer, but swollen and deep in the spring. But they weren't to that spot yet. Only one hundred and fifty yards away, those yards made a huge difference.

They cut across a field to their right. For several minutes there was no movement from the trees. But suddenly two horsemen emerged, then two more, then more until a total of ten armed men had come into view. Miralee almost laughed as they looked around in confusion to see where the three travelers had gone. They had obviously expected their quarry to remain on the road. One of the men did spot the bards and the ten turned their mounts and spread out in pursuit.

"Bandits," said Shondar. "Ride!"

"I thought bards could ride the roads unmolested," Tok cried.

"Bards or no, I think these bandits were waiting for us," said Shondar. "Now go!"

Miralee and Shondar were both good riders, but Tok was not. He fell behind, as did the pack horse, even though Miralee told it to stay close.

The ground was uneven across the meadow and the tall grass hid many of the irregularities. Miralee turned just in time to see Tok's gelding stumble and the apprentice lurch headfirst out of the saddle to the wet ground. The horse recovered and kept going, though the young man did not. Miralee swung her mare around to go back, even as the bandits closed.

She reached Tok just ahead of the closest bandit. The young man had regained his feet and was running toward her. Miralee kept low in the saddle and reached out for him when she got near.

"Take my hand!" she yelled.

He reached out and grabbed her arm. With surprising strength, Miralee managed to pull him up onto the saddle behind her. She urged the black mare on, but now she had bandits on either side of her, and one, a fat brute with a long scar across his face, moving to cut her off. She saw that Shondar had seen what had happened and had turned around as well, though he still had a good lead on them.

"Go!" she yelled to him.

The bard hesitated. He was unarmed, except for a hunting knife not unlike Miralee's. He was no fighter. To stay would most certainly mean death. To flee would mean abandoning his own apprentice to death and Miralee to possibly an even a worse fate.

"Yah!" he said, urging the stallion forward toward the bandits.

He might not be a warrior, or even smart, but he is brave, she thought. *What is* that*!?*

Now the bandits had her ringed. Her mare was stopped, as both mount and rider looked for a way through. Miralee saw movement out of the corner of her eye. She expected to see a bandit moving in on her, but instead saw a rider coming across the open field—it was the hooded man that had been in the tavern last night.

Is he one of the bandits? They aren't reacting to his presence.

But she didn't think he was a bandit. They weren't reacting to him at all, as if they couldn't see him.

Miralee had the scar-faced bandit in front of her, with one close on either side. To the left, there was another about fifteen feet away; to the right, two more about the same distance away. And to her rear, there were three bandits spread out to block her escape. The last one hung back farther still. The hooded man rode in from her right, not hurrying, with a bow in his hand.

From horseback, he strung the bow and let fly at one of the two men on the right. He immediately re-strung the bow and shot at the second bandit. Both arrows found their targets. The first bandit was struck through the back, the second through the throat.

Now the bandits reacted to the newcomer's presence. The hooded man kept coming straight ahead toward the man who was closest to Miralee's right and shot a third arrow, taking the bandit through the ribs. The man fell from his horse, leaving only Scar-face on that side. The hooded man already had him targeted. Miralee urged the black mare onward through the gap. Scar-face's horse reared as the arrow loosed. It struck the man in the shoulder. He cursed but stayed in the saddle and turned to chase after Miralee, while the two bandits that had been to her left and the three to the rear drew their swords and engaged the hooded man. He slipped his bow over his shoulder and drew his sword. The last bandit broke away from the fighting to pursue Miralee as well.

Shondar was coming full gallop toward Scar-face.

"No! The ground is too uneven. You're going too fast," Miralee tried to warn.

But as soon as the words were said, Shondar's stallion stepped into a rut and went down. From her angle, Miralee couldn't tell if the bard was hurt, but the horse was quickly up, though without a rider.

She couldn't worry about Shondar now. Scar-face had managed to catch up to her and grabbed for her reigns. Miralee's knife flashed from her pocket and she swiped at his reaching hand. The blade struck flesh and he yanked his hand back.

I don't think I hurt him too badly, but he'll think twice about grabbing for me.

Ahead, the ground looked more even. She made for it even as her second pursuer gained on her. However, he made the same mistake that Shondar had. He ran his horse too hard and the animal stepped into a hidden rut. He was close enough that Miralee heard the gut-wrenching *snap* as the horse's foreleg broke. She felt a stab of sympathy and even a brief impression of the pain itself in her left arm followed by nausea.

She reached the flat ground and looked over her shoulder. She stopped. No one was near her. She watched the hooded man dispatch one of the remaining horsemen. He must have already taken care of two, because only two of the bandits were still fighting him. But when their comrade fell, the last two turned and fled back the way they had come. Likewise, Scar-face was fleeing across the meadow. Of the ten attackers, only three escaped—and the whole fight had only lasted about two minutes.

Miralee rode the mare back to where Shondar had fallen. She found him conscious, on his back on the ground still. His right leg was twisted awkwardly. His pain hit Miralee in waves.

"Shondar!" she cried dismounting and kneeling next to him.

"My leg, I'm afraid that it's broken."

"Let me take a look at it," came a voice from not far away—the hooded man.

Only now the hood was pulled back, revealing a handsome, almost pretty, face of a young man in his early twenties with curly, shoulder length black hair. Miralee was wary.

Tok was also apprehensive about the man. He was dismounted and stood over his journeyman protectively; forgetting that he was unarmed and that this individual had just defeated ten men with ease.

"It's all right. Please. I have experience with such injuries," said the stranger. "I'm here to help you if you haven't noticed."

Following me is more like it. She took a step back and gestured for the man to go ahead. Carefully, he explored the injured limb with his fingers. When he touched a spot about six inches below the knee, Shondar winced. Gently, the man examined the spot more closely.

"Mmm, it's a clean break. It should heal well enough, but you won't be able to ride anywhere for at least a month. I can fashion a splint to help stabilize it until you get back to the village."

"The village, no. I'm going with Miralee to Edain."

"You'd never make it. I'll make a travois and your apprentice can return you to Sperry's Knoll. It's the only option."

They were distracted by a low groan from about twenty yards away. The young man stood.

"There are other wounded. I'll see to them," he said.

I still can't read anything off of him. He doesn't seem threatening, but he's definitely dangerous. I want to know why he followed us from the village. What was he doing there in the first place?

"Tok, get the water off of my horse for Shondar," she said.

Horses were milling around the meadow. Even the pack horse was standing down near the stand of trees. Miralee took out her *duduk* and improvised a song to call to the horses. Eight horses were visible, the stallion, the gelding, the pack horse, and five of the bandit's mounts, including the poor creature with the broken leg. As she played, their ears perked up, and one by one the animals came and gathered around. Only the wounded horse remained where it was, unable to stand. Miralee stopped and gave the animals a firm mental command to stay in the area. The spell broken, most took to grazing on the sweet, spring grass.

The strange man came back dragging the body of one of the bandits.

"This one was still alive when I reached him, though he seems to be expired now. His insides were crushed when his horse fell," he said. "However, he did tell me that they knew exactly who they were waiting for. Their instructions were to kill the men and take

Miralee alive and unharmed. They were to deliver you to a cottage about three miles north of the village."

"Whose cottage?" asked Shondar.

"He said he didn't know. But the land he described is owned by the en'Sperry family. He died before he could tell me more."

"I think we can surmise who is controlling and allowing these men to operate here," Shondar said.

"What about the other bandits?" Miralee asked.

"Dead."

"You have to do something for the injured horse," said Miralee.

"I can't splint a horse's leg the way I can a man's."

"I know. Go and ease its pain."

"Very well." He rose and went to do what needed to be done.

"Tok, I saw an axe on the pack horse. Go and cut some limbs, about this long," she said gesturing with her arms. "Bring them back so we can make a travois."

"Wait," said Shondar. "What if the remaining bandits are still lurking?"

Miralee closed her eyes and reached out with her senses. She couldn't feel them anywhere close by.

"No. They're gone."

Shondar stared at her uncertainly. A long moment passed, and then he decided to trust her.

"Go ahead Tok," he said.

The apprentice nodded and went to work.

The hooded man returned.

"It's done."

"Thank you. Now, who are you? Why did you follow us from the tavern?" Miralee asked.

"My name is Gabriel. Do you mind if I take care of your friend's leg while we talk?"

She shrugged.

Gabriel cut a sapling and began to fashion a splint from it and strips of cloth from the dead bandit's shirt. He cut away Shondar's boot and made slit up the side of his pants.

"I hope they're not favorites. Your leg is swelling. I'm going to reset the bone. It isn't too bad, but it will swell some more once I reset it. It should go down by tomorrow."

Gabriel took hold of Shondar's foot.

"Ready?"

"Do it."

Gabriel pulled Shondar's leg firmly by the ankle and twisted it with a strong, quick motion. Shondar gasped and stiffened. Then he relaxed.

"That should take care of it."

Quickly, Gabriel applied the splint. Miralee had to admit that he had a deft hand. When the job was done, he took a skin from his saddle and drank deeply. He offered it to Shondar.

"I have some," the bard said holding up his own half full water skin.

"Nicely done with the horses," Gabriel said to Miralee. He squatted on the ground near Shondar.

"Thank you."

"We should check the bodies and the saddlebags for valuables," Gabriel suggested.

"You can loot the dead later if you like. Right now, I want some answers. Why did you follow us from the village? What do you want?"

"I followed *you* from the village because I have been following you for days, ever since you left Brown's Ford."

She remembered the nagging feeling that had stayed with her for the whole trip.

"Why?"

"To help you. And you've needed help. Remember the troll?" Orrie wriggled in her pocket as a reminder of the encounter. "Why do you think he quit chasing you?"

"You? Did you kill him as you killed these men?"

"I did. If I hadn't you'd either still be in that cage or the troll's dinner. Nasty business that, kidnapping and eating people—I'd say he had it coming. Just like these bastards. They got what they deserved. Consider yourself lucky that I was here to save you."

Miralee bristled at the thought of having to be saved by anyone.

61

"No thanks are necessary," Gabriel said.

"Good. But why follow me in the first place?" she asked.

"Because we're the same."

"The same?"

"I can do things, like you. I sensed it when I came close to Brown's Ford, so I followed you when you ran away."

Shondar was puzzled.

"Miralee, what does he mean?"

"It isn't important right now," she said. To Gabriel she asked, "So what will you do now? Go after Rupert en'Sperry?"

"Why should I? My goal was to keep you safe. You're going to Edain. A country earl's son won't be a threat to you there."

"But, I'm going to have to take Shondar back to Sperry's Knoll."

"I think that would be a bad idea. You'll just be putting yourself into his power. The apprentice can take the bard back."

But staying here without Shondar will be putting me into Gabriel's power. Can I trust someone who just admitted to following me for several days? Is what he says true? That we're alike? He is unusual.

"Miralee, you shouldn't go to Edain with this man," said Shondar. "We know nothing about him."

"I know. But he did save our lives. Even now, if he wanted to do us harm, I don't think we could stop him. What reason could he have to lie?"

"I don't like it."

Tok returned with a load of branches. Gabriel set about fashioning a travois from them and rope taken from the pack horse.

"Miralee," said Shondar. "The only thing I agree with is that you cannot come back to Sperry's Knoll." He sighed. "This isn't how I wanted this trip to turn out."

"It's all right, Shondar. You have been wonderful. I'm sorry that you got hurt. But I'll be okay."

"I still want you to go to the conservatory. Go to my horse. In the right saddle bag is a sheaf of papers. They are apprenticeship papers. They name Master Olahan as your master, though the signature on them is mine. They are better than nothing. There is

62

also a letter of application for admission to the Edain conservatory. Take it and give it to the headmaster. His name is Master Kant. He is a friend of mine. I don't know what he will say or do. I'll send a letter to him directly as soon as I can."

"Thank you for all that you've done."

"Also, take the money pouch from my bag. You'll need it more than I will. There's about fifteen *kel* in it."

She started to protest, but his look stopped her. Nodding, Miralee went to the stallion and found the items. Luckily, there was only one sheaf of papers. She glanced at it as if reading, though the letters made no sense to her. The money pouch she slipped into her pocket without glancing at.

Gabriel completed the travois and it looked well-made. Tok helped him rope it to the gelding. The ride would be a little bumpy, but the pair should make it back by nightfall. Tok and Gabriel assisted the journeyman onto the stretcher and made him as comfortable as they could.

"Take the pack horse," Shondar said. "There is food and plenty of camping supplies. What should we do with the bandit's horses?"

"We'll keep two. A spare horse is always a good idea. The rest you can take back to Mr. Mack, swaps in case these don't make it back," Gabriel said. "And please tell him I didn't steal this horse from him, I just needed to borrow it to help you out."

Soon, Tok and Shondar were going slowly down the muddy road back to the village. Miralee was alone with Gabriel. When the two bards had disappeared from view, she turned to her stalker.

"Come on," she said. "We can ride a few more hours before we have to stop. I'd like to get out of Sperry County."

"I agree. The sooner we get to Edain, the better."

"Why?"

"I still think that you're in danger."

"From the bandits?"

"No, not from them. From the Order of the Shadow Knights. I believe the Shadow Knights want to kill you."

As they approached Brown's Ford, Mordis Silverhand rode ahead of his three knights, Joran, Janessa, and Artegan—a huge, hairy man who taught unarmed combat to the lower circle initiates. The wet, chilly day had not deterred the fishermen and bargemen who worked on the River Tandy, the first people the knights encountered. The fishermen were more curious about the four Shadow Knights than the bargemen, who saw many things in their travels up and down the river. They stopped casting their nets and lines and watched the knights pass while whispering to their neighbors. Old Medril was particularly vocal.

"They're tied in with Wolen's girl's disappearance for sure. I told you that girl was in league with demons. This lot is right in it with her, mark me. No one's safe while they're around."

"Shut up, old fool. What are you going to do, tell them to leave?" said another fisherman.

Sir Mordis was aware of the villagers' fear, but ignored it. He had his senses opened, searching with his mind for one person in particular.

"This way," he said.

Ten minutes later, the knights approached a small house on the northern edge of the village. Mordis Silverhand dismounted and climbed the three, creaky steps to the porch. He knocked on the door and waited.

"Young Mordis Silverhand himself!" Olahan said as he opened the door. "And you've brought guests."

"Master Olahan, it is good to see you. You're looking well."

"I'm not and you damn well know it. I'm old. I look old, and I feel old. But come in out of the damp, your knights too. My house isn't much, but it's warm at least."

The inside of the ex-guildmaster's home was warmer than it was outside, but not by much. The store of firewood was nearly depleted and what was left was too big for the old man to handle easily. Artegan saw this and went back outside and started splitting logs so that they were small enough for Olahan to use. Then he brought in a couple larger logs and put them on the fire, so that they would burn for most of the day. He piled the smaller pieces next to the hearth.

Meanwhile, Mordis introduced the other Shadow Knights and Olahan served everyone some thin stew, bread, and opened a bottle of good Ehrian wine.

"Forgive the state of the place. I've let it go a bit these last few days."

"Master Olahan, do you know a village girl named Miralee?" Mordis asked.

"Yes, I know Miralee. She's been my only student here since I came home. What do you want with her?"

"Well, it has been suggested that she might be a candidate for the Order. I need to meet her, and her father of course."

Olahan sipped his wine from a wooden cup. He seemed to deflate.

"I'm afraid that meeting Miralee will not be possible," he said.

"Master Olahan, Janessa seems to think that the girl might be in danger if she stays here. Ganda Nery himself said that I should come for her," said Mordis.

"He did now? I always knew the girl was special. Well, Lady Janessa is probably right. I think that things would have gotten dangerous for Miralee if she had stayed. There's been too much talk. Damn that Medril. That was why her father made plans to send her away."

"Where did he send her to?" Joran asked.

"Nowhere. She ran away before he could. About five days ago. No one has seen her since. She used to come by every day. We'd play and she would help me around the house. Mordis, were you really coming to take her to Magh Moru?"

"I was. Do you know where she might have gone?"

"Not sure. It wasn't until the next morning after she left that anyone looked for her, and not too hard it seemed to me. But they found tracks leading into Tauton Woods. That was as far as any of the villagers went."

"Any of the villagers? Did someone else go farther?" Janessa asked.

"Funny thing. From what I heard there was another set of tracks that picked up Miralee's just outside of the village, a man's tracks. Rumors have been flying ever since, including that she ran off with a bargeman or a peddlar; that she has a demon lover; and that she ran off with one of your Shadow Knights. It's all hooey. I talked to Sulloe—an old soldier who lives in the village—he ran the track and said that the man's track was fresher by a couple of hours. Someone followed her into the woods, and not someone from Brown's Ford."

It was quiet in the little house for a moment as everyone thought about what Olahan had said.

"If you had to guess, where do you think she might have gone?" Mordis asked.

Olahan leaned back and looked at the ceiling.

"She loves the forests, but she would go to where there are lots of people. Miralee is a musician. One of the best natural talents I've seen. In fact, I made her my apprentice just before she left." Mordis raised an eyebrow but said nothing. "I think she would go somewhere and try to pursue musical studies."

"Magh Moru would be an obvious choice," said Artegan. "She could have been on her way there while we were on our way here."

"Possible," said Mordis.

"Or Gedorix," said Janessa. "It's the biggest city in Istey."

"What about Edain?" asked Joran. "It isn't as big as Gedorix, but it is big. And it's closer than Magh Moru or Gedorix by a week."

"There are guild run conservatories in either city," said Olahan. "I don't think I ever told Miralee that though. She used to ask me about the guildhall however."

"I'll send messages to look out for the girl," said Mordis. "We can go and look for her trail ourselves. A few days have gone by and it has rained some, but not so much as to obliterate all signs I think.

"Before we go looking for her, Master Olahan, can you tell me about her? You seem to know her better than anyone."

The old man nodded and poured himself some more wine.

"Miralee is one of the most intuitive people I've met. You've only to show her something one time for her to know it. She has a passion that she keeps hidden."

"Why?"

"This place. She doesn't fit in here. When she plays, sometimes she glows like the sun. She has an affinity for wild things. Sometimes, she simply knows things before they happen. Because of that, she has been afraid most of her life. Afraid of what people will think of her, afraid of what they might do to her. Her father is a stern man who cares for nothing out of the ordinary. She hides herself under a rigid facade. But beneath that there is something joyous and wild."

"You think a lot of her," Janessa said.

"Yes. If I'd had a child, I would have wanted someone like her. Not that she isn't capable of being just as stupid as anyone her age. This running away is proof enough of that. She can be impetuous. She has no idea what the world is really like. I hope that you can find her before she finds out the hard way."

"We will certainly try," said Mordis.

"Good. Stay here tonight. No point in setting out till morning."

"Thank you, Master Olahan."

Morning came quickly and the knights were up several hours before dawn. Master Olahan was up as well with a fire going and oatmeal cooking in a pot.

"Mordis, I have something for you," he said, holding out a roll of papers.

"What's this?"

"I mentioned yesterday that I had made Miralee my apprentice. I meant it. The only problem was that she ran away before I could give her these. They're letters of apprenticeship to the Bard's Guild and letters of admittance to the guildhall and both of the conservatories we mentioned, as well as the one in Westport. Find her and let her have them. Actually, you might have to tell her what they are, we were so busy with music, I never got around to teaching her to read. There's no school here you know. I taught her to read music, but neglected letters."

"Master Olahan, you know that I want her for the order," said Mordis Silverhand.

"Perhaps. You haven't even met her yet. Maybe you'll decide that she isn't right. And even if you do want her, shouldn't the choice be hers?"

"Maybe she can be both," said Mordis, joking.

"Maybe she can be," Olahan said seriously.

"Master Olahan, you know that Master Berint is not going to like you taking a girl as an apprentice. He's likely to do something drastic. What if they just choose to ignore your letters, not acknowledge her apprenticeship?"

"Then they would be breaking the traditions at the same time they try to protect them."

"Okay. I'll take the papers. Hopefully, we find her soon, alive and well," Mordis said.

"I pray to Bridget, Pargestia, and your Scathach that you do."

Chapter Seven

Gabriel and Miralee spoke only when necessary until that evening. She had spent the time riding behind him studying him. He gave little away and, try as she might, she was unable to read him as she could most others—he had no aura to see; she could not sense his feelings. She knew he was a warrior. His bow, his sword sheathed at his hip, and the leather and chain armor that she had glimpsed under his cloak would have told her that even if she had not seen him defeat ten bandits singlehandedly. He was handsome and courteous and seemed to know a lot more about Miralee than she knew about him.

When dusk approached, they stopped and set up camp, consisting of two tents, a small fire—she had never seen anyone get a fire started so quickly with wet wood before—all concealed by medium-sized maples and dewberry bushes. They were off the road at the back of someone's fields, on what seemed to be a private lane that had not been frequented for some time. Among the items that Shondar had packed was a pan and some dried meat. Miralee found some chives, white mustard, and goosegrass. She used this to make a stew with the meat that was not unpleasant. There were also some cheese and biscuits in the provisions and they ate some of these while they waited for the stew to cook.

"We crossed into Corin County a few miles back," Gabriel said as he finished a biscuit. "There is a village of the same name about ten miles southeast of us, along the Tandy. We could stop there tomorrow if you like."

"How far is Edain? Could we be there by tomorrow if we ride through?"

"Forty miles give or take. If we leave early, we can arrive around dusk."

"Good. We'll do that then." She leaned forward and stirred the stew with a wooden spoon. "Gabriel, who are you? I want to know why you're following me. You said that we were alike. How do you know anything about me?"

69

"Where to start?"

"I've found the beginning is always a good place."

"The beginning. All right. Let me tell you about a boy. He lived on the fringe of the Gorewood along the Tandy with his widowed mother in a small community of woodsmen. You know of the Gorewood? Of course you do, Brown's Ford is not too far from its vastness. I'm sure you know that it is a dangerous place, but there are many people who live on its edges and take their livelihoods from it. The communities are very tight knit. Unfortunately for this boy, he was unusual. He made others uncomfortable; he always seemed to know what they were thinking. Strange things happened and the boy was blamed. When he was thirteen, the others decided that they did not want the boy or his mother to live among them anymore. They were cast out, without homes, without anything to call their own.

"Then the Shadow Knight came. He found the mother and the boy and took the boy away. He did not want to go, but had no choice. The knight took him to Magh Moru. The Shadow Knights subjected him to ordeals; failure meant death. But the boy was resourceful and survived. The knights said that he had earned the right to become part of their order. Refusal, like failure had, meant death. The boy joined.

"He had a terrible problem now, because he was in fact different. He could sense things that others could not, make things happen, do things that people, especially the Shadow Knights, would consider unnatural, even though he knew that he was just as the gods had made him. But now he was in the dragon's den. The knights, if they discovered his abilities, would think he was a demon spawn or a wizard. Then they would do what Shadow Knights do with such things and kill him. For five years, the boy lived at Magh Moru and learned the Shadow Knight's trade, learned about the Order. The longer he was there the easier it became to hide. He got better at concealing his abilities, even though Shadow Knights are adept at detecting such things.

"He advanced to the Order's third circle, not yet a knight but more than a simple initiate. The boy was squired under Lady Janessa, along with another third circle named Joran.

"One night when Janessa had taken the two on a patrol near the Gorewood, not far from where the boy had grown up, she sensed a gate open close by within the confines of the forest."

"A gate?"

"A gate is basically a hole between the barrier that separates our world from the demonic realms."

"Oh."

"Anyway, they went to investigate and found that a *pyrhol* demon had come through. The demon had been summoned by a woman, a seer, who was using its affinity with flame to help her forge a sword. They weren't harming anyone, but Janessa gave the word to attack—that's what Shadow Knights do after all, kill demons and those who consort with them.

"The battle was pitched. Between the demon and the seer, Janessa and the two young men were matched. It was a dry fall and some pine trees caught fire and the flames spread quickly. The knights found themselves trapped by an inferno.

"The boy had to make a decision. Like the *pyrhol* demon, one of his gifts was the ability to control fire. He could not create it the way the demon could, but he could affect that which already existed. He chose to use his power then to clear a path by which they could flee. He saved their lives, but Janessa realized what had happened. The boy's fears came true—instead of gratitude, she offered him the point of her shadow-blade. The boy fled into the woods and only the continued threat of the demon and the seer allowed him to get away."

He fell silent, looking over the fire toward the trees.

"And that boy was you?"

"Yes. That was four years ago. I've been running and hiding ever since. I have a death sentence hanging over me. And I am afraid that you will too."

That can't be right.

"But I've met Shadow Knights—I met Janessa and Joran! They saved me. And they knew I could do things. Joran said that I created an 'aural shield.' They were very nice."

71

But they don't know about the other things I can do. What would they think then? His story is exactly why I was afraid to go to Magh Moru.

"Nice hypocrites," Gabriel said bitterly. "Shadow Knights develop certain skills, like aural shields, that help them detect, track, and fight demons and what they call 'black magic.' And controlling flame—or talking to animals, commanding them—those are the abilities of a wizard or a witch, black magic. Do you know what a familiar is?"

She did. Miralee felt Orrie stir as the horror of what Gabriel was implying sunk in.

"But Orrie isn't a familiar. I'm not a…"

"A witch. And there is the lie. So called witches and wizards aren't evil per se. They don't choose to be what they are. They are simply people that nature has made exceptional. But the order hunts them down regardless."

Pargestia! I really am a witch. But I don't want *to be a witch.*

Miralee found herself believing Gabriel's every word. His tale echoed her own fears and something in his eyes, his voice, engendered her trust. And only the tiniest niggling of her subconscious wondered why.

Miralee's wildest imaginings could not have prepared her for the reality of Edain. Home to over two hundred thousand people and several miles in both width and length, it was surrounded entirely by a wall constructed of massive logs harvested from the Gorewood. And though the wall was easily fifty feet high, buildings higher still rose up and could be seen from outside. And the people—even as dusk drew near a steady stream of people lined up at the Canal Gate to enter the city, while just as many were coming out. In all of the world, she had not envisioned there being so many people.

Gabriel must have read her face. "Edain is impressive, but Gedorix is even more so. More than twice as many call Gedorix home. The spring festival starts in a few days, so the population will swell as the merchants and festival goers come in."

Miralee was riding a sorrel gelding now. She had insisted they release Marlon Mack's horses that morning before they had left. She missed the black mare, but the gelding was a solid performer.

They were behind a man wearing a huge pack. He had dark skin and a gold earring dangled from one ear. Nearby, a bell rang—a late barge was coming in from upriver bearing a load of timber and was signaling its approach.

While Miralee and Gabriel waited, four men on horseback thundered past everyone and rode right in. They were armored in fine chainmail and carried swords and spears. On their red tunics was a gold shell in the upper left portion and a different emblem on the right; a boar's head in one case, a trident and a sheaf of wheat were the other two.

"Who were those men?" Miralee asked.

"Knights of Duke Corgan ni'Graelly's house. The town is run by a mayor, but the duke's palace is here as well, and of course he has the final say in what goes on," Gabriel explained. "The house of Graelly is probably the strongest in Istey, next to the house of Oban, King Corliss' house. Duke Corgan sponsors the Order of the Golden Sea, which has five hundred knights in its ranks. And each knight has who knows how many common soldiers of their own. He also maintains several war vessels under both his and the king's banner. I find it best to steer clear of knights of any sort."

"Will there be Shadow Knights in Edain?"

Stupid question, this city is huge. I'm sure there is just about everything in Edain.

"Yes. The Order maintains a continuous presence here. Not to worry though. There are usually no more than three Shadow Knights here at once, sometimes only one. The first thing I want to do is show you how to mask yourself from psychic perception."

"Psychic?"

"Comes from the Old Istean word, *psyche*. It means 'of the mind'—the way we can see auras and the Shadow Knights track demons. The word probably has Golgmaran origins. Most Istean does," Gabriel said.

Miralee was still confused.

"Golgmaran? I've never heard of that country."

73

"Few people have. Golgmara was one of the ancient demon cities. Golgmara was the closest to Istey, right across the water at the very end of the Bay of Florick. All of the human languages in this part of the world came from Golgmaran. That is why Istean, Ehrian, Gellese, Florian, and even Ungmarian have so many similarities," he told Miralee.

What!? That can't be right.

"If that's true, why are you the only one who knows it?"

"I'm not. But it's history so old that most have forgotten it, and those scholars who know the truth are often forced to hide it—it's an inconvenient truth for the Shadow Knights," he said matter-of-factly, but his green eyes blazed.

"What is?"

"That demons were here first. This world was stolen from them and that's why they attack men."

Miralee had more questions. The whole thing sounded absurd, but Gabriel was very compelling. In the two days that they had traveled together, she had found that everything he said, no matter how absurd, came out sounding believable.

It might just be those pretty eyes of his. It's like I'm nodding in agreement because I don't want to see disappointment in them. Why should that matter?

The fact was she was becoming rather attracted to the young man, though she hardly recognized the fact. Because of it, subconsciously she hoped that in agreeing with his point of view she would seem smarter or be somehow more appealing to him.

They arrived at the gate. A bored looking guardsman wearing red and gold with no emblems visible charged them a copper each and another for every two horses they had. They quickly paid and Miralee got her first look at the inside of Edain.

The first thing she saw was a wide canal to her right that was full of docked barges—the same barges that often came through Brown's Ford carrying goods or timber from the Gorewood. She could see beyond the canal and the river; the city lay on either side of the water at least three miles in either direction. The street that they were on, River Road, was one of the city's widest, but it was so full of people, on foot and horseback and driving carts, that it was slow going. The smell was intense.

"It stinks worse than the pigs," Miralee said, wrinkling her nose.

Gabriel laughed. "You'll get used to it. That's the aroma of concentrated humanity."

"We need to find the conservatory. I should have asked the guard."

"Don't be so anxious. It's nearly night. We should find lodgings. We'll be able to find out all we need at an inn. Besides, I want to teach you a few things before we go out and about. It'll be safer that way."

Miralee really wanted nothing more than to go to the conservatory immediately. But she could see that there was some wisdom to Gabriel's suggestion.

I've been riding for two days and haven't taken a bath since before we were attacked. I'm a mess. The bards would probably take one look at me and show me to the door—if I got through the door in the first place.

"Okay. Where to?"

"The cheapest inns are on the north side of the river. Follow me."

They stayed on River Road, passing a bridge to the right and a few cross roads to the left. Just beyond the bridge was a large open field with risers on either end. The seats were about half full and a number of people were milling about the field.

"What's happening tonight?" Gabriel asked a sweaty, portly man who lingered near the edge of the field.

"Wrestling matches, friend. Some swamp-man from Creldon has been beating opponents from Dravin to Grane. He's going to have a go at Bull Bowman tonight. Not till later though. They have a few early matches scheduled, so there's still plenty of time to get money down on Bowman."

"I think the swamp-man, as you called him, must be Moran Galt, or the one they call 'Moran the anvil.' If so, tonight might be Bowman's night to lose. I've seen them both, Galt is stronger and larger by far, though Bowman might be more experienced."

"I don't care what you say, no backwoods swamp man can take Edain's champion," the man said proudly.

"I'm sure you must be right," Gabriel rode on. He turned back to Miralee. "That fellow was right about one thing, Galt and Bowman are both masters. It will be an entertaining match. Do you like wrestling?"

Yep, nothing I love more than to watch two muscle bound idiots grope and throw each other around all night.

"I suppose so."

"Maybe if time permits, we could come to the match."

"Wonderful."

Past the games field was a large, open air market. By now most of the stands had closed and the vendors were either gone or finishing packing their wares. They turned left down the street that separated the market and the games field, which was aptly named Market Street.

The next intersection was Tilding St. and on the right, Edain Square. She gasped.

What is that?

The square was filled with various sculptures that were unlike anything she had ever before seen. Many were human figures carved from marble and perfect in every detail, like a real person had been frozen in mid-pose and turned to stone. Other sculptures were of wood or iron. They were rougher, more abstract in their depictions of their subjects, but powerful, impressive, and in two cases quite large. There was a massive iron maiden rising out of turbulent waters that rose in turn out of the globe of the world. She was the centerpiece of a great fountain that was the heart of the square. The other sculpture Miralee loved. It was an iron guitar, eight feet long, with a huge, long fingered hand reaching out for it.

"Spare a copper, milady?"

Miralee looked down and saw that a disheveled beggar had appeared alongside her. Her first impulse was to give the man some money—she was carrying more than she'd ever had in her life—then she saw that there were other beggars ahead. In the square were at least fifty of them, men mostly, but women and children too, many with bedrolls and lean-to's.

"Get away from her, vermin," Gabriel hissed and the man shrunk back.

Miralee held up her hand. "No. It's all right. She reached into her pouch and threw down a handful of copper coins. The man pounced on them and a few others who were close did likewise. Miralee and Gabriel rode on.

"If you give them money, it just encourages them to ask for more," Gabriel said when they were past the square.

"I don't care. It's terrible. In Brown's Ford there are no beggars. Everyone works, but if they can't the village makes sure that they have a place to live and food enough."

"Not here. I've even heard that the beggars in Edain are organized, they have a guild like the bards and the other trades. Most of them don't want to work; or begging is the work. It's worse during the day; they spread out all over the city. If you give one a copper, three more will show up wanting one as well."

They took a right on Ratch Road. Here the buildings were modest. Tightly packed houses lined the north side of the road while businesses dominated the south side. At the next corner was an inn.

It was a dilapidated three stories with a weathered sign that showed a mug, a bed, and an anchor.

"We're on the edge of the Shells," said Gabriel. "This is where most of the fishermen live. It's a fairly safe neighborhood; there's a guardhouse only a block away. You don't want to wander too far north though. After a few blocks the Shells ends and a neighborhood that locals call the Shanks begins. You never see the watch in the Shanks—too dangerous."

Miralee looked at the inn dubiously, but she could hear rowdy singing coming from inside, so she nodded.

"Okay, this is fine."

Gabriel grinned at her obvious hesitation.

"Don't worry. I've stayed here before. The beds are comfortable and cleaner than most places in this city. And there is a stable in the rear for our horses. Come on."

Gabriel was right. This isn't too bad.

Her room, right next to a room that Gabriel had to share with two other men, was modest but comfortable. There was another bed, unoccupied, so she had space to spread out. The innkeeper had told them that he only had hot bathwater in the mornings, so she washed in the basin. Her dress wasn't too bad, but all of her clothes needed washing.

You know, I have some money. Maybe I could afford to buy something new, she thought, remembering some of the fashions she had seen since entering the city.

Someone knocked on Miralee's door. She reached out but could sense no one—so she assumed that it must be Gabriel.

She was right.

He looked refreshed and offered her a warm smile when he saw her. Miralee flushed and felt her face grow warm.

Why am I reacting like this? No one has ever made me feel like this.

Not entirely true—she recalled Sir Joran with a similar tingle.

"I was wondering if you would like to go to the wrestling match?"

A moment ago, she had felt very tired, but Miralee suddenly felt invigorated. Still, she was dubious about attending such a contest.

"I don't know…"

Gabriel cut her off.

"Come on. We can get something to eat and listen to the gossip. I think I might place a bet; I should be able to get good odds on Galt."

Well, she *was* hungry.

"All right. But let's not stay out too late. I want to be rested tomorrow."

"Deal."

The four Shadow Knights were camped not far from the place where they had discovered the decapitated troll. Mordis Silverhand sat statue-still, eyes closed, like one in deep meditation.

He was attempting to contact Sir Dameon en'Calo, who was one hundred and fifty miles away in Edain. It took him fifteen minutes to search out that one mind so far away and make the connection. He felt his mind touch Sir Dameon's; he gave a slight nudge.

"*Dameon?*"

"*Yes.*"

"*Mordis. How are things in Edain?*"

"*It's been quiet.*"

"*Good. I have something for you.*" Quickly Mordis filled Dameon in on the Miralee situation. "*I haven't met the girl, but Ganda Nery thought that it was important that we find her. From the direction she's taken so far, she might be headed to Edain.*"

"*Understood, Grandmaster. I'll be alert for the girl.*"

"*Good. Let me know if you learn anything.*"

Mordis let go the tenuous mental connection with his knight and opened his eyes.

"I made contact with Dameon. Tomorrow, I'll contact our knights in Gedorix."

"I took a closer look at the scene at the troll's house," said Janessa. "The cut that decapitated him was interesting. It was a single cut, very clean, made with an instrument sharp enough to have been a shadow blade. He had no other signs of injury."

"So whoever killed him caught him entirely by surprise and made a perfect attack," Artegan said.

"Yes. And that person is trailing Miralee."

"Who could it be? And what do they want with her?" Mordis wondered aloud.

"One of ours?" asked Joran. "A knight-errant who just happened to sense in her what we sensed?"

"That's the best case scenario. But I have a feeling that he isn't one of ours," Mordis said. There was nothing about this that he liked at the moment. "Let's find this girl and get back to Magh Moru."

The games field, called Gunnar's Field by the locals, was bustling, nearly full when Miralee and Gabriel arrived. Two men, evidently local lads, grappled in a ring set up in the middle of the field. People were clustered around and packed onto the risers. There was still some time until the main event.

"Wait here," Gabriel told her. "I'm going to see about placing a wager."

Miralee, left alone, felt crowded, closed in by the weight of the people. Uncomfortable, she began to ease back toward Market St. where the throng was less dense.

A carriage stopped on the road. As its occupants climbed down, the crowd parted. Miralee, overwhelmed by the carnival atmosphere, didn't notice and was standing alone and in the way as the finely dressed people came up from behind her. The first inkling she had that someone was there was when a rough hand shoved her, hard. The force propelled her to the ground, right into a cold puddle of mud.

"Get out of the way, you slag! There's real people coming through," said a harsh, masculine voice. Cruel feminine laughter rang in her ears.

"Keep her on the ground," said a haughty, girl's voice. "I can step on her to keep my shoes from getting muddy."

Miralee turned her head and got her first look at Emer ni'Oban.

Chapter Eight

She was beautiful, but with cruel, emerald eyes set in a face framed by long auburn hair. The mocking girl was petite and Miralee's age, or perhaps one or two years older. She wore an expensive green satin gown. Miralee did not yet know who Emer ni'Oban—the king's niece—was, though she was already sorry to have met her.

She was with a group that consisted of three other girls and four young men, not including the obvious employees—the drivers, the two guardsmen—one of whom was responsible for pushing her into the mud—and the foot servant. Two of the girls were laughing hysterically; one looked upset.

Miralee began to pull herself up, only to be shoved back down by the booted foot of the guardsman.

"Where you going now? You just stay still till the lady's past," he said.

"Emer, you're terrible," said one of the young men. "There's no mud on this side."

"Yes, but I want to walk on *this* side," said the young woman.

"Emer, stop it. Leave the poor thing be. Come on, let's go to our seats," said a black-haired girl

"Nonsense, Peri. This low-bred slut is happy to do this little service for her betters," Emer said.

"You…are not a nice person," the girl, Peri, understated. "I'm taking the carriage home. I'll send it back to get you."

Emer ignored her and playfully kicked at Miralee's side with a dainty toe.

She's really going to step on me?!

Whatever Emer's intentions, she never got the chance to realize them as Orrie chose that moment to emerge from Miralee's pocket. The rat leapt up onto Emer's dress. He ran up her back and under her long hair. Emer began to dance and shriek.

"It's biting me! Get it off! Get it off! It bit my face!"

No one was looking at Miralee, so she sprang to her feet and ran into the crowd. A number of people witnessed the noble girl's cruel treatment of her, and even if none of them had dared to intervene, the crowd opened up and admitted her then closed immediately. Someone tossed a shawl over her head, hiding her blond hair.

"Go on, girl. Get out of here," someone said.

She did not have to be told twice. As she ran, Miralee futilely searched the crowd for a glimpse of Gabriel.

This is his fault! He brought me here! I didn't want to come. Fine. I know the way; I'll go without him.

Cold and alone, with mud covering her dress, her face, and in her hair, she trudged down Tilding Street about as miserable as she had ever been before. She realized that she had lost track of Orrie.

I left him back there. It's the second time he's saved me and I just left him.

She began to cry, her tears creating little clean paths through the mud caked on her face. Even though she knew the general direction of the inn in Shells, distracted as she was, it was understandable that she missed the turn down Market Street. She passed Edain Square. This time, the beggars left her alone.

By missing her turn, Miralee found herself walking along the northern edge of the wharf. It was busy as sailors, footpads, and prostitutes ambled up and down the streets and lurked in the alleys. Rowdy songs could be heard coming from several different directions. For just a moment, she was turned around and unsure of the direction of her lodging. Lingering too close to the dark edge of an alley, she sensed the presence of men there, but did not necessarily see them as a threat until they grabbed her off of the street and pulled her into the alley.

"What's this? A lost bird?" said one unshaven, gin-soaked lout.

"A mud hen by the look of her," said a second man.

"I'd say we have a bit of fun with her, but look at her. I'd need a bath for sure and it's only the second week of the month," A third man said, slurring his words.

"Hey girl, didn't no one tell you the wharf's a dangerous place to them that don't know it, especially after dark? You have any money on you then? Some pretty trinkets, perhaps? Give up what you've got in your pockets and we might be inclined to let you go," the first man said.

Stupid! To let myself get so overwhelmed. I walked right into all of this. They might just rob me, but I think number one here has more in mind. If I screamed would anyone help? Probably not.

Sudden danger snapped her out of her self-pity. She had all of her earnings from Sperry's Knoll and what Shondar had given her, but she was damned if she was just going to hand it over to these drunk ruffians.

"Please, sirs, don't hurt me," she said in a trembling voice. "I have some money. You can have it all."

She slipped a dirty hand into her pocket, but not the one that held her money pouch—instead she found the hilt of her knife. Two men were in front of her, but only one behind her, blocking the way back to Tilding St.

"Good, good. Give it up and you can go. We're reasonable enough men," said the first. He stepped closer. Miralee backed up, bumping into number three behind her.

"Oh. I'm sorry sir. Here's what I have. You can have it all."

She yanked out her knife. Before it could register with the men, she slashed at the man to her rear. Her blade caught him across the cheek. He howled and she bolted for the street. A hand grabbed her dress; she yanked it and made a wild swipe with her knife. She heard cursing and tearing cloth, then she was free.

"Get that bitch back here! She cut me!" said one of the men, presumably number three.

Suddenly, she was back on Tilding Street where there were people and the occasional street lamp. Maddened, two of the men followed her out of the alley. Miralee looked over her shoulder and saw them—and ran right into Gabriel.

"They're trying to rob me," she said in explanation.

The men stopped abruptly. She got her first good look at them and was unimpressed—they were hardly cleaner than the beggars in Edain Square, hardly cleaner than she was. Gabriel had his cloak thrown back and the men eyed his sheathed sword. They had been looking for easy prey—not this. Without a word, they turned and ran back into the alley.

Gabriel moved to follow them.

"No, let them go," Miralee said. "I just want to go back to the inn."

"I'm sorry about what happened at the wrestling. I shouldn't have left you."

"No, it really wasn't your fault. I should be able to be alone for ten minutes without getting into trouble. If not, how am I going to make it here? It was that girl—they called her Emer—she really caused the trouble."

"I heard about it. That was Emer ni'Oban, the niece of our good King Corliss. She attends school at Delwyn College in Magh Moru, but must be on break to be slumming in Edain."

"How do you know all of that?"

"Ah, the tales people tell. Actually I just picked that up in snippets from the crowd at the field. I learned that she is the guest of Duke Corgan's daughter, Peri ni'Graelly, but the Lady Peri apparently was forced into it by her father. We could go back and hear more of the gossip about the wealthy."

"No," she said. "That's all right, really. Gabriel, I lost Orrie."

"I'm sorry. If it's any consolation, folks were saying a rat bit Emer ni'Oban's cheek hard enough to draw blood. Orrie, I assume?"

"Yes, he was protecting me," Miralee said miserably. "I hope he's not hurt."

"He seemed to be a rather intelligent rodent. I'm sure he escaped."

"I hope you're right. Did you make your bet at least?"

"Yes, as a matter of fact I did. I had just found someone to take it when the commotion broke out. When Galt wins, I'll go back tomorrow and collect."

"I want to find the conservatory tomorrow," she said.

Gabriel stopped and looked at her.

"Miralee, I know that the conservatory is very important to you, but I think we should wait just a few days before you go there."

"Why?"

"Tonight has proven that Edain is a dangerous place, not even taking the Shadow Knights into account, and we must take them into account. I want to teach you to mask yourself and a few tricks that will help you defend yourself before we venture out again."

"If you thought that, why did you take me out tonight?"

"I know. It was a mistake. Let's not make the same mistake twice."

Miralee stuck out her lip and began walking again.

"I'll think about it. I have to get to the conservatory. It's all that's important."

"Just a few days is all I ask. Besides, don't put all of your hopes on the conservatory. There are other ways to practice and perform music. What if they won't let you in?"

Miralee shook her head. "I'm not going to think about that possibility."

They reached the inn. The common room was still busy. Miralee and Gabriel slipped in through a side door and climbed the stairs to the second floor. At her door, he stopped her as she was about to go inside.

"So you're just going to bed now?"

"Umm, yes. After I wash. If you haven't noticed, I'm filthy."

Gabriel stepped closer and took her hand. He was so close she could feel the warmth of his body.

"Dirty or no, you're still the most beautiful woman in this entire city," he said.

Her heart was pounding and heat colored her face.

An hour ago, I was furious at him. What in Pargestia's name has come over me? This is stupid; I ran away so I wouldn't get saddled with some man.

Gabriel leaned forward and kissed her. Miralee stiffened for a second, surprised, then closed her eyes and yielded. When they finally separated, she was breathing heavy, and he was now nearly as dirty as she was. Miralee looked down at him and giggled.

"It's a small price to pay to kiss you," he said. "Good night."

Gabriel turned and left, leaving Miralee melted against the door. *Whatever it is that's come over me,* she thought, *it isn't too bad.*

85

Gabriel returned to his room after kissing Miralee. The warmth he felt had little to do with any real affection for the girl, though she was certainly pretty, an added bonus that made his job of winning her loyalty and trust tolerable. No, his real satisfaction stemmed from the ease with which he was accomplishing this task that his demanding mother had laid on him. Despite her warnings, everything was working out as he had planned.

His room was empty. Sharing the room was inconvenient. He would have to persuade the two men, strangers to each other, to check out tomorrow. And then perhaps a word with the innkeeper to dissuade him from renting the bed for the duration of Gabriel's stay. He'd pay the man for the beds of course, but he would also have a frank discussion to impress the man with his need for privacy.

It was good of his roommates to be out now, for it made things easier. He reached into his pocket and drew out a black disk of volcanic glass. It was perfectly smooth and reflected his image as well as any mirror.

Gabriel closed his eyes and concentrated.

"Mother? Can you hear me?"

It took a moment before he felt a response, like a long whispered sigh. He opened his eyes and saw that the glass had turned cloudy with a moving, heavy mist that slowly coalesced into his mother's form.

"I'm here, my son," his mother said. "What do you want?"

His mother, Delia, looked a mess. Her black hair was wild. Her firm, nude flesh was covered with a sheen of sweat. Doubtless, he had interrupted his mother in the sating one of her many appetites.

"I wanted to tell you how I am progressing," he said.

His mother waited for him to go on. After a moment, her black eyes flashed bored annoyance and she asked, "Well?"

"I have been completely successful. The girl, Miralee is her name, trusts me and is already falling in love with me. She has some ability, but she's untrained. I've been able to manipulate her emotions to the point where she will open her mind to me. I'll be able to bring her to you soon."

Delia was skeptical.

"You are overconfident as always. I told you that I sensed more than garden variety talent in this one. Her potential may be greater than your own. And she is of our lineage. Be careful with her."

"You sound worried. She is a simple farm girl. It has only taken me a few days to cause her to doubt what she has believed since childhood. A few more and she will embrace everything I tell her with her whole heart. I am going to start training her. The more she lets me into her mind, the more I will own her."

"Where are you now?"

"Edain."

"I see. No doubt you are already drinking and gambling," said Delia.

"I haven't had a drink since I left home," he protested, thinking guiltily of his wager.

"See that you don't. You are a good son and useful to me, but you are too impulsive." She changed the subject. "There are always Shadow Knights in Edain. Have you had any trouble?"

"We've only just arrived, but I will handle any trouble that comes up. I am going to begin teaching her to mask herself. And by the time we encounter a Shadow Knight, she will see them for the enemies that they are."

"Excellent. I am counting on you, my son. Don't let me down. Keep me informed."

The image of Delia faded and the disk turned black again. Gabriel felt unsatisfied, yet unsurprised. His mother was always too critical of him. Still, he had hoped that she would seem happier about his news.

From below, music and laughter still rose up from the common room. It was early. One drink would hurt nothing.

Miralee awoke to a pleasant surprise—Orrie, alive and unharmed, was asleep curled up against her chest.

She took a hot bath that morning and then she and Gabriel went to the market. The sky was an ominous slate gray with a strong wind coming in from the ocean.

87

That looks bad. Hopefully the weather will hold off long enough for me to buy some new clothes.

They were in luck. Miralee bought three new dresses and a pair of low boots. Because of the imminent weather, the merchants were eager to make a few sales and were willing to bargain. Even after her purchases, she still had more than half of the money that she had brought from Sperry's Knoll.

While they were out, Gabriel asked around and learned that Galt had indeed beaten Bowman last night after a match that had lasted nearly an hour. Gabriel led Miralee back to the wharf. He went into a dingy tavern on the waterfront, leaving Miralee standing in front, and collected his winnings.

By the time they arrived back at the inn at Shells, the wind had picked up a bite of cold, and big lazy droplets began to fall. A clap of thunder suddenly spilt the sky and the lazy rain became a torrent. They took lunch by the fireplace to warm up.

When they finished, Gabriel took Miralee's hand, sending a little thrill through her. She leaned in close, enjoying his clean, musky scent.

"We should get to work," he said after a while.

"Work?"

"I'm going to teach you to mask yourself, remember?"

"Oh, of course."

"Let's go to my room. The men who were sharing it with me checked out this morning."

Miralee nervously followed him upstairs to his room.

Stop it, she chided herself. *You're acting like one of those silly cows from home. You came here to do something more, not to fall in love with the first man to come along. What's so special about him anyway? He left you alone to be abused by that spoiled noble girl. He gambles. He's arrogant.*

"Did you hear what I said?" Gabriel said.

"What?" she realized that he had been speaking to her. "No, what did you say?"

"You must learn to pay attention to me," he said, punctuating it with a look that caused Miralee to feel a stab of guilt.

"I'm sorry. Go on."

"Have a seat," Gabriel said, gesturing to one of the three beds.

She sat demurely on the edge. Gabriel pulled up a chair and sat down across from her.

"As you know, everything generates an aura, invisible to most people, but not to people like us. A person's aura can change, but still is a unique identifier of that person."

"What do you mean?"

"Well, think of a person's face. As a person ages, their face changes. But even with those changes one's face is still recognizable as their own."

"Okay, I understand."

"A Shadow Knight can sense and track a particular aura at a great distance, unless one knows how to hide. That's what I'm going to show you."

For the next hour they practiced aura masking. With Gabriel's guidance, Miralee found it rather simple to draw in her aura so that it was invisible, even to the heightened senses of Shadow Knights. Encouraged by her success, she pressed Gabriel to show her more.

"Well, except for your abilities with animals, I don't know where your talents lie."

"What do you mean," she asked. "What kind of talents are there?"

"Well, there are both low and high order abilities. Low order abilities are possessed by most with the psychic gift, even Shadow Knights utilize some low order abilities. They include heightened sensory perception, aural manipulation, empathic abilities, and the like. High order abilities are rarer. I can control fire, which is known as pyrokinesis. You can communicate with animals. I've heard of people who could move objects with their mind—telekinesis—and others who could read the thoughts of others—telepathy. Seers possess a high order talent to see potential futures. Some people can influence weather, possess the minds of others, levitate—there are any number of high order abilities evident in old texts."

"Where do these powers come from? Why do some people possess them and others don't?" Miralee asked.

"It's our heritage."

"I don't understand."

"In time you will."

Gabriel sat next to her on the bed and kissed her. When his lips touched hers, her earlier misgivings were forgotten. She felt a flame burst to life inside of her. Pushing him back on the bed, Miralee shocked herself by straddling his well-muscled body. She kissed him hard, as a passion that she had previously only felt for music consumed her.

The rain continued the next day, so Gabriel suggested they refrain from going to the conservatory for one more day.

In the inn, Miralee learned that the conservatory was across the river near Lilting Street. She was still anxious to go, despite the distraction of Gabriel. But she allowed herself to be persuaded as a cold northeaster continued to pour rain in sheets upon Edain.

For Gabriel, Miralee's continued insistence was evidence that his manipulation of the girl's emotions was not complete. Though she obviously felt affection and trust for him, when he was not exerting a good deal of energy in *making* her feel those things, she still remembered her previous ambitions. He had to make her forget them. Ultimately, he wanted her to come with him willingly to his home in the Gorewood Forest—back the way she had come from. If he had been a truly subtle person, perhaps he could have convinced her that the threat here in Edain was so great that they had no choice but to flee immediately. But to his mother's dismay, Gabriel wasn't terribly subtle. Oh, he could be subtle when the need arose, but generally he was impatient.

That impatience led him to the decision to go inside of Miralee's mind and make it so that she could not even think of disagreeing with him. Even though, in theory, his plan meant that his own mind might be vulnerable to *her*, he did not see it as a risky endeavor. She was untrained still, and despite his mother's warnings, he did not view her as any kind of threat. She was a farm girl who could talk to animals—she couldn't even *read*!

"Miralee, I want to do something and I'll need for you to trust me. I think it will be invaluable in learning your potential and helping you to the next level," he said.

"I trust you. What do you need me to do?"

Too easy, he thought.

"Just sit back and relax. Let your mind open. When you feel a slight nudge, like a pressure on your thoughts, don't resist. Yield and invite me in. That's all."

Gabriel watched the fair-haired girl close her eyes. His inner eye registered the subtle changes of her emotions and thoughts as she relaxed. He did likewise—it took him just a second—and he sent his consciousness out like a probe into hers.

He felt only the slightest resistance as he merged with Miralee's mind. Her mind was open. He felt her love, her trust. Underneath that was fear—understandable based on the plunge into the unknown that she had taken. But her courage far outweighed her fears.

And there was her passion.

It was a massive river, hidden even from herself after a lifetime of repression. It came out in the music, but that was only a reflection of something greater. Gabriel felt his confidence slip just a little.

He tried to go deeper, but the going was not so easy.

Miralee's subconscious was locked up and tightly guarded as any treasure. He had to gain access to her most inner thoughts and emotions and manipulate these to get the results that he needed.

He sent his probe forward into the black mask that guarded her subconscious—and was rebuffed.

"Miralee, you have to yield to me."

"I am," she replied, thinking truthfully that she was doing just that.

Very well, he thought to himself so that she could not hear it, *I'll just have to break through. It should be no trouble for me.*

Miralee had no clue about Gabriel's struggle to access her deepest mind. Her experience with the merging was wholly different from what she had expected. In truth, she'd had no idea what to expect, but thought it would be more intrusive, like being examined by a healer. Instead, it was a sharing, intimate like kissing, only more so. She knew that she was supposed to passively let Gabriel do what he needed to do. He hadn't said anything about Miralee poking around in *his* mind.

But he never said not to.

It was right there after all, as close to her as her own thoughts.

I'll just take a little peek.

And in an instant she could see and feel what was on the surface of Gabriel's mind.

His thoughts were unsurprising. She felt his deep affection and goodwill for her. Bit and pieces of other thoughts and images floated around, including a memory of being attacked by Janessa and Joran. Everything she saw confirmed what he had already told her. Of course, she was only seeing what he had wanted her to see, though she did not know it. Realizing that Miralee might not be able to resist examining his mind, Gabriel had packed his surface thoughts and emotions with what he felt she would expect and want to see. He figured doing so would be more than ample protection. He planned to be in and out and, when done, to gain complete control of her.

He was wrong.

I know all of this already, she thought. *I want to see the* real *Gabriel. I won't pry too much. I'll just look for a second.*

Gently, she felt around and realized that there were many layers hiding under his surface thoughts. With an ease that would have astonished Gabriel, she drew back the top layer like a summer blanket and peered at what was underneath.

Unlike the saccharine surface emotions, what she exposed confused and disturbed her. Images and feelings flashed through her like a jumbled slideshow.

A dark house in a darker forest. A woman with glowing eyes and coal hair. A handsome demon with carnelian skin. Love. Resentment.

She saw herself, distorted through his eyes, appearing dirty and stupid. Lust. Contempt.

Frustration. A longing to drink to intoxication. The amply endowed barmaid that Miralee remembered seeing in the common room of the inn.

Gabriel taking the letters that Shondar had given her from her bag and reading them. Surprisingly, seeing them through his mind, she understood the words. After reading them through, he refolded them, and then slipped them into the pocket of his cloak.

"What are you doing!?" Gabriel's voice shouted inside of her head as he suddenly realized what was happening.

The connection broke. When she opened her eyes, Gabriel was standing over her, his eyes aglow with murderous rage.

Chapter Nine

The rage left Gabriel's eyes as quickly as it had appeared and was replaced by his typical warmth.

"Miralee, you're disoriented by what you saw. To the untrained, the subconscious can be a confusing place. Dreams and fantasies can seem like reality. That's why I wanted you to just relax and do nothing. You know I care about you. You felt that, didn't you, Mir?"

"I'm not that confused," she said, rising quickly from the bed. "Where is my letter? Why did you take it?"

"I took it to keep it safe, to protect you," he explained, putting the force of his will behind his words. "You're safe with me. You trust me."

Yes, I can trust him. I love him. He's just trying to help me. No! He's trying to do something to my mind. I feel strange, out of control. Until I know what he's done, I can only trust myself. Gods! In just a few days time, I almost forgot what brought me here.

"Give me the letter back," she said with her hand held out. "I'll keep it safe myself."

She felt his anger flash—*he's not masking*—then it was quickly tamped down. Gabriel smiled a lopsided smile.

"Of course," He produced the sheaf of papers. Miralee snatched it from his hand.

"Miralee, let's talk about what happened. I can help it make sense."

"No. Not right now. I want to be alone. I'll be in my room. Respect my wishes and stay away for now."

She did not wait for a reply. Miralee pushed open the door and almost fell into the hallway. She reached her own door and drew out her key. Her fingers tingled, and she fumbled it, caught it, and managed to open her door.

The walls of her room were constricting. Miralee's head buzzed like it was full of mosquitoes. She could hear dozens of voices whispering in her head. Whatever Gabriel had done had affected her in some lingering way. Long repressed parts of her mind had awakened. The effect was overwhelming.

Everything in the room was visible, though there was no lamp lit. The walls, bed, floorboards, everything produced an aura of some sort. The most brilliant was Orrie—the rat was surrounded by a small but sharp white radiance. He was on her bed, standing on hind legs and watching her. She went to the bed and held out her hand. He jumped on and ran up her sleeve and alit on her shoulder. Miralee sat on the bed's edge and held her head in her hands, trying to push down the sensations that tormented her.

This isn't working. I've got to relax. Panicking won't help me.

She took a deep breath and exhaled slowly. Miralee lay back on the bed and closed her eyes. She still heard the cacophony of whispers, but she centered herself and let them blow around her like a strong wind. Eventually, she became used to them as she continued to breathe in and out. They were, she realized, the voices and thoughts of nearby persons, the bulk of them being the revelers in the inn's common room. She could not separate them out, but they no longer seemed threatening, and when she opened her eyes the radiance of the room had receded to a tolerable level.

The walls still seemed too close, so Miralee decided to go out. She debated leaving the inn entirely, taking her things and just going, away from Shells and away from Gabriel. She decided against it. Her feelings toward him were confused. She realized that he had been affecting her somehow, but she felt clearheaded now. The images and feelings that she had experienced in his mind had been disturbing, but they had been no more than flashes without context. He had an agenda, of that she was certain, but she was equally certain that he knew something about her that she did not herself know. She wanted to know what that was—only not right now. She'd had enough of Gabriel for one evening. She would talk to him tomorrow.

Miralee slung her guitar over her shoulder and put Orrie into her pocket. She checked and made sure that her *duduk*, her knife, and her money pouch were all in place. She did not think it would be wise to take all of her money. With her knife she loosened a floorboard under her bed, and deposited half of her remaining funds carefully underneath it.

In the hallway, she tiptoed past Gabriel's room. Belatedly, she realized that she was not masking as he had taught her and once she was on the stairs, she paused to do so. She had not felt his presence inside of his room. He could have been masking himself, he usually did, but she just had a feeling that he was not inside.

It was dinnertime and the common room was fuller than she had yet seen it, probably owing to the weather. Still she found a small table along the wall opposite the main entrance. Scanning the room, Miralee did not see Gabriel here either.

The room was noisy, and filled with smoke and the smell of fish and the sweat of frustrated fishermen and merchants.

The thoughts in my head are louder down here, probably because I'm closer to people. Just stay calm. It's really no different than the rest of the noise in the room.

That wasn't entirely true.

A serving girl approached Miralee's table. She recognized her as the same woman who had served them lunch yesterday. As she came close the woman's thoughts came unbidden to Miralee.

Wonderful, it's the slut. Aima told me that she's been spending a lot of time in that handsome man's room over the last two days. Not even married. Disgraceful tramp, the woman thought.

But what she did was smile and say, "Hi, honey. What can I get you?"

"Umm, nothing. Thanks. I was just leaving."

Good, whores should stick to the wharf.

Miralee got up and nearly ran to the door. She pushed it open and stepped outside. Night had fallen. The air was cool and refreshing. The rain had receded to a mere mist. Without really knowing where she was going, Miralee began to walk.

Shondar, leaning heavily on a crutch, hobbled to where the knights sat. With some difficulty, he placed his splinted leg on the bench in front of him. When he was finally situated, he let out a long breath and reached for a cup of wine.

"Forgive the production, but I am afraid that the leg won't be right for at least a month."

Mordis held up his hand.

"Apologies are unnecessary. You did not have to come here. We would have happily visited you," Mordis said.

"Nonsense. I'm not going to let this slow me down. Well, maybe a little."

"Mr. Mack told us that you got that injury escorting Miralee Verity when she left Sperry's Knoll."

Shondar sipped his wine. He nodded.

"Yes. It was five days ago. I was going to escort her to Edain. I planned to take her to the conservatory there. But before we went more than ten miles, we were set upon by bandits."

Mordis frowned.

"Bandits in Graelly?"

"Unfortunately, Sperry County has been plagued for some time now. It would have ended badly for us, except a young warrior came to our assistance. Miralee accepted his offer to travel with her to Edain. I didn't like it. We knew nothing about him, except that his timely intervention certainly saved our lives. But I was injured and couldn't continue. And Miralee couldn't return here."

"You had never seen this warrior before?" Mordis asked.

"He had stayed here in the inn the same night as Miralee. Actually, he admitted that he had been following her since she had left home. He said that they were the same. I don't really know what he meant by that."

"What did this warrior look like?" Artegan asked.

"He wasn't large. About the same size and age as you," he said, indicating Joran. "He had dark, curly hair and vivid green eyes. He said that his name was Gabriel."

A look passed between the knights.

"Gabriel," Mordis said.

"That's not good," said Joran.

"No. It certainly is not," the Grandmaster agreed.

"I seem to be at a disadvantage," said Shondar. "Who is Gabriel?"

Mordis refilled his cup from the wine bottle that Marlon had left them.

"Gabriel was once a member of my order. A few years ago, he betrayed his oath, and he tried to kill two of my knights—Joran here, and Janessa."

"Gods, what possessed him?"

"He became a demon-worshipper. It ran in his family."

No one said anything for a long moment. They could hear the laughter and talk of the tavern patrons, but in the small, private room that Marlon had provided it was quiet.

"I studied as an apprentice at Magh Moru," Shondar said. "I probably saw him." He poured himself some more wine. "We're going to need another bottle."

Joran stood up. "I'll get it."

"Shondar," Janessa said, "you said that Miralee couldn't come back here. Why was that?"

"Rupert en'Sperry," he said.

Shondar shifted uncomfortably in his chair. He winced as he re-adjusted his broken leg. Then he settled back and began to tell them everything he knew about Rupert en'Sperry—Alissa Mack and the other missing and murdered girls, the reports of his sadism, the suspicious bandit activity, his interest in Miralee, the information that Gabriel said he had gotten from the captured bandit. The faces of the Shadow Knights became grimmer with each revelation.

"You've lived here for several years," Janessa said to the bard. "Do you really believe that the Earl's son is not only murdering young women, but is actually behind the bandit activity in the region?"

He nodded. "I think that it is a very strong possibility. What's more, another girl disappeared two days ago. A fair-haired local girl named Cassie Brahdie. She was employed as a maid at the Sperry manor. The Earl has suggested that she might have run off with a lover, but her parents insist that there was no one. She was known as responsible and moral young woman."

Joran returned with two more bottles. Every cup was ready for a refill. He looked around at the expressions in the room.

"What did I miss?"

"I'll fill you in later," Janessa told him. To Shondar, she said, "But what of the earl? What has he done?"

"Earl Rendel is an old man now, in his seventies. I fear he is somewhat addled. I don't think he has any knowledge of his son's activities—he has increased patrols on the roads and commissioned investigations into the murders, but nothing has come from any of it. Though if something was uncovered, I think he would strongly resist the idea that Rupert might be guilty of any wrongdoing. He thinks the world of his son. The Earl's oldest son is…well, he's a dullard. It's no secret. Everyone expects that Rupert will be the real power here when Earl Rendel is gone."

"All the more reason to try and deal with him now," Artegan said. The others looked dubious. "Of course, there is no evidence of any sort of demonic involvement. We could ask Duke Corgan, or even King Corliss to look into it."

"Yes," agreed Janessa. "If Gabriel has a hold of Miralee, we have to try to find them at once. That is our business, not investigating some rural noble's son, no matter how distasteful his activities might be."

Mordis smoothed his beard between his thumb and index finger while he weighed Janessa's words. He shook his head.

"You are right. It is even more imperative that we find Miralee. But at the same time, I can't in good conscience ride away from the possibility that a member of one of Istey's noble families is preying on the people he is supposed to protect. It is rare for the order to be involved in this sort of matter, but a there is a clause in the order's charter that empowers me as the Grandmaster to investigate and arrest nobility under certain circumstances, even if they aren't directly involved in demon-worship or black magic."

"There is?" Joran asked, surprised.

"Indeed. When the charter was drafted, during the the reign of the Whitehands, corruption of all types was rampant within the ranks of nobility. King Trell ni'Dravin, though he wasn't yet king then, added a catch all clause in the Order's charter to allow those first Shadow Knights to ferret out the serpents among the ruling class."

"What do you suggest then?" asked Artegan.

"We are going to handle both problems. Janessa, you and Joran will continue to track Miralee. Hopefully, they will have continued onto Edain, but Gabriel could have taken her anywhere. Artegan and I will stay here and see what we can find out about Rupert en'Sperry. When we are through, we will rejoin you."

"All right, but I'm not thrilled about splitting up like this if Gabriel is involved," Joran said.

"Don't worry about Gabriel," said Janessa. "I've wanted to get my hands around his pretty little neck for years."

"Hopefully, you'll get your chance," Mordis said. "Rest tonight. You'll leave at dawn."

Miralee wandered around the streets of Edain for an hour. Despite the miserable weather of the last few days, the streets of the Shells were busy. She could still hear the whispered thoughts of the people as they passed by. On Fenchel Street, she passed a tavern and, hearing music, considered going inside but quickly decided against it. The air felt too good.

She saw a shabbily dressed young woman escorting two dirty boys of ten or so. They were walking toward her at a slow pace. As they drew closer, the two boys ran forward, laughing and horse playing with one another. Miralee started to smile at their antics. Then she caught their thoughts.

They mean to pick my pocket! Why, she's not even their mother!

And yet she still felt sorry for them. The boys were hungry and tired. The woman had sore feet among a variety of other pains. A picture of a grizzled-looking older man was prominent in the woman's thoughts. She was afraid of him. He apparently beat her if she didn't return to him with an adequate sum of money.

None of this was Miralee's problem. But being privy to their thoughts and feelings made her feel as if she knew them. She didn't know what to do.

They had nearly reached her. The two boys would run by on either side, run around her, jostling her playfully. In the process they would dip their hands into her pockets and steal her valuables. She could see their intent clearly. The boy on the left, a grubby redhead in badly patched clothes, had already guessed where she was carrying her money pouch.

Then she thought of an idea—if she could hear them, maybe she could make them hear her. Concentrating on the connection that she had with their thoughts, Miralee tried to project her own thoughts at the trio.

"No! Don't steal from her! She's a poor target! Not a par on her."

The woman and the two boys paused on the sidewalk. Three heads jerked like a fly had tickled their ears. Three brows furrowed in puzzlement. They turned to each other, not one telling either of the other two what they had just heard. And not one of them commented on why they let the young woman who had, a moment before, been their intended mark pass by unmolested.

Miralee, as she walked by them, could not help offer them a wink and a smile. They simply gaped before moving off in the opposite direction to find a new target.

Miralee turned south toward the river. She found herself on Market Street, near Edain Square. She could smell the fires of the beggars and see the glows ahead. And she could feel their misery as well.

"Miss, can you spare some copper?" asked a matchstick of a man as she reached the edge of the square.

She had something else in mind. It had been days since she had played. And while tavern audiences were enthusiastic, she wanted to play now for the wretches who lived in the square.

"I'll give you a few coins, if you'll escort me to the center of the square." She showed him her guitar. "I was hoping to play a few songs."

"Here?"

He was surprised but curious, and with the promise of some money, it was a small request.

The man led Miralee through the square, warning off other beggars who tried to approach her. Still, by the time they reached the middle, there was a sizeable crowd following them.

In the heart of Edain Square stood a statue of Sir Blackthorn, the first Shadow Knight. It was atop a platform six feet tall. Several stairs led up to it. Miralee gave her escort a silver par, then she climbed up to the highest step.

"Hello," she said to the fifteen or so onlookers. Others were meandering over to see what was going on.

Without any further introduction, she began to play her guitar. She played "Far Green Hills." She played it slowly, seeing the images of the lush, rolling forests and infusing her words with all of the emotion that she could. The square was completely silent, except for Miralee's music and the soft, shuffling footsteps of the beggars and homeless people who continued to crowd around.

She played another ballad. This one about the ill-fated ship, Cowerie, and a young sailor on his first voyage. Miralee's audience was rapt, transported—they could feel the young man's fear and courage, hear the thunder claps, and feel the tremendous power of the waves as the ship was tossed.

"The Golden Fish" lightened the mood next. Miralee was totally relaxed. Riding a wave of building joy, she cut loose.

Sergeant of the Watch Kalin was showing a new recruit his beat. As they drew near Edain Square, he sensed that something was amiss. Normally at night, the beggars were spread throughout the square, two or three to a camp. Tonight, the center of the square was mobbed with people. The beggars had abandoned their camps and accounted for over half of the crowd. But a substantial number of respectable—or at least semi-respectable—citizens were present in large numbers with more steadily trickling in.

Liquid notes seeped into his ears and he found himself walking toward the source. As Sergeant Kalin drew a little closer, he saw a goddess standing on a step in the middle of the throng. She was unnaturally tall and bathed in a golden nimbus. As she sang images formed in the air above the square.

Sergeant Kalin had no idea if the images were real or only in his head. It didn't matter. He stared, mesmerized as a giant, golden carp danced high then dove down to swim just out of reach of the crowd. There was a woman with sad eyes and a lost love. He didn't notice when Miralee switched instruments—he, and everyone else present,

102

was transported to faraway castles, saw the carnage of epic battles, and the miracle of the birth of a single flower.

When the music finally stopped, he had no idea of how much time might have passed. He realized that he was crying. Sergeant Kalin tried without success to find his recruit. It was no wonder; there had to be a thousand people packed into the square. It took almost a minute for the spell to break and the wild cheering and clapping to come. Sergeant Kalin looked back to the statue of Blackthorn, half expecting it to be empty—the musician, obviously a goddess, taken back up to wherever it was she had come from. But she was there still, no longer a goddess, now just a girl.

People began to climb the stairs to her, crowding around her. The press of people became alarming. Kalin was a sergeant of the Watch; he should get her out of there.

Ahead and to his right, Kalin saw his recruit, a young local named Bent Goins. Watchman Goins was a little slow-minded, but he was a hulking figure. Sergeant Kalin pushed his way forward until he could tap the recruit on the back.

"Watchman Goins, we need to get up on that stage in a hurry. Clear a path."

Clearing a path was something that Bent Goins excelled at. Bellowing, "Watch coming through, make a hole!" and tossing those too slow to obey aside, Watchman Goins led the way and in a moment they were on Blackthorn's pedastal.

"Back up! Back up! Give her room!" Kalin ordered those closest to Miralee. "Are you all right, miss?"

"Yes. Thank you. I'm not sure what happened."

Sergeant Kalin didn't know what or who Miralee was, but she looked like a young lady in need of help and his training took over.

"Come with us. We need to get you away from this crowd." In his most authoritative voice, he told the crowd, "Show's over! Everyone needs to vacate the square right now! Go on, go home."

Shouts of protest came from the crowd. They pled for the girl to play on. Someone declared that Bridget had sent her to them to lead the beggars of Edain to salvation. This view received a surprising amount of vocal support from others.

This could get ugly, Kalin thought. He pulled out his whistle and gave it two long blows. He doubted that any other members of the watch were close by—if they had been they would have already have been there—but there was a slim chance his call would bring help. And if the crowd thought that reinforcements were nearby, perhaps they would remain at bay.

The crowd was less dense to the rear. They went that way, with Watchman Goins an unstoppable lead, the girl in the middle, and Sergeant Kalin and his truncheon bringing up the rear. Somehow, they managed to get to the eastern edge of the square. Most of the crowd was dispersing, but about fifty angry beggars were still hounding them. One, the man who had first suggested that the girl was a divine gift, came too close and tried to grab at her. Kalin, pushed him off, but it made the rest angrier.

He blew his whistle again, and then had to turn to fend off a filthy, toothless woman who tried to strike at him with a thick, knobbed cane. He did nothing to her but block her blow, but she slipped and fell, prompting howls of indignation from all around. Several men rushed them. Hands tore at his clothes and tried to pull him down. Blindly, Kalin struck out with his truncheon. Bent Goins saw that his superior was in trouble. At the same time, the first man grabbed the girl by the arm and tried to drag her off. Goins was split. Luckily, the girl yanked her arm away and kicked the man hard in the crotch. He gasped and fell over, clutching himself. Watchman Goins' indecision vanished. He roared forward and began tossing bodies away from Sgt. Kalin.

Just then, two more watchmen came running down Textile Street to help them. Even though the watch was still hugely outnumbered, Goins counted for at least five, and the beggars were used to yielding to authority. They broke and ran.

Within ten minutes another half dozen watchmen had arrived. Sgt. Kalin put them to work breaking up any remaining groups in the square and restoring order. Finally, he was able to turn to the girl.

"I'm Sergeant Kalin of the Watch. Who are you?" He had decided that she wasn't a goddess. She was tall, pretty, but now

104

there seemed to be nothing unearthly about her. She was just a girl on the cusp of womanhood.

"My name is Miralee. Thank you for helping me. I didn't realize that…"

"That you were going to start a riot. What in Golgotha was that back there? How did you create those illusions? They were illusions, weren't they?"

Miralee did not know what he was talking about.

"Illusions?"

"The images. While you were playing, I could *see* what you were singing about, the fighting, the sadness, the love—there was a bleedin' fish swimming in the air over the square."

"I don't know…I'm sorry. I was thinking about those things, picturing them in my mind. I just wanted to bring a little light to those poor folks in the square. I don't know what happened."

Kalin studied her face. It was without guile. Against every watchman's instinct, he believed her. He wanted do whatever he could to help this girl.

"Where do you live? We should get you home."

"I'm not from Edain. I have a room at the Shell's Inn."

"Goins and I will take you there."

Edain was silent. It wasn't very late, but the streets were unusually deserted. Kalin asked Miralee about her family, where she was from. Her answers were vague and so he asked her no more questions. She volunteered nothing, speaking only a handful of words until they reached the inn.

"Sergeant, Mr. Goins."

"Bent, ma'am."

"Bent. Thank you for seeing me back to the inn. I'll be all right now."

"All right," said Kalin. "But you have to promise me, no more concerts in the square in the middle of the night."

"I do promise. Thank you again."

Miralee went into the inn. Inside, the bar was packed. It was after midnight, but the Shells Inn was still doing brisk business. Miralee saw Gabriel across the room. He was laughing, a bottle of whisky on the table in front of him, the serving girl whose thoughts who had run Miralee out earlier was sitting on his lap.

She kept her hood on and stayed low. She got up the stairs without being seen by Gabriel and into her room.

Miralee could no longer hear the whispered thoughts of the people below her. Her head no longer buzzed. What she felt now was tired. She fell onto the bed without even washing. She was asleep almost immediately.

Sir Dameon en'Calo, Order of the Shadow Knights, was on Amberi Road, near the south wall when he felt the disturbance. Someone was expending a great deal of psychic energy. As he was in the southwestern corner of Edain, he turned his horse around and headed north.

Since Sir Mordis had contacted him, he'd been spending most of his time near Amberi Road and Lilting Street, where the majority of the city's actor, artists, and musicians gathered. From what Mordis had said, he thought it was a likely place to find this Miralee. But when he got back into the heart of the Arts District, he realized that the disturbance he felt, and could still feel, was not there. It was stronger now, but didn't seem to be close.

"North then," he murmured.

Sir Dameon soon passed Temple Street and crossed the Tandy via the Canal Bridge. Crossing River Road, Gunnar's Field was on his right. It was uncharacteristically empty tonight.

The disturbance seemed to come from someplace beyond the field. Just as Dameon started across, the disturbance stopped.

"Damn."

He decided to continue east in case there was anything to discover.

Halfway across the field, he could see that there appeared to be heavy foot traffic coming from the direction of Edain Square. Many of those walking looked like beggars or otherwise poor people. He turned north at Market Street, toward the square.

A few minutes later, he reached the statue filled place and discovered it empty except for a few watchmen. Was it just one of the periodic shakeups of the homeless who camped in the square? That wouldn't account for the unusual activity he'd felt.

Dameon walked his horse up to the nearest watchman, a young man barely out of boyhood whose ill-fitting helmet kept sliding down over his eyes. Dameon didn't know him, though he made a point of trying to know as many of the city's watch as he could. No doubt, judging by the man's age, he had only recently joined the watch.

"What happened here?" Sir Dameon asked the young watchman. Dameon wasn't wearing any visible emblems tonight, just a nondescript cloak. The young man didn't seem to recognize him.

"Bit of a riot, sir. The beggars were all up in arms about something. We had to close down the square."

"Who's in charge?" Dameon asked.

"I saw Sergeant Kalin a little while back. I reckon he is."

Dameon knew Kalin pretty well. The man had a good head and his observations had sometimes been valuable.

"Where did you see the sergeant last?"

"Textile side."

Dameon rode along the southern edge of the square, passing five more watchmen. When he reached the Textile Road side, the easternmost side of the square, there was a group of four more watchmen, Sergeant Kalin was not among them. One of the men had two chevrons on the side of his hat. Dameon had met him before, but was having trouble remembering the man's name.

"Corporal, I was told Sergeant Kalin is around somewhere."

"Sir Dameon. He was sir, not no more. Went off with a new recruit and some girl fifteen minutes ago, maybe a little more."

Dameon raised an eyebrow.

"No, it's not like that, Sir. He was just escorting her home. I guess she got caught up in all of this ruckus somehow. Wrong place, wrong time and all that," said the corporal.

"Do you know what happened here, corporal?" Dameon asked, hoping to get a better answer.

"Not entirely. Just that there was a big crowd in the square tonight. Started to get ugly. I guess Sergeant Kalin tried to disperse it and some of the beggars turned on him. He blew the alarm and we came running."

"And you don't know what the crowd was doing?"

"No. You know Edain, always a rally or a meeting about something. We usually hear about them in advance though. Tonight's was kind of a surprise like."

"Thank you, corporal. Good night."

Dameon flicked his reigns and his horse trotted off. He stayed in North Town for the rest of the night, patrolling the Shells, the Wharf, Mudding, even the Shanks. He hoped to feel a trace of what he had felt before, but there was nothing. He even went into some of the inns and taverns, but again he saw nothing to pique his interest. Near dawn, he went to the Ratch Street guardhouse and asked for Sergeant Kalin, but was told that the sergeant had gone off duty an hour ago. The watchman said that the sergeant would be back tomorrow night at about five.

With nothing else to do, Sir Dameon rode south. He crossed the Market Bridge just as the sun was cresting the water of the bay. On Temple Street, he turned east toward home.

Gabriel had dealt with his set back with Miralee by going downstairs, buying a bottle of whisky, and getting into a card game. He played for an hour and won big; it was easy for an empath to win at cards. He quit before anyone grew too suspicious and concentrated on his drinking. At some point, he wound up with a young woman squirming on his lap, a buxom serving wench called Tabi or something.

He failed to note when Miralee came in. A little while after that, he took to calling Tabi, "Batty." When he wouldn't stop, she got angry and left.

So he was a little more alert when the Shadow Knight came in. Still, he almost failed to recognize Sir Dameon. Gabriel thought that it was unfair that the knight wasn't wearing the order's emblem. He did recognize Dameon though and quickly made sure that he was masking. Gabriel slouched down in his chair and eased his hood up.

He felt Dameon's gaze, then felt it pass him by. Gabriel and Dameon had never actually met, but Gabriel had seen the knight on previous visits to Edain and knew him for who he was.

Dameon did not stay. After scanning the room, the Shadow Knight left. Gabriel let out a deep breath. He had to get Miralee out of Edain and to his home in the Gorewood where his mother awaited them.

"Bitch," he slurred, not sure if he meant Miralee or his mother.

It was too bad that Delia wanted Miralee's cooperation. It would have been much easier to simply truss her up and carry her back to the Gorewood.

"Tomorrow. I'll figure it out tomorrow," he said to no one. "Tonight is for drinking."

Chapter Ten

Duke Corgan ni'Graelly enjoyed a leisurely breakfast of thin pastry and orange marmalade with a hot cup of Varian coffee. He anticipated a busy day. The May Day celebration would begin soon, bringing extra problems, in addition to the usual ones.

He heard the door to his private dining room open. He sighed as he saw his daughter, Peri. She looked upset.

"Father! I have to talk to you about Emer ni'Oban."

He swallowed an impatient remark along with a swallow of coffee and instead said, "What about the Lady ni'Oban, my dear?"

"She is horrible! Since she's been here, she's done nothing but abuse the people of our city and your hospitality."

"Peri, Emer ni'Oban is of the royal family. She's Corliss' niece! Try to get along with her. It's only another week before you return to school."

"Where I have still have to put up with her. I just don't understand why she has to be here."

Corgan took a deep breath and continued as if speaking to a child of five instead of fifteen.

"She told her father she wanted to come to Edain for the May holiday. It is a great honor to host her here."

"For whom? Certainly not for me! Last night, she dumped an entire pitcher of ale over a serving girl's head in the Gray Pony."

"Gray Pony? Why were you in North Town?"

"Because Emer ni'Oban likes it there. There are no nobles in North Town; she's free to do whatever she likes. Just the other night, she had a soldier hold a poor girl down in the mud, while Emer stepped on her—like a rug! It's an embarrassment!"

"Oh yes, the Gunnar's Field incident. I saw Lady ni'Oban's face. The commoner assaulted her, I heard. I suppose I should make an effort to identify the woman and arrest her. How would it look to Corliss if we did nothing?"

"That girl did not assault Emer. A rat jumped on her. She got a few scratches."

"Still…"

Peri ni'Graelly rolled her eyes. She shook her head in resignation. Corgan began discussing the long amity between the Obans and the Graellys, but Peri didn't stay to hear. Infuriated, she stalked out of the dining room, slamming the heavy door behind her.

Miralee could no longer hear the voices the next morning. The buzzing in her head was gone. Whatever had happened yesterday when she had gone inside of Gabriel's mind seemed to have worn off. But she didn't feel normal. She felt new. It was like a door had opened, and once through there was no going back.

By nine-thirty Gabriel still had not ventured out of his room. Miralee took breakfast alone in her room and packed her belongings.

No matter what, I'm going to the Edain Conservatory today.

At ten, she decided to knock on Gabriel's door.

She went to his door and was about to knock, when the sound of a woman's voice from inside stopped her short. The words were muffled, but as she had done with the conversation between her mother and father—*no, Myra and Wolen*—Miralee blocked out everything else until she could hear inside clearly.

"Gabriel, fool son, where are you? I can hear you snoring. Drunk again, no doubt," said the woman's voice.

"What?" That was Gabriel. His voice was thick. "Mother?"

"Yes! Who do you think? You promised you would have a progress report for me today."

Miralee heard Gabriel's bed creak, something clattered to the floor, then creaking footsteps.

"What?" he said.

"Your progress. When this started, I expected you to have her here by now."

"Soon, I promise. I…used a psychic merge yesterday to gain control of her mind."

111

"So you're on your way?"

"Not exactly. She...her subconscious was protected more strongly than I anticipated. While I was trying to break through the barrier, she...she managed to access *my* mind. I had to break away before she learned too much."

"Fool! Were you drunk when you performed the merger?"

"No, mother! Of course not. I don't know what happened. She's untrained. She was even cooperating with me."

"She is of our heritage, even if it is through Phaedran. You underestimated her. Do what you must. Just get her here. Abaddon wants very much to bring her into the fold. However, if that proves impossible, it is even more important that she not go over to the Order."

"I understand. I'll bring her, even if I have to drag her home. There is one other thing—last night I saw a Shadow Knight in the inn where we're staying. He didn't see me and he left right away."

"All the more reason to bring her home quickly. Don't disappoint me—again."

"Yes, mother."

Then it was silent in the room. However the woman, Gabriel's mother, had gotten into the room, she seemed to be gone.

I'm of their line? Phaedran? What does that mean? Gabriel had said that we were alike. Does he actually know who my parents are? Who is Abaddon? It's obvious that Gabriel intended treachery all along—drag me home—indeed. But I have to know who I am. What am I going to do? It would be smartest to go back to my room, think this through before I talk to him.

Miralee could plan—she had done it when she had decided to run away. But she was always more comfortable with action. Right then her instincts were telling her to act.

She knocked on the door. The thick oak absorbed most of the noise. She kicked at it. Her boots made a more satisfying sound.

"Gabriel, open up, now!"

The doorknob turned and Miralee shoved the door open hard. Gabriel stumbled backward and nearly fell over the closest bed. He was slow to get up.

He looks terrible, smells terrible. His head is splitting—good. Either he's not masking or some lingering effect of what he did yesterday is making it easier for me to read him. I can't hear his thoughts, but his feelings are coming through clear. I seem to have the advantage at the moment, but he is dangerous. Best if I stay near the door.

"Miralee, what are you...?"

"Be quiet! You've been lying to me this whole time, but I want answers now. Start with how we're alike. What do you know about my parents? Where do I come from? Who are Phaedran and Abaddon? And what do you people want with me? I want the truth!"

Gabriel stared at her. He sat down on the edge of the bed he'd almost fallen over. He held his head in his hands, rubbing his temples.

Miralee surveyed the room. Gabriel had apparently slept in the far bed. His sword hung from the end of it, and his clothes were heaped on the floor. He was wearing just his underclothes. A bottle of amber spirits, a quarter full, sat on the small table nearest the door.

"Fine," he said. "Maybe if you know the truth you'll see why you have to come with me.

"The reason why we can do the things we do is because we share a common ancestry. I don't know who your parents were, but Phaedran is your grandfather."

"Who is Phaedran? Are you related to him as well?"

"Phaedran is a demon. There, now you have it. And no, I'm not related to Phaedran, but I have a demonic ancestry as well."

No. I don't believe it. But, I don't sense any deception in him right now. Still, it can't be.

"I don't believe you. I'm not a demon. I'm not evil. I'm just a regular girl," she protested.

"Who talks to animals, sees auras, sometimes glows, and whatever else you can do. Besides, demon is not synonymous with evil. Sit down. I'll tell you a story."

She stayed standing where she was. Gabriel shrugged. He spied the bottle of spirits and reached for it. He took two big swallows, shuddering slightly as it went down. Miralee could feel how it burned, but it also pushed back the throbbing in his head.

"A long time ago, thousands of years, this world belonged to the demons. They built great civilizations that dwarfed anything man has since built. They were proud, noble, and learned. A handsome people who bore no resemblance to the warped creature you saw slain in your village. When the demons were at their peak, humans were little more than animals. But the demons saw potential in humanity and taught humans to be more than they had been. In return, humanity served demon society."

"Slaves," she said.

"A name. Ancient men were like children, the demons like gods. Do you accuse parents of keeping their children as slaves? No, parents do what they do to protect their children."

"What about the real gods? The stories say the gods created humanity in their own image. They taught man to be civilized."

"Horse dung. The so-called gods, the elohim, were interlopers. They came to this world from…somewhere else. But by the time they arrived demonic civilizations had already existed for millennia."

He believes it. Whatever the real truth might be, Gabriel thinks this is it.

"The elohim were similar to the demons. You look surprised. They were also a strong people with an old civilization. They were fewer in number than the demons. Those elohim who appeared in our world fled some catastrophe in their own. I'm not sure what it was. But their intention was to make this world their own. War broke out between the elohim and the demons.

"It was a long, bloody affair. While the elohim were outnumbered, it took a long time for the individual demonic civilizations to unite against the threat. Much of mankind turned on the demons as well. They had grown resentful, much as a child in his teen years may grow to resent his parents. Men in droves abandoned the demons and flocked to the elohim, calling them gods.

"The war became stalemated. But then the various demon kingdoms united and threatened to crush the elohim for good. Before that could happen, the elohim completed their weapon.

"It was similar to the object that had brought the elohim here from their world in the beginning. With it, they were able to banish the demons from this world, trapping them in seven, miserable, quasi-planes where they have resided ever since."

"But if that's true, how did they get to be like, well like that thing that attacked my village?" Miralee asked.

"The hells to which they were banished have unstable, poisonous qualities that have changed them. Many among the lesser ranks have degenerated.

"They are not inherently evil. The only evil was perpetrated by the so-called gods against my people, against your people. Many of the most powerful demons, the lords among them, are unchanged. They are still the same noble people they were before they were banished.

"All of this time, they have just been searching for a way to escape the endless torture to which they were sentenced. Hundreds of years ago, when Golgotha appeared, and the first Shadow Knights fought against King Draxx, it was an attempt to right a wrong and end the demon's banishment."

"But the demons cause chaos. Even one demon can wreak havoc," said Miralee.

"When people unwittingly summon forth a low level demon and are unable to control it, yes, the results can sometimes be unfortunate. But if we can succeed in bringing them all back, the lords can control those who have degenerated, and work on finding a way to reverse the mutations."

"How can people summon them anyway, if the gods banished them?"

Gabriel laughed.

"It's complicated. Any fool can perform the rituals, but to truly understand the arcana behind the magics can take years to learn. My mother, Delia, understands it. I'm sure that she would be happy to teach you."

"I don't know…"

115

"Miralee, you can't stay here. It isn't safe. Just last night, I saw a Shadow Knight come into the inn. They're looking for you. When they find you, they'll kill you as quickly as they would any other demon. That's why you have to come to my home."

Everything else he said was the truth as he understands it, but not that. He's being deceptive again.

"You're lying. I can read you now, Gabriel. You're not telling me something."

Gabriel didn't say anything. He closed his eyes and swallowed the remainder of the liquor in his bottle.

"You obviously heard everything said between me and Delia. You know I told her that I would bring you home any way that I could," he said, a hint of danger entering his voice. "And if you can read me, you know that everything I told you was the truth. There are no more lies. Come with me and live, stay here and die."

Miralee inched toward the door.

"I don't think so. I'm leaving here, leaving the inn, and you aren't going to stop me."

"Leave the inn. You aren't going to get very far. You can't hide from me."

Sperry Manor was basically a big farm house, spacious, not huge, in need of new paint. The Earl's men wore no uniforms, unlike the warriors of the dukes and more important earls.

Mordis decided to begin with the direct approach. He and Artegan rode up to the Earl's gate and announced themselves to the man there.

"Sir Mordis Silverhand, Grandmaster of the Order of Shadow Knights, and Sir Artegan, also of the Order of Shadow Knights, to see Earl Rendel.

The man, very tall and thin with a tremendous Adam's apple, was wary. He was wary of anything out of the ordinary—this certainly qualified. He was also dubious that Mordis and Artegan were who they said that they were. The Grandmaster of the Shadow Knights did not visit Sperry County. He might as well have claimed

116

to be the King. Still, they were obviously not to be trifled with, or detained unnecessarily.

The man called out and a runner, a bushy-haired boy just into his teens, appeared. The gatekeeper gave him some quick instructions and the boy was off again.

While they waited, the gatekeeper folded his arms across his chest and stared hard at the two knights. So thin was the man that his eyes bulged out of his head making him look remarkably like an emaciated frog. Mordis spotted a fly buzzing around the man's head. He conjured a brief image of a long, frog-tongue shooting forth from the gatekeeper's mouth and had to suppress a chuckle. The gatekeeper ignored the buzzing insect, until it flew into his ear. The man smacked at the side of his head like it was on fire.

The runner and six slap-dash soldiers came trotting up to the gate. A ruddy faced, heavyset man of about forty-five years was apparently in charge. He was out of breath; the others waited on him until he recovered enough to speak.

"Sir Mordis," he said, then paused to take another breath. "My apologies for keeping you waiting. I'm Sergeant Shad. We're to escort you to the Earl." The sergeant turned to the gatekeeper. "This *is* Sir Mordis Silverhand. Take a good look you ignorant nob."

The Earl's men escorted the knights to the main house. The front room evidently served as a reception area. No one had offered to tend to their horses; it had been a short ride from the village, so they left them picketed in front.

The Earl kept them waiting for another fifteen minutes.

Earl Rendel was a stoop-shouldered man who walked with a cane. The lines, deeply carved into his face, implied he might have never smiled in his life. One eye was sky blue, while the other was milky with cataracts. He hobbled over to a plush, plum-colored chair and sat in it as if it were a throne. Mordis and Artegan remained standing, Mordis smiling amiably.

"I've combed my mind," the Earl began, "but I can think of no reason why the Grandmaster of the Order of Shadow Knights would need to see me. I've had no trouble with demons."

117

"Earl Rendel, thank you for this audience," said Mordis. "I'll get right to the point. I'm here because of the bandit activity in Sperry County."

"Since when is your order concerned with common banditry?"

"Earl Rendel, just a few days ago, bandits apparently tried to kidnap a young lady who is affiliated with the order." This was a lie, but it was close enough and sounded better than the truth. "The brigands set upon her just outside of the village. A local bard was seriously injured in the attack. Also, your son, Rupert, reportedly met and showed some interest in the girl the night before the attack."

The Earl leaned forward and rested on the edge of the chair. The six soldiers shifted uncomfortably.

"What are you implying?" the earl asked, his gravelly voice took on a distinct menace.

"I make no implications. I am simply stating the facts that have led me to your doorstep. I'd like to assist you in eliminating the bandits that have harried your county."

Earl Rendel began to laugh, a rattling chuckle that culminated in a coughing fit. Rendel wiped spittle from his mouth.

"Oh, you want to help me. As if I need your help. I can manage the affairs of my county well enough on my own. I thank you for your offer, but suggest that you leave now. Sperry County might be rustic, but I have more than enough men here to handle the likes of you. I won't be spied on by witch-hunters."

"Earl Rendel, you misunderstand."

"I think not. Goodbye, Mordis Silverhand."

The earl creaked to his feet and left without another word. The audience was over.

Sergeant Shad stood there, looking somewhat embarrassed.

"Sir Mordis, Sir Artegan, if you will accompany us, we'll see you to your horses," he said.

"Of course, Sergeant," said Mordis.

Outside, Shad dismissed the other five men and walked the Shadow Knights to their mounts himself.

"Sirs, I apologize for the Earl's behavior," he said, as if he could be held responsible. "He's become bitter in his age and the bandits are a sore spot. We've tried to locate them several times, unsuccessfully. If it helps, a number of witnesses have claimed to have seen them north of here, near White Ash Hill. It's about five miles due north."

"You've searched the area and found no trace?" Artegan asked.

"No. Lord Rupert maintains a lodge there. He's forbidden any but his own handpicked guard from entering the area. Whenever there have been bandit attacks, Lord Rupert has conducted his own searches and come up empty. His theory is that the bandits operate out of a wooded area east of the hill. But we have searched there, many times, and never found them."

"I see," said Mordis. "Thank you, Sergeant. You've given us something to think about."

"Thank you, Grandmaster. You probably don't remember me, but I was a caravan guard for a trade mission to Yellowhaven fifteen years ago. We were attacked by a demon near the edge of the Gorewood. Three of us died, and the rest of us probably would have perished as well, but you showed up and defeated the monster."

"I remember that," Mordis said. "It was a revenant—a demon inhabiting the corpse of an animal, a bear wasn't it?"

"Yes, sir, biggest one I ever saw."

"Sergeant Shad, do you have any idea where Lord Rupert is now?" Mordis asked.

"He's supposed to be up at White Ash right now. Be careful if you go up there. Lord Rupert is a cold man, and he gets upset at trespassers—doesn't matter if they're soldiers, or Shadow Knights."

"Any idea how many men he has up there?" Artegan asked.

Shad scratched his head.

"Hard to say. He's got his own resources, Rupert does. I'd say at least a score might be up at the lodge though."

The knights thanked Shad again. Then they climbed onto their saddles and rode away from Sperry Manor. They rode north.

Mordis and Artegan reached White Ash Hill by lunchtime. It was easy to see how the hill had gotten its name—it was difficult to find a tree on it that wasn't a bushy, oval-leafed white ash.

The Shadow Knights and their mounts were invisible—not actually invisible, but very hard to notice. The type of invisibility employed by members of the Order actually worked on the minds of anyone looking in the knight's direction. The eyes could see them, but the brain would insist that nothing was there. This sort of invisibility had limits. It was difficult to fool many onlookers at once. The greater the knight's skill, the more people he could affect. Also, the untrained were much more likely to be susceptible to this kind of manipulation. Still, it was a handy trick.

Mordis and Artegan began to sense people as soon as they drew close—two large clusters and several smaller groups.

"The largest grouping of people might be the lodge Sergeant Shad mentioned," Mordis suggested.

"Then what's the other group? It's fairly distant," said Artegan.

"Another structure perhaps? Or maybe they're having a picnic. Lookouts at regular intervals."

"No more than four to a group though."

"Still, let's stay off the main path. There's a lot of game around here. I'd prefer a good deer trail to take us closer."

They scouted around the base of the hill and soon found a faint trace that looked suitable. They had spotted two more man-made trails besides the main one—one obvious, one less so. They had also passed close by sentries twice, but had not been noticed.

The trace was narrow, so they went single file with Mordis leading. It took them to within a hundred yards of the largest concentration of people before turning off in another direction.

The knights dismounted and continued off of the path afoot; their horses would stay still and quiet until their riders returned.

The two men crept forward slowly, carefully working their way through the scrub bushes and once cutting through thorns as quietly as they could. Only a fool relied on passive mind tricks to go unnoticed—honest stealth should always have a place in one's repertoire. Fortunately, Shadow Knights favored light armor for greater mobility, and dark colors.

Communication was not an issue. Both Artegan and Mordis were proficient telepaths. Despite notions to the contrary, a telepath could pick up thoughts from a non-telepath quite easily, but it was much more difficult to make one's thoughts heard by a non-telepathic individual; feelings were easier.

120

They split up to get a better idea of the lay.

Mordis drifted to the north and found a rare pine that looked climbable. He lifted himself up and found a good vantage point at approximately fifteen feet.

Taking to the trees wasn't an option for Artegan—he was as big as most trees. He found a mossy sandstone boulder just inside of the tree line and used it for concealment. He had a good view of the side and front of the lodge while Mordis could see the back.

The lodge was sizeable, but not immense. It was limited by the terrain. The builder evidently had wanted concealment over defensibility. The lodge was about three-quarters of the way up the hill, on a long, narrow flat strip. The tree line came within twenty feet of the lodge's walls in most places, making it possible to sneak up rather close—as the Shadow Knights had done. Apparently, Rupert en'Sperry had felt his reputation and the lookouts posted on the trails to be sufficient protection.

"It feels to me like twenty or so inside," thought Artegan. *"Most are toward the front. I feel four in the back."*

"The back door is opening, someone's coming out," Mordis thought back.

As the Grandmaster watched, four men came outside. One of them, based on a description that Shondar had provided, the way he carried himself, and the way the others deferred to him, Mordis guessed was Rupert en'Sperry. He wasn't dressed for hunting, but looked more like he was preparing for a night out at the theater in Gedorix. His boots were shined, his breeches were of velvet, and he was wearing a cape. Rupert was excited, Mordis could sense, in almost a sexual way.

Two of the men appeared subservient to Rupert, soldiers—*or bandits*—they wore scarred leather armor and swords in scabbards that were without ornament. One of the men had a long scar across his face and a half healed gash across the back of his left wrist and hand. The other man had a pock-marked face, though much of it was covered by his beard, and eyes and a nose that were reminiscent of a weasel.

The last man made Mordis uneasy and set his mental alarms ringing. He was a small man with no visible weapons. He wore no armor, just long, black robes over more long, black robes. He joked with Rupert as an equal. Mordis relaxed his gaze to view the man's aura—it was dark and opaque as a storm cloud. And like a storm cloud, it was charged with power.

"*Artegan, I've got Rupert en'Sperry here in the back. He's got a wizard.*"

Chapter Eleven

rtegan and Mordis followed the quartet at a distance. The four went on foot toward the smaller cluster of people sensed by the knights. A faint trail led from the hunting lodge in that direction. The wizard seemed to sense something, turning several times to check their back trail and look around. Scar-face and Weasel-face were ill at ease. Only Lord Rupert acted completely confident and carefree.

There was a second structure, a small cottage, on the other side of the hill. Unlike the lodge, this one felt *old,* possibly hundreds of years old. The building was squat and made of crumbling stone that was completely overgrown by vines and weeds. Near the cottage, built into the side of the hill, was a wooden frame, its timbers blackened with age, supporting the entrance to a dark shaft, perhaps a mine.

Mordis opened his senses.

Six people in the cottage—one is terrified. No one seems to be in the shaft beyond, but I can't tell how far it extends. Something about it doesn't feel right. The air about the opening is too thick. There is a sulfurous quality to it.

Rupert, the wizard, and the two henchmen walked toward the cottage. The wizard stopped at the door. He turned and looked around one more time. His eyes lingered over the spot where Mordis and Artegan were. They were a fair distance back using conventional concealment as well as mental invisibility. After a long moment, the wizard's eyes moved past them.

As soon as Rupert and the others had disappeared inside, Mordis and Artegan changed their locations. As quickly as they could while staying cautious, the knights positioned themselves between the shaft entrance and the decaying cottage, invisible and hiding behind a sandstone outcropping from which mossy, blind faces seemed to protrude.

Ten minutes passed. Mordis and Artegan ignored the mosquitoes and gnats that buzzed around their heads, stirred up by the heat and the cessation of the rains.

Finally, the door opened. A perverse procession emerged. The wizard, now cowled so that all one could see of his face was his long, black beard, led the march. Rupert followed, then Scar and Weasel-face. Between them walked a miserable sight—a girl of about eighteen. She had blond hair and somewhat heavy features, now locked in fright. Her hands were tied in front of her and a rope was tied around her neck. Scar-face held one end and pulled her along like an animal, while Weasel-face walked behind occasionally kicking her in the back, laughing when she stumbled.

Cassie Brahdie, Mordis thought.

They had dressed her in a white, featureless robe.

The Grandmaster could hear Artegan's thoughts.

"Looks like a sacrifice."

Mordis concurred.

This group was followed by the five men who had been waiting here. It was a dirty group, loud and crude-mannered. Lord Rupert, the wizard, and the henchmen escorting Cassie Brahdie, went into the tunnel, but this group remained outside, guarding the entrance. There was little discipline among them and they obviously expected that there would be nothing to guard against.

Mordis and Artegan walked right by them, relying wholly on their invisibility for the first time since the endeavor began.

It was dark within the shaft, but not completely. Lamps were lit at regular intervals, though they did little to cut the gloom. The knights were used to operating in the shadows and were quite comfortable.

Mordis had seen a lot of sandstone in Graelly, but he noted that the bulk of the stone underground was granite.

Probably an old tin mine then.

Ahead, they could hear water dripping; sometimes droplets fell on them from above, remnants of the rains. Footsteps and muffled voices cut through the darkness at odd times.

Mordis stopped to feel ahead with his mind.

They've stopped moving. They are somewhere with some space, a cavern. Oww, something's hot, prickly at the entrance.

Hot and prickly to Shadow Knight senses meant a trap—lots of potential energy ready to be sprung on some unsuspecting intruder.

"*Trap ahead,*" Mordis thought to Artegan.

"*I feel it.*"

Mordis could make out more details as they crept closer.

Hanging in the air was a rune, invisible to normal sight, but quite plain to the knights. The rune was the ancient Golgmaran character for lightning. It felt charged with the same crackling power Mordis had felt in the wizard's aura. If anything came too close, the rune would flare and discharge its power into its hapless victim.

Doesn't look like there's any way around it. At least none that wouldn't involve hours of searching for another entrance, or carving through solid granite, Mordis thought. *No, it will have to be here.*

"*Art, what do you think?*"

"*Usually, this kind of trap is tied to the wizard who set it. Anyone, other than him, who mucks around with it sets it off.*"

"*Ideas?*"

"*One. It isn't a very good one though. Let's get a little intelligence. Maybe we won't have to go in. Maybe we can wait for them to come out. If not, perhaps something else will occur to one of us while we're figuring out what's going on.*"

"*I think we have a fair idea as to what's going on, but I agree. We can spare a few minutes to get a better idea of what we're up against. Not too long; we have to think about the girl.*"

Much in the way Miralee had done, Mordis focused in on the voices ahead to the exclusion of all else.

"Hold her. I have to secure her to the altar in a precise fashion," said a voice Mordis assumed belonged to the wizard.

"Moricai, you're certain that this will work?" asked a petulant voice.

"Lord Rupert, of course," said the wizard, Moricai. "This is the final blood required to seal the pact. Soon, you'll have power to surpass King Corliss."

Promises, thought Mordis.

The only sounds were the muffled sobs of the kidnapped girl, and then a low chant began.

"I think we've run out of time. What was your plan?" Mordis thought.

"What are the odds that the wizard's trap is the match of our shields combined?" Artegan thought back.

"Hmm, I guess we're going to find out. Put your shield around me."

"No. My plan, I get to try it out. You *put your shield around me. No time to argue."*

"Fine."

Artegan centered himself and wrapped an aural shield tightly around his person. Mordis did the same, placing his right over Artegan's. The shields could not be seen with regular eyesight, but their creation caused a ripple that a sensitive individual could feel. Indeed, Mordis sensed the wizard's alarm. Fortunately, the chanting could not be interrupted and he was unable to warn the others.

Artegan took a deep breath. Lowering his head like a bull, he charged forward.

The rune flared, accompanied by an audible crackling, which discharged in a fashion identical to any natural lightning bolt. The white energy struck Artegan square in the chest. Mordis felt his own hair stand on end. The arcane electricity coruscated all around the giant Shadow Knight. Artegan let out an inarticulate shout, but continued moving forward. He burst through into the cavern, followed closely by Mordis.

"Toa Serrakon dreng d'motis. Toa Serrakon dranic d'motis," the wizard intoned, louder and faster.

In his right hand was a curved dagger that flashed in the torchlight. Cassie Brahdie was bound on her back, upon an inclined altar so that her head was tilted down, by an intricate weave of black rope.

As one, Rupert en'Sperry and his henchmen turned toward the entrance, stunned by the flash and clap of lightning and thunder, and by the knights' appearance. Lord Rupert stood at the foot of the altar, within a magical diagram that looked like a broken star. The henchmen stood away from the altar, closer to the entrance.

Mordis and Artegan struck before their enemies could so much as gape.

If Artegan had been hurt by being struck by the lightning bolt full in the chest, he didn't show it. Without slowing his charge, he clouted Scar-face with his forearm. Scar-face was a big man, but Artegan's blow was akin to being hit in the head and shoulders by a battering ram. The bandit left his feet, thrown back two yards, before hitting the ground and rolling for at least another three. When he finally came to rest, he did not move.

Mordis took Weasel-face, dropping the surprised man with a thrust kick that planted him into the hard, mineral floor. Unlike Scar-face, he wasn't unconscious, but the kick had taken his wind and bruised ribs. He was, for the moment, out of the action.

The wizard, Moricai, shouted out words rapid-fire, trying to finish the rite even as the Shadow Knights bore down on the altar.

"Toa Serrakon dranac! Toa Serrakon dranac! Toa Serrakon KESSIC!" he screamed.

Mordis saw the dagger descend toward the helpless girl's throat. With no time for subtleties, Mordis pulled together whatever *jhi* energy he could in a split second's time and pushed it forward like an invisible hand. It caught the wizard with his blade scant inches from the girl's unprotected neck and shoved him back hard into the granite wall.

Lord Rupert was panic-stricken, looking back and forth between the Shadow Knights, Moricai, and the kidnapped, bound girl. He came to a decision and stepped out of the magical diagram and toward the altar, swinging his sword at the same time. He clearly intended to do what Moricai had been unable to do.

But Artegan had already reached him. Leaping, remarkably high and far for such a big man, the knight tackled Rupert, knocking the nobleman into the side of the altar and then to the ground.

Cassie Brahdie was unharmed.

Lord Rupert was short of stature, but a powerful man nonetheless. Still, he was no match for Artegan. The giant combat instructor took the squirming noble's sword with the same ease that a parent might take a toy from a misbehaving child.

"Rupert en'Sperry, you're under arrest in the name of the Order of Shadow Knights," Artegan said with satisfaction.

Mordis turned to the wizard. As he did, the chamber began to shake violently. Cracks appeared in the floor and ceiling. Mordis stumbled. When he recovered, Moricai was gone.

"I'll get the girl," Mordis shouted, the shaking intensifying. It was as if the demon, being denied its promised sacrifice was throwing a tantrum and was determined to tear the chamber down around their ears.

"Cassie Brahdie? Hello, I'll be your rescuer today," Mordis said, calm even as sharp, heavy shards of rock began to fall from above.

Mordis quickly cut through the girl's bonds. As soon as she was free, she latched her arms around his neck and wouldn't let go. It looked like he'd be carrying her out.

Weasel-face was conscious and up, but not Scar-face.

"If you don't want him to die, you'll have to carry him," Artegan said. "Leave both of your swords here though."

Scar-face was heavier than Weasel-face, but must have endeared himself to the other at some point, because Weasel-face, bruised ribs and all, managed to get the larger man hoisted over his shoulders.

Artegan kept Rupert next to him, controlling him with an escort position that kept the nobleman's wrist painfully locked. This way, he could control Rupert with only one hand, and could easily break the wrist if need be. In his other hand, Artegan held his great sword. He pointed it at Weasel-face and ordered him to move out.

The tremors were isolated in the ritual cavern. As soon as they reached the tunnel, the shaking lessened. Mordis and Artegan kept an eye out for the wizard, but he was nowhere to be seen.

When they got back to the tunnel entrance, they felt only the faintest rumbling.

Outside, the five bandits were still there. Eyeing the entrance curiously, they could faintly feel the rumble in the earth. Ten eyes were trained on Mordis' party when it emerged. Five swords were quickly drawn. Artegan ignored them.

"Put him down, then have a seat on the ground next to him," Artegan said to Weasel-face, who set down his comrade then sat down beside him. Scar-face was beginning to stir.

"Lord Rupert, what in Golgotha is going on here?" asked one of the men. "What happened in there? Who are they?"

"Quiet, Rupert," Artegan said, increasing the pressure on the young lord's wrist slightly.

Mordis set Cassie Brahdie down and came forward. He was relaxed.

"Gentlemen, my name is Mordis Silverhand." That got a response. It was a known name. "Lord Rupert is under arrest. Those of you who don't wish to die within the next minute or so, please put down your weapons and have a seat next to those two."

Five swords hit the ground almost simultaneously. Rupert began to swear at them for being cowards, but a slight tweak of his wrist made him choke off the words.

Cassie Brahdie was making a quick recovery from her ordeal.

"There's some irons and more rope in the cottage where they was holding me," she said. "He's had other women there before me. Place is all set up like a dungeon."

"It doesn't look that big," remarked Artegan.

"There's a cellar. It's bigger below than above," she said.

"Let's have a look," said Mordis.

They herded the eight prisoners against the front of the cottage to control their movement better. Mordis opened the door and stood there. Narrow stairs down were off to one side. He didn't note anything dangerous between the door and the stairs.

"It should be all right," he told Artegan. "Gentlemen, here is what is going to happen. We are going to take you to the cellar and lock you up. We will not be bringing you with us. By law, I could put you all to death right now for kidnapping, robbery, and aiding in a black rite. However, I am in a hurry.

"So, excepting Lord Rupert, I'll lock you up and notify the village authorities. You'll have a sporting chance. Maybe you'll hang. Maybe your friends at the lodge will find you first and free

129

you. If you get free, I suggest that you leave Sperry County immediately."

"And what of me?" asked Rupert. "Will you kill me then? My father is the law here; he won't stand for this."

"I could kill you. Under my charter, I can impose a sentence of death upon any person guilty of knowingly consorting with demons and their servants. However, it has been a long time since a noble has been put to death as a demon-worshipper. I will take you to Edain and present you to the Duke. Lucky for you, I'm already heading that way. But if I even think that you are attempting to escape, I will kill you in an instant."

Rupert sneered.

Given a chance at freedom, the bandits allowed themselves to be led to the cellar without resistance.

Cassie Brahdie had described the cellar as a dungeon. It was worse. What they found underneath the cottage was a torture chamber.

There was a rack, brands, pincers, knives, saws, and more creative instruments of pain. It smelled like a charnel house. One side of the cellar held three modest cells, sufficiently large to hold the seven men.

While Mordis and Artegan locked up the bandits, Cassie wandered to the back of the cellar to a small wooden door. Slowly, she thumbed the latch and pushed it open. An odor of rot wafted out. She picked up a lamp and thrust it inside. For a moment she was silent. Then she screamed.

Mordis rushed over. Cassie was still screaming. He pulled her back and looked inside.

Six decapitated heads stared out at him—women's heads in various states of decay, set up on wooden pedestals. A seventh pedestal was empty. Rupert en'Sperry's trophies.

"He would taunt me, Lord Rupert would," Cassie said. She was pale and sweating. "He said that when all was done, I'd have a place of honor here. Forever."

Rupert en'Sperry wore heavy irons. He waited, silent and sullen, while Mordis and Artegan decided what to do next.

"I say we execute the miserable bastard right now," said Artegan.

Mordis closed his eyes. He could still see the dead, staring gazes of Rupert's victims. The smell of death was all over him. It wasn't the first time either of them had seen death. It wasn't even the tenth. But while demons did horrific things, that a man had done it made it all the worse.

"No," Mordis said. His answer even surprised himself. "No. He'll go to the Duke. If the Duke won't take steps, I'll talk to King Corliss. The Order hasn't executed a nobleman for three generations. It would have been different if he had died in battle. But he's our prisoner. His execution can wait long enough for us to do this right."

"All right, fine. What now? Somehow, we have to get out of Sperry County with Rupert. Let someone who matters and cares know about what we found here and about the men in the cellar. We've got to get that girl back home. And what about the wizard? He's on the loose somewhere."

"One thing at a time." Mordis sighed, running his fingers through his hair; he grinned a thin smile. "What a mess. This was supposed to be a simple affair, picking up a prospective initiate and bringing her to Magh Moru."

"Simple things usually aren't."

"I'd say it's unlikely that we'll get any assistance from the earl. Let's go to town. I'd like to get a cart to transport Rupert to Edain."

Cassie had been very quiet since the gruesome discovery in the cellar. But she spoke up now.

"I have a cart."

The knights had somewhat forgotten about her.

"What?" Mordis asked.

"On my farm, my father has a cart you could use. He mostly uses it at fair time for the pigs. It's completely enclosed and can be locked from the outside."

The men looked at each other and shrugged.

131

"It's no meaner an accommodation than he deserves," said Artegan.

"And it will cut down on the time we have to spend here. Miss Brahdie, we'll have a look at that cart."

Mordis sent Artegan back to get their horses. In the meantime, he searched the cottage for provisions. As he was doing so, it occurred to him that they may need to bring evidence other than testimony against Rupert, if they wished to involve the duke or the king. It had never been necessary before; while not of a noble family himself, as Grandmaster of the Order of Shadow Knights, Sir Mordis was afforded rank to equal any of the great dukes. But Rupert en'Sperry *was* of noble blood, if only a rustic earl's son.

He began to search with a new purpose.

It occurred to Mordis immediately that he would need evidence of murder. The best evidence was in the cellar. He'd save that unsavory task for last.

To guide his search, Mordis had a word with Lord Rupert.

"There's quite a bit here," he said to the nobleman, who was currently manacled to a stout wooden chair. "I understand wanting to do for yourself. It was a good setup too. Your friends hit a traveler here and there, and in exchange for your aid and protection, they give you a cut. A pretty hefty one I'd guess."

Mordis didn't expect an answer, and he didn't get one—not in words. While trying hard to be stoic, thoughts and pictures flashed through Rupert's mind.

Okay, his cut is in the lodge, locked away. But I bet these chests and coffers contain his friend's loot.

"If not for your appetites, you might have gotten away with it for a while longer."

"My appetites?" Rupert said evenly.

"Yes. Unfortunate. I can feel so much conflict inside of you. But all of it, the lust, the anger, the greed, all of it boils down to just one thing—power. You have a demon's mind, you know?"

"*I* have a demon's mind?" asked Rupert, smiling. The idea was not unappealing to him.

"Yes. You were about to enter into a demonic pact to gain power. Not because you wanted to rule the country or even the province. Don't argue; I can see it in you. You wanted the power to expand on your other work, the work that you've been doing with the women."

He could see it there in Rupert's mind. The more Mordis talked, the more Rupert thought about the feelings he got when he killed, when he caused pain. And he fantasized about his goals—a whole castle, no, a city at least, where every person, especially the women, was subject to his every humiliating whim.

"Demons love power for the petty appetites it helps them to satisfy, just like you."

"You know nothing about me," Rupert said. He was uncertain. It certainly *sounded* like the Grandmaster knew what was in his head.

Mordis sat on the edge the table, right next to Rupert, and looked down at him.

"You kept their heads, like trophies. What else have you kept?" Mordis' eyes bored into the young nobleman.

"Nothing. Nothing at all. And I didn't kill those women!"

Journal. The fool has a journal.

Mordis hoped to find out where it was, but in response to Rupert's claim that he had not killed anyone, he began thinking of each of their deaths. Mordis could see the memories, the thrill of the hunt, capturing his prey, toying with his victims. Then, in all but one case, strangling his victim. When Rupert thought of the actual murders, the memories changed. They went from mostly visual memories combined with feelings of excitement, to memories of touch and smell accompanied by an orgasmic ecstasy.

"Why did you come here anyway? Was it the wizard?" Rupert asked.

"Moricai? You know so little about him. What did he tell you?" Mordis gave a little mental push. Once someone started talking about a subject, it was usually fairly simple to keep them talking.

"He offered to perform a rite for me that would grant me supernatural strength and make me immortal."

A lie, or with hidden strings attached. The wizard kept invoking the name 'Serrakon.' It has a familiar ring—ah yes, blood demon, a lord of the fourth hell I believe.

"Moricai is a charlatan. Doubtless, he charged you a pretty penny."

"A fair sum, but worth it. And you're wrong about him. I saw his power," said Rupert.

"And yet it was sufficient to allow him to do no more than hide from us. And where is your strength? Your power? How did you come to meet him? He approached you, I'll bet."

Mordis saw an image of a fancy ballroom, filled with people. He saw the wizard in gentleman's finery.

"No. I'll say no more."

"Okay. Just one more thing. Where do you keep your journal?" asked Mordis, watching his prisoner closely.

The man looked up sharply, but kept silent. It didn't matter. Mordis caught an image of a roll-top desk with a secret drawer. It was the same desk that currently sat in the corner of the cottage, less than ten feet away from the Grandmaster.

Mordis went to it slowly, watching Rupert's expression. The nobleman's eyes got wider the closer the knight drew to the desk.

"It's here, isn't it? Are there any surprises for me, any traps?"

The eyes narrowed.

"A poisoned needle? Really, that was the best you could come up with?"

Mordis stood to one side and forced the lock on the desk with his blade. There was a hiss as a spring loaded needle, long and heavy, was propelled forward. It struck the far wall and clattered harmlessly to the ground.

Mordis had not seen the latch for the hidden drawer in Rupert's mind, but knowing it existed went a long way. It only took him a few minutes of hunting before he located it. The drawer popped open and there was the book.

It was all written by the same hand in a narrow, tight script. Some of the lettering was in black ink, but some of it was in a dark, rusty brown. Blood.

Mordis closed the book. He would read it later.

"This will go a long way to convicting you. Let's see what else we have."

There was loot to be found throughout the cottage, money and a variety of goods stolen from merchants. In the last chamber, apparently the bedroom of the field commander of Rupert's bandits, for there was only one bed, Mordis found a cache of letters. Most of it was correspondence between Rupert and the bandit chief. Rupert had not been foolish enough to sign them, but they were in his hand, the same writing that was in the journal. Mordis tucked the letters under his shirt. He also collected a few of the looted items that he felt might be traceable to their victims.

Coming back into the living area where Rupert and Cassie awaited, he looked around for a large sack. There were several. The Grandmaster picked one that should be large enough for his needs.

"Sir Mordis," said Rupert. "I have to know, why are you here? How did you discover me? Was it the wizard?"

Mordis hesitated. Then he told the truth.

"No. It wasn't the wizard. It was your victims, one in particular."

"What do you mean?" Rupert was truly puzzled.

"Do you remember Miralee? The young lady who came through the village several days ago?"

"Her? Yes, a fine musician. What about her?"

"She's of personal interest to me and I've been looking for her for several days now. You might say that she's a friend of mine," Mordis said.

"Aaahh, I see," said Rupert. "You want her too. A little young for you don't you think?"

Mordis ignored the barb.

"Your mistake was thinking that you could victimize anyone you desired with impunity. You sent your thugs after Miralee, and that lead us to where we are now."

Mordis turned away from Rupert, wanting no more conversation. He had other things on his mind at the moment. The cellar awaited.

Chapter Twelve

Miralee wasn't sure where the dog had come from.

He was scrawny with dirty, matted brown hair. The dog had appeared somewhere near the shop where she had stopped to watch a man make glass bottles by blowing through a pipe into gobs of hot, liquid glass.

No one blew glass in Brown's Ford, and Miralee would have been interested if she did not have so many other concerns just then. The hardest to get her mind around was the revelation about her heritage.

Back and forth she went. D*emon, not a demon, how could I be? He was telling the truth. Does that make me evil? I don't feel evil; I don't feel like a demon.*

If it was true, what did it mean for her? It didn't change who she was, who she'd been for the last fifteen years, did it? Part of Miralee felt like crying. But a larger part of her wasn't going to give in to self-pity. She reigned in the Miralee that wanted to scream and shout "unfair!" She stomped the feelings down deep and wrapped them up tight. At the same time, she could feel other parts of herself unraveling. She decided to ignore it.

"Pargestia, help me," she whispered. "Whatever happens, happens."

Another concern was Gabriel. So far, he did not seem to be following her. It was only a matter of time. She knew that he would come for her, and she had no idea what she would do then.

By the time she had collected her belongings and gone to the stables, Gabriel had already left, and he had taken both horses with him. So Miralee had left on foot, lugging her belongings, along with all of her new clothes, on her back.

Adopting another animal was not in her plans. But these things just seemed to happen.

She saw the scruffy thing near the glassblower's shop, but gave it no real thought. When she reached the edge of the wharf, close to the spot where she had been nearly robbed, the mutt popped out from an alley behind her. It barked once, and then sat on its haunches and whimpered.

"*I'm hungry,*" he was telling her.

He was too. Miralee could feel his hunger.

"I'm sorry," she told him. "I have a lot going on right now. Can't you find someone else?"

"*Please, please, please. I like you. And I'm so hungry. Just a little something? I can smell food in your pack.*"

That's how Miralee heard it, though it actually sounded like— *whimper, whimper, whimper, ruff, pant, pant, whine, ruff!*

"Oh, all right. It is lunchtime. But the things in my pack are old. Let's get something fresh."

They were near the docks. Miralee had not seen the ocean yet, so she walked to the water front.

It was a beautiful day, after the days of rain, and the docks were bustling. North of the river was the merchant side of the harbor. It was full of ships of all sizes and styles. Many of the ships flew the flag of Istey, but just as many were from foreign lands—Ehrian, Gelit, and Florick were all represented. There was also a crew of pale and grim sailors from Ungmar, and exotic, dark-skinned crews on ships from Varia and Tyne.

She smelled roasting meat and found an enterprising tavern owner with a small stand set up just outside of his establishment. He was selling whole turkey legs, and skewers of beef and chicken. Sailors, tired of dried meat or fish, flocked to the stand. Some just bought lunch, some who had liberty drifted inside for a beer or something stronger.

Miralee got in line behind a pair of mahogany-skinned sailors who wore gold earrings and colorful, if faded, trousers and scarves. When it was her turn, she bought a skewer of meat from the smiling, ruddy-faced man behind the counter.

She took it to a shady spot, behind a lone maple tree. She sat down, and the mutt sat beside her. When Orrie climbed out from her pocket, the dog stiffened and growled. Miralee chided it.

"Stop that! This is my friend Orrie. He's hungry too. If you want to be friends with me, you will have to get along with Orrie."

137

The dog stopped growling. He slowly extended his head and sniffed the rat, which stood defiantly on his hind legs trying to appear bigger than he was.

They ate. Miralee portioned off the meat for herself and each of the animals. She went into her pouch and found a piece of cheese. She cut off one portion that had grown a greenish, fuzzy mold. They ate the rest. She also found a somewhat hard, half-loaf of bread that she added to the meal.

While they ate, Miralee stared rapt at the ships and the vast water beyond. Never had she imagined the ocean could look so *big,* just endless water to the horizon. She knew that on this side of the island, the water was not in fact endless; Ehrian, on the mainland, was maybe fifty miles due east. Still, it was impressive. One could step onto a ship and go anywhere.

I could take a ship from here to Sinoom, if I wanted, or even to Marya.

The dog placed a dirty paw on her leg. He was still hungry. So was she for that matter. She went back to the stand and bought a second skewer.

A few minutes later, she was back under the tree, alone with the animals and her thoughts.

Maybe I should do that, get on a ship and leave Istey. I'd like to see Gabriel or the Shadow Knights find me in Ehrian. I probably don't have enough money left to book passage to Ehrian. I could perform for the crew in exchange for passage.

But she knew that she wouldn't get on one of those ships, not yet. She had promised herself and Shondar that she would go to the conservatory. When she had gotten up that morning, she'd promised herself that she would go today.

So what are you doing sitting here watching the ships for? Because you're afraid. You latched onto the Edain conservatory as a goal, and when they reject you—which they probably will, letter or no letter—then what do I do?

Gabriel knows that you're going to the conservatory. Still want to go?

Yes. No excuses now. Time to go.

Miralee got up to leave. She sensed that there was someone walking up behind her. They radiated excitement.

"It's you! Bridget, come to save us!"

Miralee turned and looked into the eyes of the same beggar who had started much of the trouble last night. He was thin and stooped with a mouth full of rot and the odor of fermented feces about him.

"I'm not Bridget and I can't save you. Please, leave me alone," she said, picking up her burdens from the ground.

He didn't seem to hear her and came shuffling closer. Even without empathy, she could tell the man was not in his right mind. He was a pitiful wreck, and Miralee could sense no threat from him. But adoration spurned could quickly turn to hostility. She wanted to be away from him as quickly as possible.

Ruff, ruff, ruff! Grrrrr.

The dog, her new friend, had interposed himself between Miralee and the crazed beggar. He had his hackles up and was showing teeth, warning the man away.

The dog was nearly as emaciated as the man, but at least he had a full stomach.

The beggar took notice of the snarling canine and stopped short.

"Please, Bridget! Don't abandon us!" he cried out falling to his knees. A few curious sailors stopped what they were doing and looked.

Miralee shouldered her belongings and walked away. When she did, the dog fell into step beside her. Miralee was much more fleet than the beggar. But the man gamely shuffled along behind her as best as he could.

Many beggars were along the waterfront today. When the man would pass one, he'd yell out.

"It's her, Bridget from the square! Come, come!"

Whether they believed him, or just had nothing better to do, by the time she reached the market, Miralee had a ragged tail of maybe twenty of Edain's beggars.

The market was packed with people. Miralee ducked between two stalls and wove her way through the crowd. She cut between stalls again to the next aisle, and repeated this three more times. The

139

wave of beggars seemed to break on the crowd. For the moment, she lost them.

Miralee reached Market Street, the far edge of the open air bazaar. She hurried south. The bridge was just ahead. She crossed it and went into South Edain for the first time.

Down River Road, a stooped beggar with a mouth full of rot watched her cross. Slowly, he shuffled along after her.

The conservatory was a grand, three story building built of tan brick with marble columns. A four foot mosaic of the guild's triangular emblem was mounted above the double-doors of the main entrance. It was on Lilting Street, a winding road with lots of space, trees, theaters, and concert halls. The fair weather had brought many people outside. Painters painted landscapes. Small groups of musicians sat on well-manicured lawns and practiced in the shade.

It seemed magical.

It had taken Miralee two hours since crossing the bridge to find the conservatory. Everything around it was esthetically designed and beautiful. Miralee became very self-conscious as she drew closer. Her clothes were clean, even her travel cloak, but she felt very rustic here. And no one else was being followed by a shaggy mutt badly in need of a bath.

I doubt anyone is carrying a rat in their pocket either.

"I should probably leave you out here," she said to the dog. "Go lay down under that tree. I'll be back soon."

Taking a deep breath, she pushed open the doors and went inside.

She walked into a wide foyer with a green marble floor polished to a reflective shine. Flowering potted plants flowed out of recesses in the walls. A statue of a bard holding a scroll in one hand and a lute in the other dominated the center of the room. Stairs were on either side of the entrance, and the foyer had no ceiling, letting Miralee see all the way up to the roof, which was a stained glass image of a man receiving a book from a woman on a throne. She had flowing hair that was red and gold. Across her lap was a guitar.

Bridget. It makes no sense. The goddess of music is a woman, but they don't allow women into the Bard's Guild. I don't understand men.

Speaking of men, she was surrounded by them. The foyer and the halls that she could see were full of activity. Men and boys, mostly wearing bard's green and black, hurried about in all directions. They carried instruments of all sorts, as well as books and sheet music. Many were wearing medallions like the one that Olahan had given to her. Miralee pulled her own medallion out from under her dress and wore it openly.

There were a few women in the hall. They were not wearing green and black, but were dressed simply. She saw one woman watering plants. Another came through carrying a mop and bucket.

Of course, women aren't good enough to be in the guild, but we are good enough to clean it. I'm sure that there are women in the kitchens too.

An older bard, with a drooping gray moustache and a massive round belly atop two matchstick legs, saw Miralee standing there and stopped.

"Miss, the servant's entrance is around back. You can try Mrs. Norris if you'd like a position." He spied the medallion around her neck and the guitar slung over her back. "What are you playing at with those?"

"Sir, my name's Miralee. I was told to see Headmaster Kant."

He looked skeptical. "Told by whom?"

"Journeyman Shondar in Sperry's Knoll. I have a letter for the Headmaster."

"You can give it to me then. I'll see that the Headmaster gets the letter."

"With respect, no sir. I have to deliver it myself. You see, it's about me."

"What's that? Nonsense, the Headmaster is very busy. He can't just stop what he's doing for some girl." He glared at her for close to a minute, as if he could make her go away just by staring hard. When she didn't disappear, he *harrumphed.* "Very well. I'll see if he'll see you. Wait here."

The bard marched off, no, *waddled* was a more apt description, leaving Miralee standing there feeling foolish. No one else paid any attention to her until a few minutes later, when a boy about Miralee's age approached her. He seemed nervous and eager.

"Hello. Master Prodley told me to take you to the Headmaster's office. Follow me, please," he said.

Headmaster Kant was seventy-six years old and had seen a lot, therefore, he was not easily surprised. But today would prove to be interesting, if not all out surprising.

Master Kant was in his office signing a purchase order for ink, quills, and parchment, when Master Prodley came in. The vein at the top of Prodley's bald head was visible, a sure sign that the bard was irritated. But since the man was a well-known curmudgeon, Kant ignored it.

"What is it Prodley? We're somewhat busy here," said the Headmaster.

The other half of the 'we' was his secretary, a man named Grigg. While not a musician—the man could not carry a tune in a bucket—Mr. Grigg was invaluable to the guild in that he excelled at keeping those things organized and on track that Master Kant was, speaking generously, less good at keeping organized and on the proper track.

"There is a girl here to see you," Prodley said.

"Me? Are you sure? Mrs. Norris usually…"

"She's not a servant, I guess, more of a messenger—a damned impertinent one. Says she has a message from the journeyman at Sperry's Knoll."

"Ah, Shondar, a solid man."

"Well, certainly. But she insists on delivering it to you personally. What's more, she seems to think that she's a bard."

"How's that?" Kant asked.

"Well, she's wearing a guild medallion and carrying a guitar across her back."

Grigg leaned in.

"Headmaster, it sounds like it might be the girl that Sir Dameon mentioned."

"Oh yes. He did say he was looking for a young lady with some musical ability, didn't he?"

"He did. Coming from the west no less."

"Well, from here, everything is to the west," said Kant.

"Did the girl mention her name?" Grigg asked Prodley.

"Yes, she said it was Merrily, or some such. Sounds like a harlot's name."

"Miralee," said Grigg. "That's her. Sir Dameon asked to be notified if we came across her."

"Very well. Mr. Grigg, send a runner to Sir Dameon's residence. In the meantime, I suppose I'll meet the young lady."

"I told an apprentice to bring her up," Prodley said.

Grigg got up and left to find a messenger.

Without being asked, Master Prodley plopped down onto a chair, which creaked in protest, and sighed deeply. Apparently, he had decided to stay and see what Miralee's message was. The girl had annoyed him so he wanted to show her that he was important enough to hear any message Shondar might have for the headmaster.

Well, thought Kant, *I'll decide if that's true after I read it.*

He heard the outer office door open. A moment later someone knocked on the door to Kant's inner office.

"Come in," he said.

An apprentice, Tullison was his name, escorted into the headmaster's office a girl who was both very pretty and rather tall, easily the tallest person in the room.

She looked nervous.

He took in the medallion and guitar, both just as Prodley said. Additionally, she bore a heavy pack that might have contained all of her worldly possessions.

"Sit, please," Kant said, gesturing to a plush chair across from his desk. "Put down your burden. I'm Headmaster Kant. So far, I have yet to bite anyone."

Prodley shifted his bulk forward.

"Headmaster, that's not entirely true," he said.

143

Kant winced, remembering the incident years ago that involved an upstart stage manager.

"Yes, well, there was one. But he had it coming.

"Anyway, I understand that you are acquainted with Shondar Skale and have a message from him for me."

Miralee nodded.

"That's right, sir."

She reached into her cloak pocket, not the one where Orrie liked to nest, and drew out the letter, which was now somewhat crumpled. Saying nothing, her mouth was too dry for words, she handed the bundled papers to the old headmaster.

Kant accepted the papers, smoothing them out on his desk. The parchment was slightly damp, but the ink was legible. He recognized Journeyman Shondar's neat, compressed hand. These days, Kant had to sit back several feet, at a precise distance, to read anything. He found his range and started to read.

Headmaster Kant, Greetings…

So far so good.

I hope this letter finds you well. The last time we met, you had eaten three day old halibut and, well, I just hope your humor's improved.

I am writing to you in regards to the young lady bearing this letter. Her name is Miralee Verity from the village of Brown's Ford.

Kant recognized the name of the village.

I had the pleasure of hearing and then playing with Miralee in Sperry's Knoll as she was making her way to Edain. I was extremely impressed by her ability. I was so impressed that when she told me that she was apprenticed to Master Olahan, I believed her immediately.

Headmaster Kant read the last sentence three times. He looked up, just managing to keep his face neutral, and glanced at the young woman sitting across from him. She was staring at her hands, which were clasped tightly in her lap. Still, Kant had the impression that she was closely attuned to him somehow, watching his reaction. Prodley openly stared at him, impatient to know what the letter said. Kant kept reading.

Miralee had no real direction when I met her, other than to come to Edain and study music. She has tremendous raw skill and an intuition for music rarely found. She is a great asset to our guild.

The awkward part, other than the obvious one, is that she left Brown's Ford in a hurry and had no apprenticeship papers per se. I have taken the liberty of providing her with papers of apprenticeship, showing Master Olahan as her master. I have included them. They are in my hand and bear my signature, so obviously Master Olahan will have to confirm. I will send a messenger to Brown's Ford as soon as possible.

I have sent Miralee to you hoping several things: that my opinion is held highly by you; that you will accept my documents on behalf of Master Olahan until he can be contacted; and that you will overlook Miralee's gender and admit her to study at the conservatory as an apprentice of the guild.

Miralee was born a woman through no fault of her own. If she was a boy, she would be the bright star of her generation. I feel that it is time for our guild to abandon traditions that hold us back. Listen to her. See if you agree.

I can hear the objections from here; the biggest being that the guildmaster would never allow it. Olahan was guildmaster once, and he hears in her what I hear. Whereas the current leadership in Magh Moru is conservative, I trust in you to be open-minded enough to do the right thing. Maybe by the time the guildhall learns of her, she will be established enough, with enough support, to overcome the limits of traditional conservatism.

Your Friend, Shondar.

Kant finished reading. He did not look up. Instead, he shuffled through the rest of the parchments. There were two more sheets that comprised the apprenticeship papers mentioned. Kant only pretended to read these. He was deep in thought. He even went back to the letter he had just read and pretended to read it over again.

He had absolutely no idea what he was going to say. At first he wondered if it was a joke, but looking at the nervous, hopeful young woman, he knew that it was not. Then he felt angry at Shondar, despite his fondness for the young journeyman, for putting him in this position.

There's just no way, he thought.

Grigg came back into the room then, nodding almost imperceptibly to let the Headmaster know the message had been sent.

Perhaps this decision will be out of my hands.

But he had no way of knowing how long the Shadow Knight might take to respond. In the meantime, it behooved him to keep the girl at the conservatory.

"Miralee," he said. "You have read this?"

"No, not as such, sir."

"But you know what this letter says?"

She nodded.

"Then you know this is no small thing for me to decide." She remained stone still. "What I propose is an audition. It is nearly dinner time. You look tired, and I'm certain you must be hungry. Mr. Grigg, for the next few hours, Miralee is our guest. Provide her with food and facilities for refreshment. After dinner, you will play for me and a few of the conservatory instructors. Agreed?"

"Yes sir," she said meekly.

Grigg led Miralee out. Kant sighed. He was getting too old for this sort of thing. With luck, Sir Dameon would hurry, take the girl wherever he intended to take her, and this problem would go away.

"Ahem."

It was Master Prodley. He seemed about to burst.

At the same time that Grigg was showing Miralee to a small guestroom, Sir Dameon en'Calo located Sergeant Kalin as the man came in for the night watch. The sergeant told Sir Dameon about Miralee, and that he had taken her to the Shells Inn. Dameon thanked Kalin and went to the inn forthwith. When he arrived, he was disappointed to learn that both Miralee and the young man with whom she had been seen had checked out of the inn, leaving separately.

With no other leads, he thought about heading to his home on the harbor, just south of the mouth of the Tandy River. He had just come from there though and decided to patrol North Town for a while in hopes of picking up the trail. He had no way of knowing that a message telling him exactly where Miralee could be found was soon to arrive at his house.

Janessa had contacted him earlier, estimating that she and Joran would arrive at midnight through the Canal Gate. He'd stay in North Town at least that long to meet them.

Silently, Miralee chided herself for being so nervous during her meeting with Headmaster Kant. Being accepted into the conservatory was important to her, but her nerves would only get in the way. She'd been so worked up that she hadn't been able to get much of a read on the headmaster.

Relax, she told herself. *They haven't kicked you out yet.*

She ate, washed, and even managed to go out and feed the dog, which was out of sight, but appeared as soon as Miralee stepped outside.

An hour later, Miralee was in a small hall, standing in front of an assembled group of ten masters and journeymen. Her stomach flip-flopped as she felt the stares, most were disapproving, a few merely curious.

However, the instant that she placed her lips to the mouthpiece of her *duduk* and began to play, her nervousness vanished.

She played a song whose name she did not know.

When Olahan had first given her the *duduk* he taught her several songs from the eastern lands where the instrument was native. One of those songs Miralee had always loved. To her, it was wind on a lonely hill, snow covered pines gently rubbing their branches together, the roar of a flooded river—it was passion, and it was fury. It was beautiful. She hadn't played it in over a year, but she played it now.

Miralee had promised herself that she wouldn't let go. She didn't want random light shows and images causing a stir. But she felt the energy blossom inside of her all the same. Directed inward, the cracks in the self-forged chains that fettered her core-self widened, until just a single link held her in check.

The buzz of voices in her head came rushing back.

147

By the time she finished, to polite, surprised applause, and started her next song, the thoughts of the bards were practically being shouted at her.

Amazing, I have to find out what that last song was, a journeyman thought.

What a lovely girl, thought a middle-aged master bard. *As good as she is, we can't have a woman here. With the likes of her around, nothing would ever get done...*

That rapscallion, Rafe, said the street people of North Town were all talking about a statuesque, fair-haired woman said to be Bridget incarnate. Can this be her? I could certainly believe it, another thought.

If I was thirty years younger...

This is absurd. Guildmaster Berint would see us all drummed out of the guild, no matter how good she is...

She is good, very good. I almost wish I hadn't notified the Shadow Knights that she is here.

That last thought belonged to none other than Headmaster Kant.

It changed everything.

Miralee's dream of the conservatory was destroyed by that one overheard thought.

She would have to keep running. She could have cried.

But she didn't. She didn't even stop playing. Whatever was unraveling inside of her was a tempest that the music fed.

There was no holding back now.

The notes she played were just notes. But each note shot forth like an arrow propelled by the strength of her mind. Even though she was playing indoors, an actual wind started to blow. The lamps in the room dimmed then blew out.

What happened next brought varying accounts by the bards in the room.

Some swore that the night sky, full of stars, appeared where the ceiling had been. They saw the stars begin to whirl in hypnotic patterns, before falling, one by one, to gather around Miralee like fairy dust. Others saw the entire hall drop away and become a snowy forest. From not too distant the howling of wolves created a terrifying chorus. A few just saw Miralee, standing in the hall

148

playing. But even these swore that she seemed to grow before their eyes, and they saw her begin to glow brighter and brighter, like the moon and sun together, until they had to avert their eyes.

And then she was gone.

The hall was just a hall. The depth of the silence was abysmal.

It took several, long moments before anyone spoke. When they did, it was all at once. Confusion, wonderment, talk of witchcraft, all blended into a frantic babble.

Headmaster Kant had a better idea what the Shadow Knights wanted with the girl.

Now I see the source of Shondar's infatuation, he thought. *She's a witch*.

Chapter Thirteen

The tempest pushed Miralee to the edge. Yet rather than allow herself to be blown into the chasm, she caught herself at the last moment.

It was within her to tear the hall down at the crescendo of her song—it wouldn't even be hard. And part of her wanted to do just that, sing a song of destruction to wipe away the pain in her heart.

The headmaster had betrayed her. Shondar had told Miralee that Kant was a good man, that he would help her. Shondar had been wrong.

And Miralee was ready to unleash a storm that would wipe it all away, wipe them away. Something that had been unchained inside of her cried out for destruction, and hungered for their fear and pain.

But Miralee was stronger than that. Her first instinct had always been to help, to protect. When the demon had attacked, she'd been ready to sacrifice her life to save the lives of others.

The strength of her other side frightened and surprised her, but she would not let it get the better of her.

She soared on the music, her song as wild and irresistible as a hurricane. Momentarily, she saw herself through the eyes of one of the bards in the audience.

She was beautiful and terrible, in the way that a tornado or lightning storm can inspire both awe and terror—that was how she looked. Not human at all.

Seeing herself looking so alien, shocked her like a splash of cold water to the face. It brought her back.

She cut off her song mid-phrase.

"Don't see me!" She thought at the stunned bards.

And they didn't.

Without training, Miralee made herself invisible in the same manner that Shadow Knights could.

She ran from the hall, not knowing if they could see her or not, and kept running until she was outside. No one molested her, or even seemed to notice her. The only exception was the stray dog. It fell into step beside her as she ran toward a modest patch of woods that was across the street directly across from the conservatory.

In her pocket, Orrie stirred. The rodent had slept through the entire performance.

Miralee's wooded refuge was almost a perfect circle with a diameter of no more than one hundred feet. She clung to the cool shadows like a child with a favorite blanket. A few well-tended paths wound through the trees, but there was no one there now. Miralee knew it. She could hear the whispered thoughts, sense the feelings and see the auras of everyone within a quarter mile.

She moved off of the path and sheltered in the hollow of a large oak near the middle of the copse. Orrie crawled onto her shoulder and rubbed himself against her ear. The dog cocked his head to one side and looked at her with sad eyes. Miralee held out her hand. The dog touched it with his wet nose then gave it a quick, affectionate lick. He seemed to know that Miralee was distressed. He sat close and laid his head in her lap.

"Thank you," she told him.

His presence, and Orrie's, helped. The animals grounded her. Miralee relaxed. She did not try to fight what was happening. The voices receded to a wash of white noise. The feelings she shut out by focusing on the comfort of her animals.

Orrie already had a name, but not the dog. Right then, Miralee decided to call him Solace. It seemed very appropriate.

With Orrie and Solace to keep her warm, Miralee slept.

.

.

.

She came awake suddenly.

What am I doing? I can't stay here. It's too close. I'll be found for sure.

She checked the pocket where Orrie liked to sleep and found him well.

"Come on Solace."

Fifteen minutes later, Miralee stood on a very crowded Amberi Street.

Edain's Mayday celebration had begun.

151

In Edain, Mayday was actually four days long. There was Mayday itself, and the three preceding days, beginning at sundown of the first night. The city would be given over to a celebration of the fertility of spring. Many marriages would be consummated over the next four nights and days. Life would be celebrated through music, song, dance, theater, and more erotic pastimes.

While Lilting Street was home to Edain's *fine* arts, Amberi Street was where the arts met the common man—though not too common, it was still South Town. Amberi Street was blocks full of theaters, taverns, galleries, and coffee shops, frequented by gentlemen, wealthy merchants, and the sons and daughters of the city's nobility. Of course, those who preyed on or catered to the wealthy and comfortably middle class were present as well—pick pockets, flim-flam artists, and entertainers.

Of entertainers there were all sorts. Musicians busked on street corners under the warm glow of oil lamps. They played in the coffee shops and taverns. Additionally, fire-eaters, jugglers, mimes, acrobats, actors, dancers of all kinds, and more exotic entertainment abounded. Miralee saw a man with a bucket and a dog. People were throwing coins—mostly tin or copper, but money still—on the ground. The dog would come over, take the coin in his mouth, offer a paw to shake with the donor, and then would place the coin in the man's bucket.

I can make money here. I just have to be careful. I can't have another incident like last night. And there's Gabriel to think of. And as much as I hate to admit, it looks like he was right—the Shadow Knights know about me and are looking for me. I don't have a choice, I'm going to have to leave Istey. I'll make what I can and hope it's enough for passage to Ehrian.

She might have started right away, but she was exhausted and first wanted someplace safe to stay for the night.

She found an inn toward the southern end of Amberi Street. The front facade was dominated by a painting of a red dragon seated upon a mountain of golden cups. The dragon was drinking from a keg that it held like a mug in its clawed hand. Below the painting was the name of the place.

"The Dragon's Flagon," she read.

She stopped abruptly.

How did I just do that?

Miralee had never been taught to read, yet she had looked at the letters on the sign and they had made sense to her. In part, she seemed to be pulling the words from the minds of those around her, but not entirely. She thought of reading Shondar's letter when she had shared Gabriel's mind. It seemed that she had learned to read because he knew how to read. Had she retained that knowledge, and it was just manifesting now, as things happened inside of her that she did not understand?

If that's true, it's about the only good thing to happen to me since I met Gabriel.

Miralee had to take a room sharing a bed. The cost was twice what she had paid for a private room in the Shells. She had to give the innkeeper three more pennies to allow her to take Solace to the room.

Her roommate was absent when she arrived in the room, which was hardly bigger than a closet. There was a bed, just big enough for two, a wash basin with brownish water, and two lockers at the foot of the bed, one of which Miralee possessed the key to. She stuffed all of her belongings into the locker, except her guitar, which did not quite fit, and her money and her knife. These stayed safely on her person. Miralee decided to take the far side of the bed, closest to a small, dirty window.

"Solace, you can sleep on the floor next to me. Keep an eye on my guitar," she told the dog, leaning her instrument into the crook of the bed and the wall. "And we're sharing the room, so don't get excited when someone comes in and gets into bed."

Miralee lay down and was asleep almost immediately.

She awoke as soon as the first gray light found its way through the window. A woman was on her back, snoring on the bed next to her. Miralee quietly got up. Solace was already awake, watching her patiently. No doubt, he needed to go out.

Her roommate was middle-aged, a few years older than Miralee's mother perhaps.

Not my real mother…I miss her so much.

Miralee had a vivid memory of helping Myra in the kitchen. Miralee had been about eight. She had burned her hand when she'd turned over a pan full of hot grease. If it had been Wolen (*like he ever cooked*), he would first have admonished her for making a mess and possibly ruining dinner. But not Myra. She'd rushed over to Miralee in an instant and examined her burned hand. Blisters were already forming. Myra put it in cold water for a few minutes, then she applied a salve that she made from Casper Root and Jewel Weed. It both numbed the pain and promoted healing. Myra had wrapped the injured hand loosely with a dry, linen bandage. Then she had taken Miralee in a tight embrace and kissed both of her cheeks, which were wet with tears even though Miralee had refused to vocalize her pain, beyond an initial, surprised yelp. Only then did her mother concern herself with the mess.

My mother…the only one I've known, even if it isn't by blood. Stop it! This isn't helping. I can't go back home. It isn't an option.

I just didn't realize being alone would be so hard.

I wonder what Olahan's doing right now.

Miralee looked down at her hand. Today, no mark of the accident was evident. She wiped tears from her eyes, surprised to find them there.

Solace, true to his name, nuzzled her leg with his head. She scratched behind his ears appreciatively.

"Let's find out about breakfast and a bath," she said to both of her animal friends.

As soon as she stepped out of the room, Miralee was greeted by the smell of fresh coffee and frying bacon.

Downstairs, very few patrons were in evidence. The few she saw looked haggard.

A young woman, pretty, but with an all-business demeanor, was behind the counter. Unlike the other girls that Miralee had encountered in the taverns and inns since leaving home, this efficient-looking woman seemed decisively in charge.

"No! And while you chat up your friends all day, I keep this place running. So don't argue with me about the menu. Just do it!" She yelled at someone in the kitchen as Miralee walked up. "How

154

can I help you?" she asked, going from bossy to benevolent without missing a beat.

"I'm in room four. I wanted to take the room for a few more nights. Also, what are the chances of getting a bath?" Miralee asked.

The woman smiled. It seemed genuine. Miralee realized that she *could* read the woman's thoughts, but was able to block them out. Such prying seemed rude if one could help it.

"You're in luck. The bathwater is just heating up now. You can have it hot and fresh. Not many early risers during Mayday."

Miralee thanked her and paid for the extra nights.

"Is that your dog?" the woman asked.

"Yes," Miralee said, preparing to hand over more money for Solace.

"He seems very well-behaved. There are some steak bones left over from last night's dinner. Can I give him one?"

"Of course! Thank you. My name is Miralee."

"Jolie. After your bath come back and get some breakfast. Hang on, I'll get that bone."

A few minutes later, Miralee luxuriated in a hot tub of water, while Solace, equally content, gnawed on a steak bone on the floor next to the tub. Orrie took the opportunity to explore the small bath house.

Relaxed, she considered her problems.

I don't have much money left. I'll have to earn what I can over the next few days, but not draw a lot of attention. I'll have to stay in control. Just play music, nothing else, like when I was at home. It's too much to hope that Gabriel will forget about me. Once he sobers up, he'll try to find me. And the Shadow Knights. And I guess the bards. Seems they're in league. Why can't they just leave me alone?

After her bath, Miralee returned to the dining room. The coffee smell had almost covered the odor of stale beer that lingered from the previous night. A few more customers were in evidence, but the room was still mostly empty.

She sat on a stool at the bar. Jolie saw her and came over.

"How was your bath?"

"Wonderful. I feel like a new person."

155

"I've got bacon, eggs, biscuits with gravy, and coffee for breakfast."

"Sounds good," said Miralee.

Jolie disappeared into the kitchen. She returned a moment later with a heaping plate and a cup of coffee.

The breakfast tasted as delicious as it smelled. Even the coffee, something for which Miralee had never really developed a taste, was perfect.

Jolie lingered while Miralee ate.

"Are you in town for the festival?"

"Not really," Miralee said between bites. "I…had business here, but it sort of fell through."

Jolie nodded. She seemed to see right into Miralee, who resisted the urge to peek into the woman's mind.

"But you are staying for the festival or you wouldn't have rented the bed for three more nights. You'll be going home afterwards?"

Miralee hesitated to disclose her business to a stranger, but strangers were all she had these days. And even though she was refraining from reading the woman's thoughts, she could not help but feel the woman's emotions. There was no maliciousness or duplicity, just an intuitive concern.

"No. I'm planning on finding a ship that will take me out of Istey. I hope to earn enough money during the festival to book passage on a trader, maybe to Ehrian."

An unshaven, red-eyed man sat down at the bar, a few stools away. Jolie brought him a cup of coffee. Having done so, she came back to Miralee.

"Did you kill anyone?"

Miralee was shocked.

"What? No. I mean…"

"Okay, it's just that for a woman as young as you to be fleeing the country without too much care about where she winds up, well, you must be in pretty bad trouble," Jolie said, slowly wiping the counter with a towel.

It occurred to Miralee that the concern she felt in the other woman might be worry that Miralee would bring her troubles to the Dragon's Flagon. She didn't want that, so she wound up telling

Jolie the entire story—well, most of the story. She said how she had wanted to be a musician and how Olahan had made her his apprentice. She said that she had run away when Wolen wanted to send her to another village to marry her off. And how Gabriel had rescued her, and how she had liked him, but he turned out to be no good. Miralee described Gabriel as a fallen Shadow Knight who had somehow turned the other Shadow Knights against her. She ended by saying that she had gone to the conservatory, but had been rejected. She implied that the reason was her gender; no mention was made of her gifts.

Throughout the story, Jolie listened attentively. As she heard how the bards had rejected Miralee, she began to nod vigorously.

"I know what you mean. This is my inn, but technically my brother owns it. I'm the one who runs it and does all the work, but he gets all of the credit. All because I'm a woman, and because of backward Istean inheritance laws. Unmarried women can't inherit real property, you know."

Miralee didn't know; in Brown's Ford, it never came up. Pretty much all of the girls were married by seventeen.

"As for this man, you're better off without him. But why are the Shadow Knights looking for you? If he's no longer one of them, they can't have much love for each other. It doesn't sound like them to get involved in someone's romantic affairs. And they don't care about runaway girls."

But they would if she was a demon, Miralee thought glumly.

"I don't know, but I overheard the headmaster saying that one of them had asked about me and wanted to be notified if I showed up."

Jolie looked thoughtful.

"It would probably be Sir Dameon. He's the only one of them that lives here on a permanent basis. There aren't a lot of them you know, Shadow Knights I mean. I heard there are only like a hundred. Sir Dameon has a manor on the harbor. I've only met him a few times, but he's always struck me as a good man."

"I'd rather leave before I find out for myself if he is or isn't," said Miralee.

"Mmm. You're kind of noticeable. That's good, I suppose, for a musician. But not for one who's also trying to hide. I have an idea."

157

"What?"

"No. Come on. I'll show you. Jesur, watch the counter! I'm taking a break." The last was shouted into the kitchen, presumably toward her brother.

"You aren't helping with the cooking. You never help with the cooking."

A large, lethargic-looking man appeared. He muttered something that Miralee couldn't hear. Whatever it was, Jolie decided to ignore it. She came around the counter, took Miralee by the hand and led her off to the owner's suite.

The top floor of the Flagon was given over to storage and also contained a spacious three bedroom apartment with an open living space. The furniture was older and worn, but comfortable.

Miralee followed Jolie, and was followed by Solace. To Orrie, Miralee gave a firm mental command to stay put. As nice as Jolie seemed, she was an innkeeper, and what innkeeper wanted a patron who brought a rat into the establishment?

"Have a seat," Jolie said, pointing Miralee to a plush sofa. "Okay, here's my thought. Like I said, you're noticeable. There aren't many six foot tall, pretty young women with long, fair hair who are musicians, even in Edain. But a six foot young man, with short, dark hair isn't uncommon at all."

Miralee saw what Jolie was getting at, but she was doubtful. It showed on her face.

"No, hear me out. I think it could work. You're tall enough that you could fit into a pair of my brother's pants and wear one of his shirts. For the hair, I can put yours up, and you can wear this."

Jolie ran into her room and came out holding what looked like a limp, possibly dead, animal of some sort. It was a dark brown wig.

"This will work," the innkeeper said eagerly. "Can I?"

Maybe it will. It won't hurt to see.

"Okay. What first?"

"Great. Stay here. I'm going to get some things."

In a few moments, Jolie brought a pair of men's pants, a man's shirt, a comb, hairpins, and some strips of linen, such as those one might use as bandages.

"We'll start with those," Jolie said, pointing at Miralee's chest. "You're not very bosomy, but we should do this right. Take off your clothes."

Shrugging, Miralee laid her cloak down on the couch and pulled off her dress. Since they were in Jolie's living room, she prayed that Jesur didn't walk in. She reached out and checked. He was still engaged downstairs. Solace seemed disinterested in what was going on. Out of the corner of her eye, she saw the pocket of her cloak move—Orrie. She hoped that Jolie hadn't noticed.

"Now what?" asked Miralee, hoping she sounded casual, standing there in her underwear.

"I'm going to take a few of these linens and wrap them around your chest, make it look more masculine. Hold your arms up like this," said Jolie.

Miralee held up her arms.

"Goodness, look at your arms. You look strong enough to be a man," Jolie said. "Don't get me wrong. You're beautifully feminine, but such muscles."

"I grew up on a farm. I'm used to hard work."

Even as Miralee said it, she thought that there was more to it. Since she left home, she had felt stronger, especially in the last few days. Might it be not just her mind that was changing, but her body as well? Maybe she was simply maturing. She was of an age where she might not yet be done growing.

"There," Jolie said, bringing Miralee out of her thoughts. "Not too tight?"

"No, it's comfortable."

"Okay, try the shirt and pants."

The shirt was a little big in the shoulders, the pants tight in the hips, but loose in the waist. All in all, the clothes looked pretty good. Miralee had never worn trousers before. They seemed a little constrictive, but strangely liberating.

"Not bad," Jolie said, nodding appraisingly. "Now for the hair."

Jolie combed out Miralee's long, yellow hair, pulled it together and pinned it up on the top of her head. She set the wig on her head and pinned that in place. Then Jolie combed the wig out and arranged it so that it looked natural. It was actually fairly long, though much shorter than Miralee's own hair. It hung past her ears and touched her shoulders in the back, a length worn by many Istean men.

Jolie took Miralee into her bedroom and stood her in front of a large mirror. The image she saw was herself, certainly, but remarkably dissimilar to the Miralee she knew. Just the addition of trousers and the change in her hair radically altered her appearance.

It just might work, she thought.

"Nearly perfect," Jolie told her. "But one more thing is needed. Here take this."

Jolie handed Miralee another of the linen strips. This one she had rolled up in a tight bundle about the size of a fist. Miralee took it from her, mystified as to what she was supposed to do with it. Reading Miralee's face, Jolie laughed and pointed down.

"Put it down the front of your pants," she explained. "You know, you're a little light down there."

"Oh!" said Miralee with sudden understanding.

She tucked the wadded cloth down the front of her pants as instructed.

"There we are now, as handsome a lad as a girl could want," Jolie announced.

In spite of all that had happened and the dangers she still faced, Miralee giggled. It was infectious, and soon the both women were laughing until they were red-faced and out of breath.

"Thank you," Miralee said, sitting on the edge of the bed and wiping a tear from her eye. "Though I don't see why you should go to all of this trouble for a stranger."

"Nonsense. I see a lot of myself in you. This was a little thing. And, anything to serve a customer and all of that."

Jolie's face was serious then broke into a grin. There was more laughter.

"So, did you have a plan? Do you have any venues in mind?" the innkeeper asked her.

"No. I thought I'd start on the street and go from there."

"That's certainly an option. However, I happen to be in need of an entertainer for my lunch crowd. Would you like a job?"

Miralee was unsure. She didn't want to bring her troubles to the Dragon's Flagon. But Jolie knew (*mostly*) what Miralee's situation was. She glanced into the mirror again. Maybe it would be okay. They were looking for Miralee after all, not...

Who should I be?

She spied her guitar sitting on the couch in the next room. She thought of how she had gotten it.

Brex, I'll be Brex Lorexson. It's as good a name as any. No one will know it here.

"Okay, I'd love to."

Chapter Fourteen

Sir Dameon was glad for Janessa's and Joran's company. However, there had been the disappointment of, after having greeting them at the city gates and returning home, getting the late message from Headmaster Kant. Still, he had hoped that the bards had found some way to keep the girl at the conservatory. He and his fellow Shadow Knights had arrived at the conservatory at almost four in the morning. The girl was long gone.

And now, after only a few hours rest, Dameon and his guests were seated on the back patio of his home, which overlooked the harbor, deciding what to do next.

Janessa had her feet up on a chair, sipping coffee and looking out at the ships moored on the water. Overhead, seagulls screamed.

"At least she's no longer with Gabriel, it seems," Joran ventured.

"A pity," Janessa said. "I'd love to see that traitor again."

"I wish that I'd been able to locate this girl before the festival began. With the festival started, the city's population has swollen. It will be that much more difficult to find her until it is over," Dameon said.

"There are three of us to look now," said Janessa.

"And we'll be five when Artegan and Mordis arrive in two days," Joran said.

Janessa shook her head. "I'd really like to find Miralee before they get here. Perhaps Gabriel is no longer with her, but he's about. The sooner we find her and return to Magh Moru, the better. If we locate her before the festival ends, we can get on the road as soon as the others get here."

"Do we know that she'll want to go Magh Moru?" asked Dameon. "What if she says no?"

Neither Janessa nor Joran had really considered the possibility. It gave them pause. Finally, Janessa shrugged.

"She might, but it doesn't change our duty to find her. So let's find her. We'll worry about the rest once we do."

"Okay, how?" asked Joran.

"Her strength seems to be growing. There was a strong residual energy at the conservatory."

"And I felt her power manifest from miles away the other night," Dameon offered.

"So we spread out and wait. We'll try to cover those places where she is likely to be."

"That would probably be Lilting, Amberi, the Shells, and maybe near the Market or Gunnar's Field."

"She might try to leave the city," suggested Joran. "Her goal, as far as we know, was to go to the conservatory. Without that, she might not stay in Edain."

Janessa sighed. "You're right. Joran, I want you to patrol Lilting, Amberi, and adjacent neighborhoods. Dameon, take North Town. I'll keep an eye on the gates. Dameon update me periodically and give a telepathic shout if you find anything. Joran's telepathic abilities aren't fully developed, so I'll act as a switch board—I can make myself heard and hear him if he shouts loud enough.

"Also, for the next few days, I want to keep two of us out in the city all of the time, meaning we sleep in shifts and keep it short. Let's find Miralee."

Gabriel spent the day Miralee had left deeply immersed in drink. He'd had the good sense to leave the Shells Inn for a rougher accommodation in the wharf. He had left in a hurry, beating her to the stable and taking her horse. Then he had quickly sold it to a Varian trader. After that he had tried to lose himself. Unfortunately, no amount of drink had been sufficient to bring the oblivion he craved.

He wanted to forget the whole endeavor. He fantasized about climbing on one of the ships in the harbor and sailing away to Jarrow, P'el, or farther, someplace where his mother would never find him, where he could be free of her machinations.

But he hadn't left, wouldn't leave. Deep down, he knew that. But he could dream. And he could drink.

At some point, near dawn, he had passed out.

163

Now his mother's angry, demanding voice penetrated the blanket of slumber that was his refuge from his responsibilities.

No.

Gabriel's feeble wishes did nothing to halt the shrill tirade coming from the black, stone mirror in his pack. Groaning, he forced himself upright. Eyes half closed, Gabriel fumbled through his belongings until his hands fell on the smooth mirror.

"What, mother?"

Delia was a picture of barely controlled fury, not an unusual state for his mother.

"What is your status?" she asked after a long moment.

"My status?"

"Don't play dumb. You have been traveling with the girl for almost two weeks. After we spoke yesterday, I thought you understood that I expected you to begin back immediately—with her cooperation or without. So?"

Should he tell the truth, he wondered?

"I have her. I managed to dominate her mind as promised. We are a day out of Edain," he lied.

His mother's eyes narrowed.

"Show her to me."

"What?!"

"If you have conquered her mind as you say, it will do no harm to show her to me in the glass."

"I, uh, mother..."

"Fool, you can't lie to me; you never could. Where is she really?"

"She's...she's gone. She left the inn yesterday."

"And you let her go. I should have known better than to trust you. Formidable as you are, you're worthless to me. Your weakness of character is an embarrassment."

"Mother, please! I know where she has gone. I am going to collect her today. I wanted to take her by surprise. Things are well in hand, I promise," Gabriel said, hating how whiney his voice sounded.

"Your promises mean nothing. What is the word of a drunkard worth? Fortunately, I knew that you would fail me."

"Then why did you send me?!"

"Oh, initially it was my hope that you had developed sufficient self-control to avoid your vices. That's the pity of it really. You could be an excellent agent of our people, but you lack constancy. It was clear to me days ago that this was beyond you. So I have arranged for you to have help," said Delia.

"What help?" he asked warily.

"Ghorach."

"No!"

"Yes! I already have an ally who has found a host and will perform the rite tonight."

Ghorach was a high order demon and Gabriel's uncle. Gabriel had always found him rather unnerving. He was a hunter and a killer, things Gabriel did very well. But while Gabriel took pride in his proficiency, he felt no special joy in terrorizing those he hunted or killed. For Ghorach, pain was his sustenance, causing terror, his art. For a second, Gabriel blanched at the thought of Miralee at his uncle's mercy. He pushed the thought from his mind. She meant nothing to him; their intimacy had merely been a ruse.

"I thought the girl was valuable," he said to his mother. "Ghorach will ruin her."

"She has power, considerable power. Abaddon wants her power in his service. Some time in my brother's hands might make her more malleable. If not, I know he can be counted on to keep her out of the grasp of our enemies. Plus, Ghorach will find the girl, and when he does, she will not escape."

"I'll find her before tonight," he said.

"Maybe. But either way, Ghorach is coming. I want no more mistakes. And you should know, if he arrives and finds you drunk, I've given him permission to discipline you however he sees fit," said Delia.

Gabriel shuddered.

"Don't worry, mother. There will be no mistakes."

Emer ni'Oban checked her hair. She looked unhappily at the scratch on her face and the tiny bite mark left by the rat—*a rat!*—

that had attacked her when she'd been having her bit of fun with that peasant girl the other night. She would have to talk to the Duke before going out to the festival and see if his inquiry had produced anything. Despite that prig Peri's protests, Emer and Duke ni'Graelly agreed that commoners cannot be allowed to go around assaulting nobility. He had promised to begin an investigation and to have the girl arrested and punished.

The Duke was a fine man from a fine, old family. Emer had discovered that she had a lot in common with the man, and she was glad that she had decided to come to Edain for her holiday from school.

But how Peri came from him, I'll never know.

Emer made her way from her suite to the Duke's conference room and found him there. The guard outside announced her.

The room was empty but for the Duke and another man, unusual for this time of day. Perhaps the Duke had suspended normal business because of the festival. Emer recognized the man as Moricai, who was some sort of advisor. She had met him the day she had arrived and not seen him since. He was handsome in a dark sort of way, quiet, but with a disturbing gaze. Today, he was not at his best. His face was palid. Emer could see small scratches on his forhead and a dark bruise on his cheek. He was whispering something to the Duke as she entered.

The Duke waved Moricai off and smiled as Emer entered the room.

"Lady ni'Oban, how good to see you," he said. "My advisor was just…no, it isn't important. He was just leaving."

"Of course, My Lord." Moricai left, giving Emer a glance and slight nod as he passed. She felt a slight shiver, not unpleasant, in response.

"Duke ni'Graelly," said Emer once they were alone. "I wanted to ask if your investigation has succeeded in locating the criminal who attacked me."

"Not yet, I'm afraid. I've had the guard questioning people ever since. No one has been able to identify her. There are quite a few tall, blonde women in Edain. I can't arrest them all. There was even an incident in Edain Square two nights ago that involved a tall, fair-haired young woman…"

"What? That's only a few blocks from the field. Did your men detain her?"

"I'm told it was impossible. A riot was in progress at the time and…"

My Lord, you assured me that you would arrest the girl," said Emer.

"I will. But with the festival in progress…"

"How do you think my father would like hearing that I was assaulted by a commoner in your city and you did nothing about it? How do you think my uncle, the King, would feel?"

King Corliss was known as a fair man. He might even fall in line with Peri's opinion on the matter. The Duke did not say this to Emer though.

"Lady ni'Oban, you have nothing to worry about. The matter will be taken care of. My daughter mentioned that you and she would be going out into the city today. Go, enjoy your Mayday."

Emer was far from mollified, but decided that she would gain nothing at the moment by pressing.

"Yes, we'll be leaving soon. Somehow, I let Peri talk me into staying in South Town today."

"Well, my daughter loves music, and the best musicians are down here. Because of the swollen crowds, I'm going to send an extra half dozen guardsmen, under your command of course, as a personal bodyguard."

"As if I'll need them in South Town. Duke ni'Graelly…"

"Call me Corgan."

"Corgan, that's very kind. Of course, commanding common guards is too coarse a task for a lady. Perhaps you could assign one of your knights as well. He can deal with the guards so I don't have to interact with them directly," Emer said.

Actually, she didn't mind commanding the guards herself. Bossing people around was her specialty. It was just that she had her eye on one young knight.

"Consider it done."

"I think Sir Kaden en'Ulster would make a suitable choice," she suggested.

"Yes. Certainly that can be arranged."

"Thank you, Corgan. If they could be ready in an hour that would be splendid."

Emer left the Duke's conference room feeling optimistic about her day. It would be mid-afternoon when they went out. The festival would be in full swing. Even in South Town, she should be able to find some fun. The presence of the attractive and attentive Sir Kaden would help. Emer didn't even mind the necessity of bringing the Duke's daughter, Peri, along. Sometimes the girl's righteous outrage was amusing.

Quickening her step, Emer went to see if her friends were ready to go.

Deg pressed his thumb to his temple trying to push down the constant whisper of voices that plagued him. Filthy as he was, even on crowded Amberi Street, no one came within several feet of him if they could help it. Normally, he would be approaching the well-to-do festival goers, begging for alms or regaling them with the prophecies of destruction the voices fed him. That was why, on the streets, he was known as the Doom-crier.

Today, he was doing neither of those things.

He was on the hunt.

He had trailed the goddess across the bridge, but had lost sight of her on Temple Row. But this was where she had been coming to. She was Bridget, where else would the goddess go except to this part of the city? Well, perhaps her temple, but Deg had gone into the temple of Bridget shortly after losing track of her. She had not been there, he'd sensed it. It had not mattered that two effeminate priests had thrown him out. Deg had gone willingly. He knew the goddess was elsewhere.

When she had played two nights ago in the square, her music had cut through the voices, dispelling them for the first time he could remember. Her song had brought him peace for the first time ever.

168

He had to find her. She was his salvation.

He'd been looking for hours, eyes darting to and fro hoping to catch a glimpse of her, his ears straining to hear her voice.

Deg had nearly reached the southern end of Amberi Street, again. If he failed to find her this time, he would go to Lilting Street and resume his search there.

He would keep at it until he found her or he died.

Mostly, people were happy to get out of Deg's way; just the smell was enough in most cases. But when he saw a group of young nobles, including the Duke's own daughter, arrive in a carriage that was surrounded by at least a dozen guardsmen and a knight or two, Deg spun on his heels and headed north. Deg and nobility did not get along, especially when said nobility was escorted by a large armed contingent. He was perfectly willing to continue looking for Bridget until he died, but he had no desire to hasten his demise.

Miralee's first set had gone well. She played to an enthusiastic lunch crowd that had tipped reasonably generously. She had kept the music simple and light, and nothing had gone wrong. The songs kept out the whispered voices of the crowd, or absorbed them rather. They were still there, but as different color threads in the tapestry. She had relaxed and felt in control the whole time. She had not started glowing. There had been no lightshows. And at no point had Miralee been tempted to tear down the inn.

Her disguise had worked well. No one had suspected that she was anything other than a young, talented lad from parts unknown. Not just a lad, but a fairly non-descript one. She had stuck to playing her guitar. The *duduk* was too unique, too memorable.

She finished an early dinner, taking time to feed Solace and, discreetly, Orrie. Providence smiled on Miralee, as the bard who was scheduled to play at the Dragon's Flagon that night begged off with the excuse of a guild commitment. Miralee accepted Jolie's offer to play all night if she wanted.

She climbed back onto the stage, really no more than a small wooden riser, maybe four foot by six foot, against one wall.

169

The room was full; everyone's spirits were high. Things were going well. Already a few coins had been tossed into her bowl on the edge of the stage.

Then there was a commotion near the back. Uniformed, armed men pushed their way into Flagon. Elevated, Miralee could see Jolie hurry over to them. She didn't seem unduly worried. The men seemed to be escorting a party of well-dressed people.

Like in Sperry's Knoll, she thought.

The resemblance to her night in Sperry's Knoll became even more pronounced as Jolie's brother emptied two tables of irate patrons close to the stage. The group made their way to the tables, and Miralee's heart skipped. She almost, almost, fumbled the progression she was playing as she saw that this was the same group that had engineered her humiliation at Gunnar's Field. And in the center was Emer ni'Oban, the pretty girl with the auburn hair and cat's eyes that had been about to use Miralee as a rug, before Orrie had intervened. Miralee had only seen her face momentarily, but it had been etched in her mind, along with the young woman's venomous aura.

Stay calm. I'm not me. I'm Brex Lorexson. I didn't even have my guitar with me that night. She won't recognize me.

And it seemed to be true. Miralee finished her song to hearty applause from most of the crowd and polite clapping from the nobles. Feeling some relief, she launched into her next tune.

Deg arrived back on Amberi Street about an hour after dusk. So far, his search had been fruitless, but he was undaunted. He believed with his whole heart that she was near and that she could end his pain.

And as he reached the southern end of the street, the voices in his head were banished. From one of the taverns came the clear voice of the goddess. Eagerly, he followed the blessed sound until he came to an inn with a large painting of a dragon on the front.

Deg pushed his way inside. Normally, he would be thrown out of a South Town inn in a matter of seconds. But tonight, he was in the hands of destiny. The innkeeper and several employees were preoccupied with a large party on the far side of the room. Deg saw that the party was the same group of nobles and guards that he had avoided earlier. They no longer mattered. His goddess was here.

Deg looked to the stage. For a moment, he was confused. A young man was on stage. Where was she? Then the musician resumed singing and the voice was hers. Of course, Bridget could take any form she wished.

"Bridget, I'm coming. Here I come," he muttered, pushing his way through the crowd.

Fumbling and banging his way past the knots of drunken revelers, Deg drew closer and closer.

Miralee had just gotten comfortable when she sensed something amiss. She was four songs beyond when the group of nobles had come in, and they had shown no sign of recognizing her. Miralee had even peeked into the thoughts of a few of the people at the tables and confirmed it.

She was feeling pretty confident when disaster struck.

First, it was a thought that stood out from all of the others, as if it was meant for her.

"I'm here," it said.

She jumped and stumbled over the line she was singing.

Gabriel's found me, she thought at first.

But it didn't sound like Gabriel, even though the tone of the thoughts was familiar. She tried to pin point the source, both with her eyes and her other senses. The Flagon was too full. It wasn't until he appeared at the edge of the stage that Miralee realized from whom the thought had originated.

"Bridget," the beggar croaked, bumping into a burly man and spilling the man's ale as he stepped onto the riser, reaching for Miralee.

"Hey! Filthy bum!" said the man whose beer had been spilled. He stepped up after the beggar and shoved him in the back.

The beggar pitched forward, hands outstretched. Miralee shrank back, but the beggar ran into her just the same. His hand struck her head as he toppled, snagging the wig and pulling it most of the way off. It hung by a few pins on the side of her head, and all of her blond hair spilled out.

"Bridget, please, give me your grace. Free me from my torments," said the beggar, looking up at her from his knees.

Every eye was on the stage, including that of the nobles. Emer ni'Oban stood up, gaping.

"That's her! That's the piece of trash who assaulted me! Arrest her!" Emer yelled to the guards.

Seven armed men pushed forward and surrounded the stage.

One of Emer's companions, a pale young woman with black hair also rushed forward.

"No! Sir Kaden, order your men to stand down! I was there. This girl assaulted no one," she said.

"I'm sorry, Lady Peri. But your father specifically told me that this girl is to be arrested if located. Please stand aside."

Solace appeared on the stage growling at the guards, who drew their swords in response.

"Solace, no!" Miralee ordered, adding a mental command for him to flee the tavern. Orrie had been exploring the room, but she felt him run up her pant leg and she told him to be still and hide as they would likely search her at some point.

Across the room, Miralee could see Jolie. Her new friend looked horrified, but helpless to do anything in the face of so many armed men. Miralee hoped that her presence here didn't bring any reprisals onto the innkeeper, who had simply tried to help a stranger. She didn't want to bring any more trouble to anyone, even to the guards, who were basically innocent, just men trying to do their jobs. She decided to surrender.

Miralee set down her guitar and held up her hands. Two men came forward and took hold of her arms. As soon as they touched her, Miralee felt a flash of hot anger and heard an animalistic shout. The beggar was suddenly up, spitting and striking at the two guards.

"No!" she shouted.

The guards were surprised by the attack, so overmatched was the beggar against even one of the armed men. A few even chuckled. But the knight wasn't amused. He stepped up onto the small stage and clouted the beggar behind the ear. The raggedy man

172

staggered and slumped up against the wall. Quickly, before Miralee could even think about helping, the knight drew his sword and stabbed the beggar through the chest.

The beggar stared at the sword uncomprehendingly for a moment. The knight pulled the blade out and the beggar fell to the side.

Miralee caught the man before he struck the floor and lowered him gently down.

"Goddess…" he spoke, blood already bubbling up out of his mouth.

"Shh," she said. "Tell me your name."

"Deg, mistress."

"Thank you, Deg, for trying to help me."

Finally, the voices were stopped as he died in her arms, content.

Miralee felt sick. She had seen death recently, more than she had ever wanted, but none had made her feel as miserable as this. A lump formed in her throat. Tears rolled freely down her cheeks.

"Enough of this," the knight said. "Get her up and let's get out of here."

Hands gripped her and stood her up. The front of her clothes was soaked with Deg's blood. She didn't resist as she was marched across the room, which was now mostly empty of patrons, and into the cool night air of Edain.

Moricai climbed to the top of his tower. The hour was almost here. In Sperry County, he had barely managed to escape the Shadow Knights and transport himself back to Edain.

That had been bad luck. He had made promises to the demon prince that he had not fulfilled. Serrakon would see to it that he was paid in full, likely taking Moricai's life as partial payment, but only after subjecting him to exquisite torments. Serrakon was a blood demon and, as such, relished the lengthy and painful suffering of sacrifices.

Delia's request had been a blessing. The seeress had considerable influence in the demonic realms. She had promised to intercede on Moricai's behalf if he assisted her. He was happy to.

173

What she had asked was a simple enough matter—perform a rite that would allow the demon Ghorach to manifest in possession of a human host. Ghorach was a powerful demon, but Delia had promised his cooperation. Once the demon was free and in possession of a human form, Moricai's task was over. In exchange, Delia promised the wizard at least a moon's grace in appeasing hungry Serrakon.

The most difficult part of the whole affair was locating a person who would not be missed to act as the demon's host, for rarely did a person survive possession. For Moricai, this was a minor obstacle. In Edain, he had considerable influence.

In this case, getting a host had been easily accomplished. The unlucky victim was a Varian sailor who had been arrested for public drunkenness and affray, to wit, starting a bar brawl in the wharf and then vomiting beer and mutton on the boots of a night watchman. His captain, if the man was missed at all, likely would not look too hard—Edain's wharf district was notoriously dangerous to the foolish or unwary.

Moricai's ritual workspace was at the very top of the tower, above his personal quarters and library. Duke ni'Graelly knew of its existence. He seemed to consider what he called 'dabbling in the arts' to be a requisite for a spiritual advisor, which was Moricai's official title.

The ritual space was circular and twenty-five feet across. In the center was an engraved pentagram. Currently, in the center of the pentagram, the Varian sailor was prone on his back, wrapped in black silk that was tied in a very specific manner. He was conscious, but paralyzed due to the effects of a potent draught brewed from the toxin of the Sinoomian bird spider.

The preparations were the hardest part of summoning Ghorach. The actual ritual, as long as the demon cooperated, was easy. Moricai doused all of the light in the room. Standing at the apex of the pentagram, the wizard began to chant in Old Golgmaran. It was hardly even a chant really, just ten lines. A blood sacrifice was required, in this case a dove. With a curved blade, Moricai beheaded the bird and let the blood drip down onto the face and head of the Varian.

The sailor's body began to jerk and flop like a fish left to die on the shore. After a minute, the movements subsided. The temperature in the room went up by several degrees. The five candles set up at the points of the pentagram ignited.

The Varian stood up. In his eyes was a red fire that had nothing to do with the reflections of the candles.

Ghorach had arrived.

Chapter Fifteen

iralee was dragged outside and held under guard until a prisoner transport wagon could be brought from the Lords Road guard house. It took over thirty minutes to arrive, and a large crowd of onlookers watched from a safe distance.

While they waited, the dark haired girl named Peri, got into a heated argument with Emer ni'Oban. Peri demanded that the guards release Miralee. When they refused, she tried to appeal to Emer's sense of decency and pled with her to order the guards to release Miralee. Two other young noble women and three young noble men watched, smirking and whispering to one another.

Miralee could tell that Lady Peri's pleas would not be successful. In fact, they only encouraged Emer to be that much more adamant. Peri's distress was almost as satisfying to the young woman as tormenting the poor and helpless.

"Please, Emer. I'm asking you one last time to let this poor girl go. She has done nothing to you," Peri asked. She seemed close to tears.

Emer pretended to consider it.

"Well...perhaps if you were to beg me to let her go," Emer said, smirking.

Anger flashed across Peri's dark features, but she quickly banished it and nodded.

"Fine. I am begging you to let her go. Please let her go," she said.

Emer and all of her friends dissolved into laughter. Peri's face turned red and tight. She took a step closer to Emer, who stood her ground.

"You bitch! You are an embarrassment to all of us!" she yelled. "I am going to talk to my father. You haven't won!"

She turned and stalked off to their carriage. Without looking back, she climbed in and it drove off. Emer watched her go, looking unimpressed.

"Sir Kaden, we'll require another carriage. I think I'd like to go to North Town. In the meantime, leave enough men to guard this slut. The rest of you will accompany us down the street. I'm getting bored here," Emer said.

She and the other nobles walked north with half the guards clearing their way. People were quick to move out of their path. The remaining guards kept Miralee surrounded.

She said nothing the whole time, except once.

"Sir," she said to the guard who seemed to be in charge—he had two chevrons on his sleeve. "Could I bring my guitar with me? I dropped it inside."

She could feel the man's sympathy for her, but his answer was, "I'm afraid not miss. I'm sure it will be fine."

Miralee didn't argue.

She wondered idly as she sat there if she could escape. She thought that she probably could. All that had come loose within her remained so. The thoughts and feelings of the men were open to her. And she felt the potential for so much more. She just wasn't sure that, once started, she would be able to control it. These weren't bad men. She might hurt them seriously, or worse.

So when the wagon arrived, she let herself be placed into the back. It had thick wooden walls and a door on the back that was reinforced with iron. Miralee's ankles were locked into cuffs that were attached to an iron bar on the floor by a short chain.

The wagon began to move. There were no windows in the back, so Miralee could not see her surroundings. She could tell though, that after a few turns, they were on a street with considerably fewer people than Amberi Street. The wagon picked up speed.

And then it stopped.

"Hey you, get out of the road!" she heard the driver yell. "Last chance. If my men have to move you, you'll be lucky if you're just..."

There was a roar. And screams. Miralee felt a blast of heat, even in the rear of the wagon. She heard a second then a third roar and more screaming. She felt the anguish of the guards. They were dying.

Maybe I should go now.

177

She concentrated on the ankle cuffs. She tried to relax and really feel the essence of the metal, like she could when she was playing. She felt the power inside of her and visualized the cuff opening. She reached out with her mind.

Click.

The cuff fell open.

I don't believe it! Okay, now for the door.

The door clanged open.

But I didn't do that.

A figure filled the doorway. Gabriel. He had his sword in hand. He looked sober and grim, like he had when she had first seen him.

"Come. It's time to go. I'd rather not hurt you, but I will without hesitation if you don't cooperate with me," he said.

She could tell he meant it.

Slowly, she climbed down from the wagon. She gasped at what she saw. All six guards were dead, as were the horses. All of them had been burned to death. The front of the wagon was on fire. Gabriel had told her about his pyrokinetic powers, but she had never seen them in action.

"The fools, I used the wagon's own lamps as a source for my flame."

He pulled her onto the horse so that she sat in front of him. She didn't resist. There was plenty of fire around for him to use, and she didn't feel like matching her knife against his sword. As soon as she thought it, he reached into her pocket and removed her knife.

But I have other weapons, don't I? I just opened that lock. But so does he. I'd better wait for the right moment.

He held her tight and galloped away from the scene of the attack as fast as the horse would take them.

The mood of the crowd on Amberi Street subtly changed. Sir Joran felt it as he rode slowly down the north end of the street. An increased excitement and agitation were more precisely what he felt. He saw a knot of men having an animated discussion and rode by them, his ears straining to hear them over the carnival atmosphere.

"You're crazy. Bowman could take him in a rematch. My brother knows Bowman's trainer, and he told me that Bowman was sick when he wrestled Galt," said one man.

"Sick with old age," sneered another. "Bowman's over the hill. It's time for him to retire…"

Sir Joran rode past, disappointed. Nothing seemed to be happening at the north end of the street, other than the usual drunken shenanigans one associated with Mayday. Maybe to the south.

"It was horrible! He died right there in front of us," he heard a woman say.

"Just a beggar from the look of him," replied a man.

"But what about that girl? What do you think she did to get arrested like that?" said the woman.

"Must have been something heinous for her to go about disguised as a lad and all."

Joran stopped and looked around for the speakers. He saw them just off to his right, walking in the street on the edge of the busy sidewalk. They were a young couple. The man looked like the son of a successful merchant, or perhaps an artisan. The woman looked slightly younger than the man and dressed in respectable, middle-class fashion.

"Excuse me," Joran said as he maneuvered his horse along side of them. "But may I ask what you're talking about?"

The couple looked up. Joran was wearing a dark cloak that hid his order insignia. The man regarded him suspiciously. The woman had no qualms though and immediately began to relate the events at the Dragon's Flagon.

"She was a musician you say? Tall and fair?" Joran asked.

"Yes, a skilled musician, so much so that I never questioned that she was a man," said the woman.

"I had my doubts," the man interjected.

"Oh, you had no idea," the woman replied back.

Joran had heard enough.

"Thank you both. You've been very helpful."

He urged his mount forward, as fast as was safe in the heavy traffic.

179

Several knots of people lingered in the vicinity of the Dragon's Flagon, but the street here was much emptier than further north.

Joran tied his horse in front of the tavern and went inside. There were some patrons clustered around the bar and in the back of the tavern, but considering that it was Mayday festival, the place was practically deserted.

He spied a young woman mopping the small stage; he smelled the subtle metallic odor of recently spilled blood. She looked like she had been crying. Except for a harried barmaid, no one else looked like they worked for the Flagon.

He approached the woman by the stage. As he came close, she glanced up at him with barely controlled fury.

"What?! I'm a little busy just now," she said.

"Madam, I'm sorry to interrupt your work, but I was hoping that you could tell me whose inn this is," he said.

"I'm Jolie. It's mine."

"I'm Sir Joran. I'm trying to find a girl named Miralee. I think she might have been here tonight."

She leaned against her mop.

"You're too late. The city guard arrested her. They just left out front a few minutes ago. Damned girl, she told me that Shadow Knights and the bards might be looking for her; she never mentioned that she was wanted for assaulting the king's damned niece."

"She knows we're trying to find her? You see, I'm of the Order of Shadow Knights," said Joran.

"Of course she does. She said that you were in cahoots with some blackguard named Gabriel. Seems like the whole city is looking for her. And I was fool enough to think I could help her. Instead, someone got killed in my bar and she got arrested. I'm sure they're taking her to the palace; you might still be able to get a piece of her."

"Miss Jolie, you misunderstand. I've been trying to find her to keep her from Gabriel. I feel certain he means her harm and the Order wishes to extend her protection."

"Call it what you like."

"That guitar, is it hers?"

"Yes."

"May I take it? I'm going to find her and help. When I do, I'll return it."

"Sure, take it. Take it and go," Jolie said, returning to her mopping.

Back outside, Joran climbed onto his horse, thinking.

The quickest route to the palace is east through Graelly Green, but if I remember correctly, the rich that live there dislike things like prisoner transports. Amberi Street is crowded. It's more likely that they would cut down to Lords Road. If they don't have too much of a lead, perhaps I can overtake them.

And then what? I rather doubt Sir Mordis would appreciate it if I helped a legitimate prisoner of the Duke escape custody. Find her first, worry about that second.

Like a wave crashing over him, Joran felt a sudden surge of power to the northeast. Lords Road was east of him. It ran north to south. He urged his mount forward.

He overcame the wagon sooner than he expected.

Joran looked grimly at the burnt out wagon and the corpses of the guards. The back of the wagon was empty.

Could Miralee have done this? No, it must have been Gabriel.

Joran wasn't a strong, or even moderately strong, telepath, but he knew Janessa would hear him. He called her now. Her response was immediate.

"Joran, what have you found?"

He quickly told her about his discovery.

"I should be able to get a track from here," he finished.

"Good. I'm near the West Gate. I'll make sure that Dameon is watching the Canal Gate. Keep me updated," she thought back.

Joran took a deep breath, relaxed, and opened his senses wide. Residual *jhi* energy was visible outside of the wagon with a hint of it inside. He was looking for something else though.

There. He had it—two shimmering aural trails, like softly incandescent ribbons hovering in the air. One was faint, and Joran recognized it as Gabriel's. The fallen Shadow Knight was sure to be masking, but that simply made his traces less noticeable. One always left evidence, like a lingering scent.

The second belonged to Miralee, of course. It was stronger than Gabriel's, quite a bit stronger. But even Miralee's trail was muted as if she was masked as well.

She's learning to use her gifts, and she's getting stronger.

Like a cloud of perfume, the aural trails would dissipate with time. In the wilderness such evidence of passing could last for hours, or even days. But in a crowded city like Edain the trails would be obscured quickly. With that in mind, he started after them at a good pace, though not so fast that he would ride into an ambush.

Very soon Joran would meet Gabriel again.

He was looking forward to it.

He's nervous.

Even without empathic senses, simple observation would have told her as much. Gabriel's eyes continually darted back and forth. Every minute or so, he turned back and looked over his shoulder. Miralee's knife was gripped tightly in his right hand, always close to her back.

The streets were busy again as soon as they turned off of Lords Road. Their progress slowed. She considered just calling out for help, but decided that even if she survived, such an action would place the lives of those around her in great danger.

The only little bit of cheer she received was when they passed a carriage, which was stopped and unloading passengers. One passenger, as she stepped out onto the sidewalk, turned and looked right at Miralee. It was Emer ni'Oban. Her eyes grew wide and her jaw fell as she recognized Miralee.

Miralee didn't see what Emer did after that, but the one look made her smile, even in her current predicament. If Emer had rallied pursuit, it had been too slow in setting forth to overtake them in the Mayday crowd.

They arrived at the gate sooner than she had hoped. A small row of carts was exiting the city—peddlers who had come into the city for the day to sell their wares to festival goers. Some guards, who looked like they would much rather be among the revelers than standing duty, watched with bored expressions as the carts filed out. Otherwise, no one was in the immediate vicinity of the gate.

No, that's not true. Someone is there, in the shadows. They're mounted. Why didn't I see him—her, it's a woman—before? It's like my eyes want to slide away from her.

She suddenly realized who the woman was.

Janessa!

Miralee made no outward sign, but had to fight down her inner excitement. Gabriel didn't seem to notice. Miralee focused her mind on hiding her thoughts and feelings specifically from him. However, she thought hard at Janessa, *"Help me!"*

Right then she did not care if the Shadow Knights wanted to harm her. When she had met Janessa and Joran, Miralee had gotten the impression that they were both good people. They were certainly a better option than Gabriel.

Gabriel didn't appear to see Janessa, yet he sensed something. He stopped maybe two hundred feet from where the Shadow Knight waited. Eyes narrowed, he scanned back and forth trying to see why his instincts were warning him away. After two minutes of this, he abruptly turned the horse around and started away from the gate, away from Janessa. Miralee could not see if the woman was following them.

Miralee became aware of their horse. The horse sensed Gabriel's nervousness and didn't like it. Gently, so that he wouldn't notice, she encouraged the horse's nervousness like blowing on the smallest spark to make a flame.

The horse grew so tense that, when three blocks back in the direction from which they had come, Joran suddenly appeared from around a corner, and Gabriel pulled back a little too hard on the reigns, the animal reared back angrily. As soon as it did, Miralee drove her head back. Her skull connected with Gabriel's face, and both riders fell over the animal's rump and into the road.

It only took a second. But for Miralee, who was waiting to feel sharp steel plunge into her back, it seemed much longer.

The expected stab never came.

183

She tried to stay on her feet, but she and Gabriel got tangled up. He landed on his back, she on her stomach on top of him, with her legs up by his face. She felt a sharp pain in her right knee.

Miralee saw her knife laying on the cobble stones four feet from her hand. She lunged for it. Gabriel cursed and grabbed her, catching her by the belt. He tried to draw his sword with his other hand, but it was tangled in his cloak and partially blocked by Miralee sitting astride him.

She kicked back once, hit something, and twisted around to face him. Gabriel looked surprised. He was even more surprised when Miralee rammed her fist into his face. His nose flattened under her knuckles and she heard a very satisfying *crunch.*

"Leave me alone!" she yelled and drew back her fist to hit him again.

"Miralee, it's all right. I've got him." It was Joran. The handsome Shadow Knight was standing next to her. His bright sword was drawn, and he pressed the tip of it against Gabriel's neck.

"Though it looked like you were handling him pretty well by yourself," said Janessa, who had arrived from the rear just a moment after Joran. "And it wasn't necessary to shout at me. I saw you. I'll have a headache for hours."

Janessa's own blade was bare. She stepped up and held it on Gabriel from the other side.

"Miralee, slowly get up and step back," Janessa said.

Miralee did as she was told, hobbling somewhat. She looked down and saw that her pants were torn and her knee was bleeding from a jagged gash. It didn't hurt much yet, but no doubt it soon would.

Janessa kept her sword covering Gabriel while Joran removed his sword belt and checked him for other weapons. From his saddle bag, Joran produced a length of rope and wrapped it several times around Gabriel, binding his arms to his body.

Just as he finished, a third Shadow Knight arrived. Miralee knew him for what he was because, unlike Janessa and Joran, who were in plain black, he wore the Order's emblem openly on his cloak. About thirty, he was a small, but fit-looking man, with a needle-thin moustache and goatee.

"Dameon, blindfold him. Gabriel's pyrokinetic abilities are sight dependent," Janessa said.

Miralee picked up her dagger and backed up a few steps to let the knights work. It didn't occur to her to try and flee. She'd done enough running lately.

My guitar!

She spied the neck of her guitar sticking out of Joran's saddle bag and immediately recognized it.

Would he have bothered to get that for me if they meant to kill me? Maybe they don't know I'm a demon.

"Make a hole! Watch coming through!" said a loud voice.

The crowd reluctantly parted and six city watchmen came through.

"What's all this then?" said the sergeant. "Oh. Sir Dameon, didn't know you were involved in all of this. Just heard there was a fight in progress."

"We've got things under control sergeant," Dameon said.

"Sergeant," said Joran. "About fifteen minutes ago, this man attacked and killed several members of the watch on Lords Road. If they have not yet been discovered, you should go there now."

"Killed watchmen?" said the sergeant, whose suddenly grim expression was mirrored by those of his men. "You'll have to let me take him then."

Miralee had no doubt of what the sergeant wanted to do with Gabriel.

"No, sergeant. This man is extremely dangerous. He was once a member of the Order. We'll hold him at my compound until he can be tried for murder," Dameon said.

There was some grumbling among the guards.

They think the knights are trying to protect him as one of their own.

"I'm sorry sergeant, but I can't take a chance on this one escaping," Dameon said.

"Sir Dameon, if he killed city watchmen, I want him. Corporal, go back to the station and put out word. I want two squads here immediately." One of the men detached from the group and ran off through the crowd. The sergeant picked out two more men and sent them to Lords Road. "There, I'll have a dozen more men here soon, plenty to handle one man. With all due respect to your order, this is watch business. But I appreciate your assistance in apprehending him."

"Sergeant, I disagree. This man's crimes go far beyond his latest murders," Dameon said. "However, he will be tried for them. But we are taking him to my home, now."

Gabriel's horse was close. Joran led her over. The animal became fidgety when Gabriel was brought near. Miralee went and spoke softly to the horse, and it calmed down.

She felt something stir in her pocket.

Goddess! Orrie! I forgot to check him after the fall!

She reached into her pocket and pulled the rat out, fearing he might be hurt. However, the rodent looked like he was just getting up from a nap and was quite well.

Joran and Dameon hoisted Gabriel onto his horse and tied his wrists to the saddle horn.

"Miralee, will you ride with me?" asked Janessa.

She thought for a moment that she'd like to ride with Joran. *He's even cuter than I remember.* But the sergeant of the guard was looking on with barely controlled anger. Miralee sensed that he wouldn't try to take Gabriel yet. But if they were still there when his backup arrived, it would be another matter.

"Fine," the sergeant spat. "Take him, Dameon. But I'll be along in a bit to collect him from you."

Dameon did not reply.

Miralee accepted Janessa's hand and swung herself up and behind the female Shadow Knight. They fell in behind Dameon, who was closely following Gabriel's mount, which was being led by Joran on a very short lead.

"Are you all right?" Janessa asked, once they were underway.

"Yes. I banged my knee, but it isn't serious," Miralee said. After a moment, she asked, "What are you and Joran doing here?"

"Looking for you. And you've led us on a merry chase," Janessa told her. Miralee's heart skipped and her stomach flopped. She'd actually been happy to see Janessa and Joran, even now she felt friendly toward them, but Gabriel had been right about one thing— they were searching for her.

"Me? Why were you looking for me?" she asked in a small voice.

Janessa laughed. Miralee wasn't sure at what.

"We want for you to join the Order, of course," she said as if it was obvious.

Miralee was baffled.

"The Order?"

"Yes, the Order, you know, the Order of Shadow Knights?"

"But, wait…"Miralee began.

"Yes?"

"Umm, but, oh nothing. I think I'm tired."

"We'll talk about later then."

Miralee nodded and said nothing. Instead, she tried to focus in on Janessa's thoughts, hoping to learn if the knights really meant her harm. She could see nothing, nor hear nothing.

Of course, stupid. Janessa is a high ranking Shadow Knight. They have to be able to defend themselves against demons, like me.

The sound of barking caught her attention. Miralee looked over her shoulder. Solace appeared from out of an alley and was chasing after the horse.

"Solace!" she said, nearly squealing. "Sorry. He's kind of my dog. I thought I'd lost him when I got arrested."

Janessa smiled and slowed a bit so the dog could catch up.

Dameon's "house" was a polygonal stone keep situated at the mouth of the river and surrounded by a twelve foot high stone wall. It was probably seventy feet tall and fifty feet wide at the base. It was the largest building Miralee had ever seen.

"It's huge," she remarked.

"It's not bad," Janessa agreed. "But only a quarter the size of the duke's palace, which is maybe a fifth of the size of Magh Moru."

"I can't even imagine something so big. Does the Order own it?"

"We do now, thanks to Sir Dameon. He's rich you know, son of the Earl of Calo. This was a naval outpost. Sir Dameon arranged to buy it from Duke Corgan and gifted it to the Order. Of course, we had to agree to man the keep and defend the mouth of the river in case of an invasion. Often, Sir Dameon is the only Shadow Knight here and, as good as he is, probably couldn't stem an invasion all by himself. So he keeps a retinue of fighting men from Calo just in case. We also have three ships docked just beyond the keep. You can see them when it's day."

Dameon rode ahead and ordered all the lamps, torches, and any other fires that they might pass put out. When that was accomplished they rode inside of the compound walls. There were dozens of armed men nearby. Miralee sensed them, rather than saw them. With the fires out, she could barely make out the outline of the keep now against the black, night sky. Gabriel did not offer any trouble though. Dameon and Joran led him away, Miralee imagined to a cell somewhere.

Inside, the keep smelled of clean wood smoke and leather. No one made any hostile moves and Miralee started to feel more comfortable.

While the thoughts of the Shadow Knights were closed to her—though she could pick up the occasional image or emotion from Joran—those of most of the other fighting men at the order's keep were not. Miralee surveyed several warrior's thoughts; no sinister plans were revealed.

Maybe they don't know. But then why would they be looking for me. Janessa said they wanted me to join the Order. Me, a Shadow Knight? How? I'm a musician. I can't fight.

Pictures flashed through her mind: the demon attacking Brown's Ford; escaping the troll; the fight outside of Sperry's Knoll; the attempted robbery by the wharf; even her very recent altercation with Gabriel. She had always been physically strong, uncommonly so even for someone used to farm labor, and lately she felt stronger still.

Well, maybe I can...

Sir Dameon's home was on Caudefeld Street, which was dominated by the shipyards that serviced the Duke's fleet, Edain's main watchhouse, and squat naval barracks. It was honeycombed with nooks and shadowy recesses.

In the shadows at the top of a narrow cellar staircase, stood Ghorach, nearly invisible except for his eyes, which glowed angrily faint, dark red, like blood reflecting the moonlight. Gabriel and the girl were both in the hands of the Shadow Knights.

Gabriel is a fool. I should leave him to the mercy of the Shadow Knights. But I may need him. Now that the knights have found the girl, she'll have to die. That's safest. Pity, I had hoped to have some time alone with her.

Ghorach slipped down the street, back toward the palace. The wizard, Moricai, might be useful now. Ghorach felt certain that he could think of some way to compel the wizard's further assistance.

Chapter Sixteen

The next morning, a chilly fog rolled in off of the bay, so Miralee was invited to breakfast in Dameon's private dining hall, along with Janessa and Joran. The hall was cozy and tight, and was kept warm by a fireplace with a green marble mantle.

"Miralee, last night I told you that we have been looking for you," Janessa said.

Miralee had a mouthful of bread and apple jam, so she nodded.

"And I told you that we wanted you to join our order and come to Magh Moru.

Magh Moru, I hadn't thought about that. Of course they would take new initiates there. What I still can't fathom is that they would want me.

Practically the whole time since she had left home, Miralee had been in fear of the Shadow Knights, which she hated as she had loved the stories of the knights since childhood. It was time to leave fear behind.

"Janessa, you've saved my life, probably twice now. But you might have been better off letting me die."

Janessa looked startled, Joran puzzled.

"What do you mean?" Janessa asked.

"I think I'm a demon. I think that's why I can do the things I can do." There it was out. Miralee felt better for having said it. No more running. "I'll understand if you lock me up with Gabriel."

"What?" Joran said. "Miralee, I think you had better start at the beginning."

Head lowered, Miralee relayed about learning she was adopted and everything that Gabriel had told her. When she finished, they looked at one another. Joran sat back, frowning.

"Phaedran? I'm not familiar with the name."

"I am," said Janessa. "In Ehrian, Phaedran is known as a demon who sided with the gods against his own kind. His name was inscribed in Scathach's temple at the foot of Silver Mountain."

"A connection?" Dameon asked.

"It would seem so, though I'm not sure what the connection is," Janessa said. "I am curious to find out though, especially since Miralee has no clue to her parentage.

"Miralee, it is very possible that what Gabriel told you is true. No, wipe that horrified expression from your face. It is equally possible that at least one of the three of us," Janessa said, indicating the Shadow Knights, "has demonic heritage."

"But you're Shadow Knights! That makes no sense," protested Miralee.

"Right. And Shadow Knights have abilities that allow us fight demonic threats. Why do you think we possess special abilities and most people do not?"

"I, uh, I don't know," Miralee said.

"Once, it was not uncommon for humans to breed with both demons and gods," Janessa explained. "The resulting offspring were exceptional, possessing qualities of both races. Many think that every person today who has talents like we have, owe it to having the blood of the gods, or demons, in our veins.

"Of course, most people can't trace their lineage exactly. Too many generations have passed, and often the god or demon in question would have relations disguised as someone, or something else. It's rare to have such an ancestor so recently removed, but not impossible. There are still gods that live among us; and there are still demons that find their way into our realm, more often than I'd like."

"So you weren't looking for me to kill me?" Miralee asked.

Joran laughed.

"Kill you? Perish the thought!"

"Miralee, what I told you when we were riding was true; we would like to invite you to join our order," Janessa told her.

"A Shadow Knight? I'm not sure. My music...do you really think I could?" Miralee asked.

"Absolutely. I think that you would make a fine Shadow Knight. And based on what Joran and I told him, Grandmaster Mordis agrees. He's on his way to Edain. He should be here by nightfall."

"With a surprise," added Joran. "One Lord Rupert en'Sperry."

Miralee gasped.

191

"Lord Rupert? Why?"

"Relax, he's Mordis' prisoner, arrested on multiple charges of kidnapping, murder, and participation in a demonic rite."

"Goddess!"

"He made a mistake when he tried to make you his victim," Janessa said.

Miralee shuddered, remembering the incident in Sperry's Knoll.

"Maybe, but truth be told, he probably would have succeeded if it hadn't been for Gabriel. If he hadn't intervened then, I don't think any of us would have escaped."

"That may be true...do you feel sorry for Gabriel?" asked Janessa.

"That obvious, huh? I...no, well, maybe a little. I mean, I know he's done a lot of bad things, but I was inside of his mind. He's tormented."

"Be that as it may, he will be tried for his crimes, I can't do anything about that."

"I know. I'm not suggesting otherwise."

"So Miralee, what do you think of our offer?" Joran asked. "Will you come to Magh Moru with us and join the Order? You know, the Bard's Guildhall is there as well; you could still pursue your music if you wished. Or did you have other plans?"

"No, I was going to leave Istey. It's just...it's just been terrible here. I didn't know what to do." She laughed. "Yes, I'll come to Magh Moru with you. Thank you."

"Wonderful," Joran said.

There was a knock. The door opened.

"Sir Dameon? Forgive my intrusion but you have guests," said a portly-looking man-at-arms.

"Who is it?"

"Major Jeric and Sir Kaden en'Ulster."

"Do they have men with them?" Dameon asked.

"Three knights and a score of watchmen. Except for the major and Sir Kaden, I left them waiting at the gate."

"Good work. Show them in."

Miralee recognized Sir Kaden immediately. His own eyes hardened when he saw her. He leaned over and whispered into the ear of the other man. Major Jeric was a fit, white-haired man with broken vessels running through a crooked nose.

Dameon and the other Shadow Knights stood, so Miralee followed suit. Jeric nodded amiably to Dameon. To Miralee, he felt tired. Sir Kaden was rigid and aloof.

"Major Jeric, a pleasure. Kaden," said Dameon.

"Sir Dameon. I wish it was pleasure I was here for," the major said. "But as you know there was some nasty business last night, some of my men died."

"I know. I'm very sorry about it. I know most of the watchmen in this town; they're good men."

"Thank you. And I'd like to thank you for assisting in taking those responsible into custody." He glanced nervously at Miralee. He reached into his shirt and pulled out a sheaf of papers. "Sir Dameon, I have arrest warrants for the man you took into custody and for this girl here, along with release orders signed by the Duke requiring you to surrender both of them to me immediately."

"Major, the man I'm holding in my dungeon is the man responsible for the deaths of your men. But this young lady had nothing to do with it. She's innocent of any crime, and is under the protection of the Order. I won't release her to you. Gabriel, we can talk about. I brought him here because he is extremely dangerous."

Sir Kaden's face had slowly turned red while Dameon spoke.

"This *innocent* woman assaulted a member of the royal family!" he said. "Then after she was lawfully arrested for the crime, she escaped from custody, and was caught in the company of the man you claim was responsible for the deaths of her escort. If she was innocent, she would be dead along with those men—not trying to flee the city with him!"

Dameon stayed calm in the face of Kaden's outburst.

"Sir Kaden, I admit that it could look that way. But appearances, in this case, are deceiving. Miralee was not killed in the attack because she was the target. She was not fleeing with Gabriel; she was being kidnapped by him."

Major Jeric shifted on his feet uneasily.

"Sir, the Duke's warrants…"

193

"Yes, as I said, I have no issue with turning Gabriel over to you, other than security, of course. I propose that we begin preparations to transfer him over to you. It will take time, you understand, what with the necessary briefing to familiarize yourself and your men with the threats he can pose, preparing the route, and such. And then the actual transfer. In the meantime, I propose that Miralee remain here. You have my word that she will not leave Edain until the matter is resolved. I would expect dealing with Gabriel will take most of the day, certainly until Grandmaster Mordis arrives."

"Sir Mordis is coming to Edain?" asked Jeric.

"He is. He should be here by dusk, with an important prisoner, I understand. Perhaps his arrival might help facilitate this matter."

Jeric nodded slowly.

"Yes, yes, I think you are right. We should address the matter of this Gabriel, if he is as dangerous as you say. Best to proceed slowly."

Sir Kaden's face turned red and his lips tightened.

"Major, I find this unacceptable! This is Edain—the Duke's authority is the highest. We must take both prisoners now. I'll take the girl myself. You and your men can worry about the man."

"Kaden, you should have come to Delwyn College to study," Janessa said. "Then you would know that dedicated strongholds of the Order of Shadow Knights are sovereign soil, not subject to the King's rule, or the Duke's for that matter. And Sir Dameon's keep is a dedicated stronghold."

Kaden took a step toward Janessa. Miralee could feel the frustration and fury radiating from him like heat from a winter stove. She wanted to shrink away from his hot anger, but instead, she took a deep breath and forced her body to stay still and relaxed.

Just as she began to exhale, Sir Kaden turned on his boot heel and strode away from Janessa, who hadn't moved at all. He reached the door, threw it open hard, and disappeared through it.

"I'm sorry about him," said Major Jeric. "It wasn't my idea to bring him along. I personally think that it is a bad idea to bring this man to the castle, but the Duke was adamant. I think the girl is an afterthought, begging your pardon ma'am. If not for Lady Emer, Duke Corgan wouldn't care a whit about her. Sir Dameon, I've

194

known you a long time and trust your word. Kaden, however, is a hothead. Worse, he is smitten by Lady Emer. He'll do what he must to impress her."

"Emer isn't impressed by anything but power," said Janessa. "She's been at Delwyn these past years and left quite an impression on *me*. I don't think Sir Kaden is a big enough fish for her. But that won't stop her from playing him on the line for awhile."

Sir Dameon offered the major a cup of wine. The man waved it off, then reconsidered and took it.

"I can't wait for the festival to end," Major Jeric said, taking a healthy gulp from his cup. "Lady Emer and her friends should be leaving then."

"And then she becomes our problem again," said Janessa.

In a pitch black cell, Gabriel sat upon a bed of damp straw, knees drawn up with his head buried in his arms. Though motionless, his mind was churning. He had always thought well of himself, despite his mother's frequent criticism. Now he felt like a fool.

This whole affair had been a disaster.

The job had sounded so simple when his mother had given it to him. Find Miralee, win her trust, bring her back to Delia in the Gorewood.

How had it gone wrong?

It was his mother's fault. If she hadn't harried his every step, Miralee would never have overheard their conversation. That was the point when everything started to unravel. It wouldn't matter; she would blame him.

Now he was the Shadow Knights' prisoner. One of two things would happen. Either they would kill him, or he would escape. Dying would be easier; at least he would be rid of his mother. No, that was unlikely to happen. He would probably escape, though he couldn't see how at the moment.

Ghorach was out there, somewhere. He would create an opportunity for Gabriel, if he could. And Gabriel would take whatever chance that might present itself. He knew he would. He could accept death if it was unavoidable. But even as disgusted as he was with everything in his life lately, he still loved life. It was funny, for days Gabriel had been morose and depressed. But the longer he sat in his cell, the angrier and more energetic he felt.

I have to control myself though.

Gabriel took a deep breath and covered his anger with a featureless mask. He would hold it in check until the time was right.

As if on cue, light filtered into the cell as a door opened down the corridor. He heard the footsteps of several men.

"Open up the door," one of them said.

Gabriel heard the lock click and the door slowly swung open. Men with crossbows lined the hall. Sir Dameon stood center, his shadow blade bare and ready. Leg irons were tossed into the cell.

"Put them on or you'll be shot," said Dameon.

Gabriel looked the Shadow Knight in the eye, smiling. He put the irons around his ankles. Dameon wasn't bluffing. It didn't matter.

There would be an opportunity.

"Janessa, Artegan and I are in Edain now. We're going straight through to the palace. How are things there?"

"Fine, Mordis. Gabriel was successfully transferred to the Duke's dungeon. Miralee is here. One of the Duke's knights is outside of Dameon's keep with twenty men to make sure that we don't sneak her out."

"I'll talk to Duke Corgan about Miralee while I'm delivering Lord Rupert into custody. I want to get this resolved tonight and be on the way in the morning."

Due to the thick festival crowds, Mordis and Artegan took over an hour to reach the palace with their prisoner. It was full dark by the time the Grandmaster drew up to the gates. Major Jeric had warned the guards of his impending arrival, so the knights found the portcullis being raised without having to announce themselves.

Major Jeric met them as soon as they came onto the grounds.

"Grandmaster Mordis, Duke Corgan is waiting to receive you."

196

"Thank you, major. This is Rupert en'Sperry. I've arrested him on multiple counts of murder, kidnapping, and participation in a demonic ritual. Have him escorted to the dungeon."

"Yes sir. These men will see him safely locked up. I'll…"

"You can assist them, major. I'll escort Sir Mordis and Sir Artegan to see my father."

"Lady Peri. I didn't see you approach. Yes, certainly. Milords."

Major Jeric took Rupert away. Peri ni'Graelly deflated a little and smiled up at the two knights.

"Peri, you look well. Not out enjoying the festival?" Mordis asked.

"Hardly. This has been a dreadful holiday. I would have stayed at school if my father hadn't insisted that I come home."

"Hmm. I seem to remember hearing that Emer ni'Oban was taking her holiday in Edain."

"Shanda en'Marsk and Diagrane ni'Grane, as well," Artegan added.

Peri shuddered imperceptibly. Her smile became a bit more drawn.

"Yes. They're all here. Two more days…" She took a deep breath and exhaled forcefully. She turned and walked into the palace. Mordis and Artegan followed. "Sir Mordis, did I hear you correctly that your prisoner was Lord Rupert en'Sperry, and that you arrested him for murder?"

"Yes, among other things. He…well, his crimes were horrific, not really fit for discussion."

Artegan shifted the large sack he carried uncomfortably. Peri did not seem to notice.

"As you wish. I'm not really surprised. I've met him before. He always struck me as odd…the way he would stare at me…like a snake looking at a mouse. Of course you know my father isn't going to appreciate having this placed in his lap."

"Who would? Rupert is the first noble to be arrested for trafficking with demons in decades. I wouldn't blame your father if he passed the responsibility onto King Corliss."

"My father has been kowtowing to Emer in the hopes that it will somehow bring him Corliss's favor. He's even gone so far as to

197

order the arrest of some poor girl at Emer's say-so, even though I saw everything and told him that she was innocent. He didn't care. She was taken into custody last night, but I haven't been able to learn anything about her whereabouts. Poor thing."

"Her name's Miralee and she's at Dameon's keep. She's the main reason that I need to speak with the Duke," said Mordis. "I've accepted her into the Order and intend on taking her back to Magh Moru."

"Really? That's wonderful! Emer will absolutely hate it!"

They arrived at the Duke's private room and found him already eating. He wiped his hands and rose when Peri and the knights entered.

"Grandmaster Mordis, welcome. And Sir...?"

"Artegan, Your Grace."

"Of course. Please gentlemen, be seated. Thank you, Peri."

"It was nice to see you, Peri," said Mordis. The young woman offered a half-curtsey, and then left.

The two Shadow Knights sat and accepted food. Both were famished after a long day of travel. As they ate, Sir Mordis told the Duke about Rupert en'Sperry and the horror they had encountered. Corgan's expression became incredulous, then deeply troubled. He lowered his head, rubbing his temple with his index and middle fingers.

"Enough, please. Do you realize what this will mean for me?"

"I realize what it meant to all of those girls who were tortured and murdered," said Mordis. "Corgan, I do understand what a sensitive situation this is. However, I think our course is clear."

"Clear? Earl en'Sperry is a long time supporter of mine. Our families go back hundreds of years. The penalty for Rupert's alleged crimes..."

"Alleged?!" exclaimed Artegan. "Your Grace, we saw his crimes with our own eyes. He..."

"Sir Artegan! Duke Corgan, I realize that this is a delicate issue and as such, evidence should be presented to support testimony. This is a journal in Lord Rupert's own hand. In it he discussed his crimes in a manner one might call passionate."

Corgan took the book, holding it as if it might suddenly bite. He thumbed through it. As he read, his eyes narrowed and his nose wrinkled up. After a few moments, he slammed the book shut and almost threw it onto the table.

"That is certainly the product of a, deranged mind. But I saw nothing in it to tie it to Rupert. There is no signature, no name," he said.

If Mordis bridled under the Duke's doubts, he gave no sign.

"There is other evidence. Of course there is the young woman we rescued. She could testify. But there is another thing I brought, which I recovered from Rupert's personal lodge that might make that unnecessary."

"If you have more convincing evidence, let me see it."

"Very well. I was hoping to spare you. Sir Artegan, show the Duke the evidence."

Grim-faced, Artegan brought forth the sack. It was leather, large, and lumpy; when Artegan stepped forward and opened it a putrid smell wafted out. The Duke wretched as soon as the odor hit him. Artegan thrust the bag forward. Corgan did not want to look inside, but he had no choice. He leaned forward slowly, covering his nose and mouth with his hand. He peered inside for just a second before closing his eyes and falling back into his chair.

"Close it! Get it out of here! Mordis what possessed you to bring that in here?"

Artegan closed the bag and took Rupert's grisly trophies from the hall.

When the were alone, Corgan said, "Okay. You've made your point. What do you suggest I do? Execute the son of one of my earls? I suppose I could confine him in the dungeon. Or place him under house arrest."

"Duke Corgan, this needn't be your problem. I can try him under my own authority, though I thought, in consideration of his position, that the involvement of government was desirable. I suggest en'Sperry be sent onto Gedorix. What needs to be done can be done under the King's banner. That way there can be no conflict of interest."

Duke Corgan brightened some at that.

"Yes, I see your logic. Rendel can hardly be upset with me if Corliss is responsible for Rupert's execution."

"I would have taken him myself, except I am engaged in another matter and Gedorix would have been too far a diversion. And actually, my other purpose in Edain concerns you as well."

"How so?"

"I left Magh Moru many days ago in search of an exceptional person to invite into the Order of Shadow Knights."

"So? Isn't that what you do? Traipse about the country looking for exceptional people, as you put it?"

Mordis smiled and sipped his wine.

"Something like that. But in this instance, I was searching for a specific person. The trail ended here in Edain. My knights located the person in question of course."

"Wonderful. So why should that involve me?"

"Because you have issued a warrant for her arrest and sent knights and soldiers to apprehend her from Sir Dameon's keep."

"Ah."

"Yes. Ah. Her name is Miralee and she has been accepted into my order. I would view it as a favor if you would rescind the warrant and allow me to return to Magh Moru with her, without any further delays."

"She is accused of assaulting a member of the royal family."

"Yes. An incident which your own daughter witnessed and said did not happen."

"Hmm, well. Though, perhaps…"

"Corgan, I know Lady Emer, and I know King Corliss knows his niece reasonably well. He is aware of her nature. He would not be impressed by prosecuting an innocent girl to placate Emer's vanity. But, he most certainly will be impressed when you deliver Rupert."

Corgan nodded slowly.

"Perhaps you are right. Very well, take your Miralee back to Magh Moru. I'll tell Lady Emer…well, I'll tell her something. As for the warrant, consider it rescinded."

"Thank you, Corgan. I owe you."

Ghorach, still wearing the body of the Varian sailor like a poorly tailored suit, waited impatiently for Moricai's return. Finally, the wizard arrived. He looked troubled. Ghorach didn't care.

"Has Gabriel arrived?" he asked.

"What? Yes. He's here. But that isn't all. Rupert en'Sperry is in the dungeon as well."

Ghorach's expression was blank.

"The one for whom I made the rite to Serrakon."

"Oh yes, the aborted rite that so angered Lord Serrakon. What of it?"

"He knows me, as a wizard, not as the Duke's advisor. He can compromise me."

"Kill him then. No, wait. Bring him here along with Gabriel. I may be able to use him, but you will have to complete the Serrakon rite."

"What!? Serrakon is already furious. I promised him a feast, but left him hungry. I only helped Delia, because she promised to intercede with him until I could placate him somehow."

"And we will placate the bloated bastard. Instead of one sacrifice, we'll give him five."

"And where will you get five young women to sacrifice?"

The Varian face grinned in lopsided fashion.

"From here in the palace, of course."

Moricai nodded; he had known the answer.

"I suppose it would be too much to ask that you take care not to be discovered. I want, if at all possible, to remain the Duke's advisor when this is all over. I'm much more useful to your kind here than I would be reading tea leaves for farmer's wives off in some hinterland."

"I understand. And if you can free my nephew and en'Sperry from the dungeon, bring them here, and still remain undiscovered, then perhaps you can remain here. But if you fail to obey me in any way, or at any time, the loss of your position will be the least of your worries. Have them here in an hour. I'll get the women."

The late hour meant the palace halls were mostly empty. *Mostly.* The palace of Edain never wholly slept. Moricai was aware of every churl, guardsman, and drudge he passed while making his way down to the dungeon.

If I make it through this unscathed, it will be a miracle. Not that freeing them from the dungeon will be difficult, there is still too much that can go wrong as long as Ghorach is here. Corgan is tolerant, but there are limits.

Moricai reached the stairs down to the dungeon where the prisoners were held. Instead of descending, he continued on until he came to a closet door. Making sure no one was about, he opened the door and went inside.

Soon, he heard heavy footsteps. The wizard held his breath. The knob turned. Dim light from the hall filtered in, illuminating the features of the dullard who cleaned the ash from the fireplaces of the dungeon every night at this time.

Moricai pounced, casting his spell before the man even knew he was there. The simpleton's features grew slack; his eyes closed. Moricai pulled him into the closet and stood the servant in the corner. He cast one spell that would prevent him from being affected by any sort of drug for the next hour or so. He cast another elementary spell that cloaked him in an illusion, making him the servant's double. Taking up the other man's bucket and tools, he started for the dungeon.

The guards opened the thick, banded doors as soon as he appeared.

"Brund, what's the good word today?" one guard asked jovially.

Moricai's illusion did not change his voice, so he grinned moronically and hefted his ash bucket. That seemed to satisfy the guard who went back to conversing with his fellows.

There were a dozen guards in the dungeon tonight, twice the usual number. But they were all clustered together around a table near a fireplace, while the prisoners were down a narrow corridor where the cells were. Moricai moved toward the fireplace, ignored by the guards. They did not see him toss a handful of powder onto the fire, before he began to scoop out the ash below. And not one of them noticed the faint odor the powder produced.

Inside of a minute, every guard had nodded off into an induced slumber.

Moricai dropped his illusion and fetched the cell keys.

The cells were pitch black; no fires had been lit in the hallway. He uttered a low syllable and a small, flameless light appeared in his left palm.

He came to Rupert en'Sperry first. The man was asleep on a hard plank, snoring loudly.

"Lord Rupert, get up. Your salvation is at hand."

Moricai opened the cell and went in. Rupert did not stir, so Moricai kicked the side of the wooden cot.

"Lord Rupert, get up."

"What? What do you want with me?" Rupert asked, shielding his eyes against the light.

"It's your wizard, fool. I'm here to rescue you."

Gabriel was sitting silent and alert in the last cell. He did not look surprised, or even interested in Moricai.

"Sir Gabriel, Ghorach is here and sent me to fetch you."

The young man simply stared, but when the wizard opened the cell, Gabriel stood and exited. He didn't speak, just started walking out to where the guards slept. Moricai, a few paces behind, found him examining a large locker.

"The keys," Gabriel said.

"We really should go. They should sleep, but someone may come."

"Give me the keys."

Moricai passed over the keys. It seemed to take Gabriel forever to find the right one, though in truth, it took just a few minutes. The iron lock clicked open and Gabriel pulled the doors open. He removed a pack, his chain shirt, and a sword.

"Sir Gabriel, may we go now? Ghorach is waiting."

Gabriel stood motionless for a long fifteen seconds. Just when Moricai thought he might refuse to accompany him, the young man nodded.

"Fine, take me to my uncle."

"Good. If both of you will stand next to me, I'll transport us there. It is too risky to walk through the palace."

The two men stood on either side of the wizard. There was a brief moment of disorientation and breathlessness, and then they were in Moricai's tower.

Rupert looked queasy.

Ghorach was present. As promised, he had five women with him, the sacrifices. They were bound and gagged with cloth, dumped in one corner of the room. Three appeared to be unconscious, two were awake. Terror was writ across their faces as they squirmed helplessly in their bonds.

"Quickly, make the preparations. At least one of these girls is already missed," the demon said.

"What? You were supposed to be stealthy! Is that Kadence Horn? Her father is a lieutenant in the guard!"

"Irrelevant. We needed five. She was in the wrong place at the wrong time. Get on with it wizard."

Moricai began inscribing the necessary sigils around the inscribed pentagram on his floor. Rupert en'Sperry edged closer while he worked.

"So, er, what do we do now?" he asked. "I assume that you have a plan for getting me out of here."

"Talk to him," Moricai said, gesturing at Ghorach. "Rescuing you was his idea."

Rupert turned and eyed Ghorach warily. His Varian body was beginning to deteriorate. The healthy brown of the skin showed purple blotches. Here and there, small, pus-filled blisters had formed, like the skin was being burned from the inside.

"I'm Lord Rupert en'Sperry. You are…?"

"Your master and your benefactor. I have a deal for you, Lord Rupert. Right now, the wizard is preparing to perform the Serrakon rite for you, at my request. I will have him complete the ritual, granting you all of the strength that Serrakon promised. But in return, you will aid me in completing a task."

"If I refuse?"

"No hard feelings. I'd simply have the wizard return you to where he found you, in a dank cell awaiting the headsman's axe."

"I see." It was obvious that he did not care for that option. "What's the task?"

204

"The easiest thing, to kill someone, a young lady."

"Well, I like the sound of that."

"It's Miralee," said Gabriel. He was opening cupboards and cabinets. "Do you have anything to drink in here?"

Ghorach turned on him. "You will refrain from imbibing until this is over."

"Or what? You'll tell my mommy?"

"No. I'll deal with you myself."

"I don't know. You aren't looking well, uncle. That body is already wearing out."

"It will last a few more days, at least. You will listen to me. Once we've done this task, you can do as you like."

"Very well."

"Wait!" Rupert interjected. "Did you say Miralee? The pretty one who sings?"

"Yes," said Gabriel. "I believe you're acquainted with her."

"Oh yes, she was a beauty, a special beauty. You've got a deal, but only if I get to kill her."

"She'll be protected by Shadow Knights," Gabriel told him.

Rupert paused and looked down, pursing his lips.

"I'll have demonic strength? And what do you two do? Shadow Knights have powers; they're not human."

"Well, my uncle is a major demon, and I killed the ten men you sent to kidnap Miralee."

"Hmm. And what about you, wizard? Are you going to help? Or are you going to run again."

"I'm…"

"He will help in anything required of him," said Ghorach. Moricai said nothing.

"Okay then, I'll help you."

"Of course you will," the demon said, smiling.

Chapter Seventeen

Solace yawned at Miralee's feet. Orrie, for once not having to hide, nestled up against the dog's stomach while Miralee played a song for the Shadow Knights. No longer afraid, she played with abandon, merging herself totally with the environment. She brought the light and shadow under the influence of her imagination. Currently, a misty image of Cassan, bereft by the sea, floated like a ghost above her head.

She had been nervous when Grandmaster Mordis had arrived. What would he think of her? What if, after meeting her, he changed his mind about having her at Magh Moru? Maybe he would just give her over to the Duke.

None of that had happened. Mordis had greeted her like a friend and made the offer for her to join the Shadow Knights himself. And he had come with the good news that the Duke had lifted the order for her arrest. And an hour after Mordis brought the word, a message from the Duke ordered Sir Kaden and his men away from the Shadow Knight keep.

Feeling better than she had in weeks, Miralee had been eager to play for the knights and Sir Dameon's men-at-arms. Now it was midnight and she wasn't even tired. As the last notes of "Eyes of Cassan" faded, she lowered her *duduk* and reached for a glass of water. The ghostly images faded and applause, slow to start, rolled over the room like a wave as the spell broke.

She set down the *duduk* and reached for her guitar, but Mordis stopped her.

"Miralee, that was amazing; you have a gift. But it is getting late and we should talk."

Miralee sat at the table between Joran and Janessa. Around the room, conversation resumed and some of the men began to get up, excusing themselves from the hall.

"Miralee, you led us on a merry chase, but I'm glad that we have finally found you and that you have agreed to join us. Janessa and Joran's instincts were spot on; you'll make an excellent addition to our order," Mordis said.

"Thank you, sir."

"I know that you've had a difficult time, but if you're able, I'd like to leave for Magh Moru in the morning."

"That's fine, sir, though I'd like to stop by the Dragon's Flagon and see if I can collect my things."

"I could send someone by there if you like," Dameon said.

"Thank you, but I'd like to talk to Jolie, the proprietor. I need to apologize to her."

"We can do that," said Mordis. "We'll go by before we leave Edain."

"There is one more thing," Miralee said. "Is there any way that we can go to Magh Moru through Brown's Ford? I think I need to see…Wolen and Myra, and Olahan. When I ran away, I was angry at them, and scared. But the last few days, I've really missed them. They're the only parents I've known. I want to let them know that I'm all right and where I'll be. And I want to know where I came from."

Mordis regarded her thoughtfully. He nodded.

"It will tack on an extra two days of travel, but I have no problem doing that. Though I think we might want to avoid going back through Sperry's Knoll."

Miralee laughed. "Agreed. Though I'd like to see how Shondar's leg is healing."

"Write him."

They left an hour after dawn. Miralee, Joran, Janessa, Artegan, and Mordis. Miralee had her own horse, a fine chestnut stallion, order-bred. She wore a black shirt that Dameon had found in his stores, and a pair of black riding pants that belonged to Janessa. They weren't a perfect fit; they were a little short and too wide in the hips, but close enough.

Miralee was able to get her belongings, meager as they were, back from Jolie. The innkeeper had a hollow look in her eyes as she fetched them and listened to Miralee's apology, making no reply.

Apparently, seeing someone murdered in her establishment had been too much for her. And whether or not she blamed Miralee, the association was there. Miralee was saddened but understood. She thanked Jolie again, and then Miralee and the knights rode away.

They departed Edain through the West Gate and rode along the city wall north till they reached the river. They followed the south bank, riding along a wide, muddy trail along the top of the steep valley.

Around lunchtime, Miralee saw the Village of Corin across the river. Men fished with nets and lines from the shore, reminding her very much of Brown's Ford. And on either side of the river were well-tended farms with all of their familiar smells and sounds.

She was anxious to go home, but nervous as well.

Mordis called for a break just beyond the village. They found a spot where they could ride into the valley and water their horses. There was good grass for grazing. They ate light and fast, jerked beef and dried fruit. Filling their water skins, they rode on.

Conn's Crossing was the next village, and it was several hours later before they arrived. It was even more similar to Brown's Ford than Corin. Miralee looked at the staring faces as they rode through and wondered if any of them were the kin with whom she would have lived had she come.

The knights chose not to stop in the village, and Miralee was pleased. They only rode through to take advantage of the bridge there and crossed the river.

By the time they made the north bank, the afternoon light was getting long and they began to look for a likely spot to camp.

They found one in a hollow off the main valley, near a creek and a stand of pin oaks. They built a small fire and ate a stew that Artegan made from smoked beef cut into cubes, water apples—a root which grew in southern Istey that resembled a potato—and some herbs from his saddle bag.

Miralee, whose stomach had been growling for at least an hour before they stopped, found it delicious and had two bowls, though not before making certain that Solace and Orrie were taken care of.

All were tired and no one called for singing. It was just as well, Miralee could scarcely keep her eyes open.

"It'll be a little further of a ride tomorrow if we want to reach Brown's Ford by sunset," said Mordis. "I suggest we turn in. I'll take the first watch."

"Wake me when you're tired," Janessa said.

Miralee made her bed with the blankets that Dameon had given her. Fortunately, it looked to be a cool, dry night. Once she was set, she let Orrie and Solace both climb under the blankets with her. In moments, she was asleep.

Something woke Miralee from a sound sleep. She stayed still and opened her eyes. She was suddenly aware that Solace was standing, stiff and staring into the trees, growling softly. She sent calming feelings toward the dog and the growl subsided, but he remained alert.

She could not see Mordis, who had been on watch when she had fallen asleep. She opened her senses and felt for him, but could not locate him. He was shielded, like the other knights, and Miralee too.

Janessa was sleeping next to her, so Miralee gently touched her arm. The knight's eyes came open, but she stayed silent.

"I think something is out there. I don't see Mordis," she thought to the knight. To Miralee's surprise, Janessa nodded. She had heard her.

"Stay still," Janessa thought back.

Miralee did as she was told. She relaxed and closed her eyes and let her mind open fully.

The fire was out, but she felt the warmth of the remaining coals. She felt the cool wind and heard the creaking of the trees. She heard the bubbling of the creek. She found the horses; they were fine, but alert like Solace. Then she sensed…hunger and lust, consuming unmasked emotions, though the aura of their possessor was hidden. And not far from there, the hint of a familiar presence. Even though he was masked, Miralee had intimately experienced his mind and knew it even now.

"Gabriel's out there. I can feel him."

Again Janessa nodded.

"Stay still and wait. Mordis is in touch with me. He says there are four of them. When the fighting starts, move back and let us handle it."

Miralee coaxed Solace back to the blanket and hugged him with one arm. The dog allowed it, though he was still on edge.

And they waited.

It was strange; everyone was awake and ready, but pretending to be asleep. Half-an-hour went by and Miralee began to get sleepy for real and had to force herself to remain alert.

It was another half-an-hour still before the attack came.

It was a few hours after sunset when Gabriel and his three cohorts found the Shadow Knight's camp. It was not terribly defensible, just a small clearing in a hollow. They did not appear to be expecting trouble.

But whereas Rupert en'Sperry was eager, and even Ghorach seemed optimistic, Gabriel had a bad feeling about the whole endeavor. The feeling had been with him since the wizard freed him from the dungeon. He would have abandoned them if not for his uncle's presence.

After he had retrieved his belongings, which had included his stone mirror, his mother had screeched at and berated him for nearly an hour when he had been foolish enough to contact her.

Gabriel was pretty certain that the wizard felt the same as he did. For someone who was neither knight nor demon, Moricai did a good job of controlling his emotions and his aura, but Gabriel got the distinct impression that the man would rather be anywhere else.

Ghorach stopped on the trail and pulled Gabriel out of his thoughts.

"They are just ahead," he said. "They're masked, but I can smell the horses. Stay here; I'm going to scout."

Ghorach moved into the woods, silent and nearly invisible. Gabriel spied a downed tree trunk and had a seat. He wanted to talk to Moricai, but Rupert, twitchy and wild-eyed now, would not leave them alone.

"I am so hungry! I have to taste her," Rupert said.

"Lower your voice," said Gabriel. "The senses of the Shadow Knights are keen. We will be in battle soon enough. You should rest some before the fight, over there."

Rupert shook his head.

"I can't rest. The way I feel, I'll never want to rest again. I hope he hurries; I can't wait to sink my teeth into her flesh."

Gabriel sighed and closed his eyes. He sent out his senses. He could feel the knight's horses as Ghorach had said, but he couldn't sense the knights or Miralee.

I taught her too well, he thought.

His uncle returned about ten minutes later.

"There is one watch. The rest are asleep. The girl is on the far side of the camp," Ghorach said. "I will circle around. Wait thirty minutes and attack them from this side."

"I can't wait that long," Rupert protested.

"Obey me. Gabriel, lead them. Don't disappoint me."

Gabriel inclined his head a fraction of an inch. Then Ghorach was gone again. Gabriel waited a few moments.

"All right. Let's move into position. No more talking until we attack."

Here they come, Miralee thought.

One arm held Solace, who was still tense and growling. The other held her knife. Cold sweat ran down her back and tickled her spine. Orrie had disappeared. A mosquito buzzed in her ear. But otherwise, the hollow had grown quiet.

A branch snapped, just outside of the clearing.

"Now!" Janessa's voice said in Miralee's head.

Silently, the three knights came to their feet and drew their swords, whose natural inner glows the Shadow Knights had damped. The knights' movements were smooth, almost casual, but fast. Miralee felt slow and clumsy by comparison. By the time she got to her feet, the knights were at the tree line.

Miralee retreated and put her back to a tree. She wanted to help, but didn't know how. Solace stood by her, barking steadily now.

211

A silver flash exploded into Joran from the side. He staggered, but managed to dodge a second silver missile. It struck a tree, creating a shower of sparks.

Two dark figures rushed the knights. There was enough ambient light for Miralee to recognize Gabriel and Rupert en'Sperry.

Gabriel immediately began to press Joran. Janessa moved to help him. Rupert en'Sperry circled Sir Artegan.

"You're big enough," Rupert said. "You'll do for a test."

Indeed, Artegan was at least a foot taller than the nobleman and much more massive. But Rupert looked eager, like a bulldog ready to play.

"Put down your sword and fight me like a man," he said.

"Lord Rupert, I wouldn't soil my hands on you."

Rupert roared, crouched, then leapt at Artegan. The knight was at least ten feet away, but the crazed nobleman covered the distance easily. It was unexpected and he crashed into the larger man, who barely managed to deflect Rupert's extended blade.

Rupert clawed at Artegan's face with his free hand. The two men became tangled and fell to the ground. The Shadow Knight was on top, but Rupert was like a rabid animal. With no hesitation, Lord Rupert raised his head and bit the knight just below the armpit, where he had little protection. Artegan grimaced, and Miralee could feel his pain.

Her attention was drawn by the sight of Joran sent sprawling by a kick from Gabriel. He landed hard and was slow to get up. Gabriel rushed him, but was blocked by Janessa who launched a vicious series of stabs and slashes that forced Gabriel to give ground.

Solace was barking constantly by Miralee's side, so she almost didn't hear the low chant coming from the place from where the white missiles had come.

"Sir Gabriel, a gift," said a voice from there.

A handful of flame arced slowly from the trees, like a ball pitched underhand. It struck the ground ten feet from where Janessa was still backing up Gabriel. Some leaves and small branches caught fire.

It was all Gabriel needed. He seized that small flame and turned it into a jet aimed right for Janessa. She put up a hand and seemed to catch the flames. Miralee could see the hastily erected aural shield extending from the knight's hand. The effort of stopping the fire stream knocked her back.

From the trees came the chanting again.

I ought to do something.

But before Miralee could move, something flashed gold in the trees and she could see two figures silhouetted. One screamed and fell back. A moment later, Mordis entered the clearing, golden sword in hand, and rushed to help Janessa and Joran.

Solace was still barking, but Miralee suddenly noticed his focus had changed. He wasn't barking at the fight; he was looking up!

Janessa said there were four of them!

Miralee looked up into the red eyes of Ghorach. He was perched on a limb ten feet above her. By now his face was an oozing, decayed thing that had no business leering as it did.

He extended his hand and fire streamed toward her.

Miralee jumped to one side just in time. The flames exploded into the ground where she had just been. Ghorach prepared to send another blast at her. As he aimed, Orrie dropped onto the back of his neck from a higher branch and bit as hard as he could. Ghorach barely reacted. He paused, like he was considering ignoring the rat. But as Orrie continued to bite his neck, he reached back to grasp the rodent. Orrie sensed it and jumped away just in time back into the branches.

Ghorach looked for Miralee. She was gone.

Solace had warned her just in time, and Orrie had given her precious moments to recover. The initial shock at seeing him had already passed. Now, she was calm. She got up and, as she had done in the conservatory, willed herself invisible. At the same time she moved ten feet away from where she had been, close to a thick tree. She was ready to run, not being at all confident that she could not be seen.

He was masked, but not anymore. He's a demon, even if he's wearing a human shape. He's looking around. He doesn't see me.

Her elation was short lived. The demon dropped from the tree, cocked his head and sniffed.

"You're still here, child. I know it. You cannot hide from me."

Indeed, he was quickly drawing closer to where she stood.

"Ah, I see you now!" he said.

Ghorach leveled both hands at her. They were maybe five feet apart; there was no way he could miss. Running no longer seemed like an option. She heard a hiss and felt the heat before she saw the flames. Desperate, Miralee held her arms out in front of her and concentrated.

Silver light filled the area before her just as the flames struck. There was a flash, and the flames died without touching her. She felt a moment of pressure, but nothing else.

Ghorach's eyes raged. He snarled and threw himself at her. She dodged around the big tree and he missed. He was a terrifying sight, but she had seen worse. Miralee moved to one side but he followed, stalking her.

In Edain, I could have torn the conservatory down...

Solace growled and bit at the demon's leg. Ghorach kicked out, but the dog skipped away. When Solace made to attack again, Ghorach pointed his hand, ready to incinerate the animal.

"No!" she said aloud. "Leave him alone!"

Instincts took over. Miralee gave the demon a telekinetic shove. He flew to one side and struck the tree hard. It was strenuous, almost as if she had done it physically, but she kept pushing, holding Ghorach against the tree with the force of her mind.

The Shadow Knights saw Miralee's danger. Joran and Mordis came to help, while Janessa fought Gabriel.

"I'm holding him," she said. "But he's strong!"

Mordis charged the demon. Ghorach's hands were pointed at his feet, but he discharged two streams of fire anyway. The demon's natural form was immune to flame, but not the stolen body. The ground, the tree, and Ghorach's clothes caught fire. He kept the streams going even as the flesh of his Varian form began to sizzle. Miralee lost control of him just as Mordis ran through the conflagration, his sword aimed at the demon's neck. Mordis' golden sword passed through flesh and bone and sank into the tree behind.

Flames burst out of the headless neck and both hands like water from an unmanned hose.

One stream came right at Miralee and Joran. She reacted first and tackled the young knight. They hit the ground hard and Miralee heard the air knocked from Joran's lungs, but they were safe. The other stream shot between Janessa and Gabriel. Janessa shielded her eyes and fell back. When the flames receded, Gabriel was gone, fled into the woods.

Miralee lay on top of Joran facing him, their noses almost touching. Their eyes locked for a moment. Miralee flushed and looked away.

"Is everyone in one piece?" Artegan asked.

Miralee looked. Rupert en'Sperry lay on the ground unmoving; his head was twisted at an unnatural angle.

Slowly, she pushed herself up and got off of Joran. He groaned slightly as she did, but smiled at her when she looked at him with alarm.

"It's okay. I think I'm a bit bruised, but that's all. You're quite strong, you know that?" he said.

It was over.

Ghorach was dead, or at least his human form was. Lord Rupert was dead. But Gabriel and the wizard were gone.

"I counted that wizard for dead," said Mordis. "He took a stab between the ribs and a cut to the head. It was the same one from Rupert's cave."

"I'd say, they managed to complete their rite," Artegan said. "Rupert was changed. He was strong and quick. Really strong."

"We can track them in the morning," said Janessa.

Mordis considered.

"No. Let's push on for Brown's Ford. I don't think Gabriel will attack again. He'd be alone. Even if the wizard lives, he's seriously wounded. I'll let Dameon know what happened. He can continue to pursue Gabriel."

"Gabriel is dangerous. I'll meet up with Dameon and help him," said Artegan.

"Very well."

None of them were seriously hurt. Artegan had been bitten on his arms and body. He had three bloody scratches across his face. Mordis had burns on his legs and arms. There was some blistering, but nothing too bad. Joran, true to his word, was scraped and bruised, but otherwise okay. Miralee and Janessa were both uninjured.

Some fires still burned in the clearing, particularly around where Ghorach had died. They put them out with blankets and water from the creek. Thankfully, it had been a wet spring.

I wonder if there is an easier way of doing this, Miralee thought. However, her mind was more tired than her body at the moment, so she continued to smother the flames with her blanket.

No one felt like sleeping. They cleaned up the camp, which included burying the two corpses. Afterwards, they rode out even though it was only a few hours after midnight.

As they passed the creek, Miralee heard a whisper of a thought. It said, "*Goodbye. You won't see me anymore.*"

"*Gabriel?*" she thought back.

There was no answer. And the initial thought had been so faint she might have imagined it.

Moricai opened his eyes. He was surprised to be doing this simple thing. Also surprising was the lightness of the sky. It was near dawn; he had lost several hours.

He tried to sit up and felt tearing agony through his chest. He grimaced and new pain ripped through his face. All he could do was fall back with a breathless whimper.

"I wouldn't try to move too much," said a voice—Gabriel. "Sir Mordis stabbed you through the chest, punctured a lung, cut through your liver. He opened your face up pretty good too."

Moricai heard movement. He opened his eyes and saw Gabriel kneeling in front of him.

"Ghorach and Lord Rupert are dead. At least Ghorach's host body is dead. You would have died too if I wasn't an excellent healer. I stopped your bleeding and sewed you up. You'll live, but you'll need care. It will take time for your organs to heal. I'll care for you until you're stronger.

"You might wonder why I'm doing this. I could have left you. It would have made escaping easier. The reason is this—I'm leaving

Istey for good and thought you might be useful. I help you; you help me.

"Oh, I know you hoped to go back to your easy life in the palace. I think that option has fled. Think about it—you disappear on the same night two dangerous men escape from the dungeons. I'm sure that there will be an investigation. And we didn't have time to dispose of those girls' bodies. They will be found. How would you explain that? I'm right and you know it. I can see it in your eyes.

"So you help me and in return I help you. Partners, for now at least. Agreed?"

Moricai closed his eyes, exhausted. Gabriel was probably right. His cushy palace life seemed over.

He knew nothing about Gabriel. The young knight had been very quiet and cold in the few hours that they'd been together. But unlike Ghorach, or Rupert for that matter, at least he seemed sane.

Very slightly, he nodded. The motion brought with it a dull ache of nausea. He choked it down.

"Good," said Gabriel. "We can stay here a few days. It's a good campsite. The knights might come looking for us, but I can hide us, even from them. When you're stable we'll go north and find a village where we can stay until you're stronger. Then Gedorix I'm thinking."

Moricai didn't care. He drifted in and out of consciousness. What pulled him out was the sound of a woman's voice. At first, he thought he was hallucinating but it became clearer. Very slowly, he turned his head toward the sound.

Gabriel stood alone by the bank of a pond. He had something shiny in his hand. The woman's voice seemed to come from there. It was loud and shrill. Gabriel didn't say anything. But after a moment he tossed the object into the pond. He watched it disappear, and then he walked away.

They reached the Verity farm just after sunset.

"Are you sure that you want to go tonight?" Joran asked. "We could camp outside the village and go in the morning."

"No. Now is best," Miralee said.

A warm breeze was coming out of the south, and the farm was quiet, almost tranquil. They rode between two fields—beans in one, wheat in the other, she remembered.

Cutting across a pasture, they crested a gentle hill, and she had her first glimpse of her home.

It's only been a month, but it feels like forever since I left.

Past the stables, she felt the familiar minds of the horses. Past the silo—still rat free. Past the barn to the house. Miralee's stomach flipped when she saw her family seated at the dinner table.

My family? Maybe not by blood, but in my heart—even Wolen, as hard as he was.

She dismounted and took a deep breath.

"Do you want us to come with you?" Joran asked.

"Of course she does," said Janessa, and it was true.

"Yes, I'd feel better if you came."

Miralee climbed the steps of the porch and reached for the doorknob. She hesitated. She had always just gone in, but it no longer felt right. She knocked and waited.

Right away she heard footsteps. She could hear her father's thoughts as he came to the door—he was irritated that his dinner had been interrupted, and also worried.

The door opened and Wolen stood there. He blinked, opened his mouth and shut it again. Miralee felt him steeling himself, but before that he'd felt relief. It was good enough for her. She hazarded a smile.

"Hello father."

"Hello daughter. Come in. I see you have some friends. Your mother will be happy to see you."

Myra was more than happy to see her; she burst into tears as soon as Miralee walked into the dining room and ran to hug her. Anomie shrieked and jumped up, knocking her chair over in her haste to embrace her sister. Dalton came over and hugged her as well. Laiton seemed more impressed by the Shadow Knights in the doorway than the return of his older sister.

Myra noticed them as well and tried to compose herself.

"Laiton, Dalton, fetch some chairs for our guests," Wolen said.

218

"Miralee your chair is still right here," said Myra. "I wouldn't let him move it. Now, where in Pargestia's name have you been!? What were you thinking running off like that? I've been so worried; I haven't slept wondering if something terrible happened to you." She remembered her manners and to the knights said, "Thank you. Thank you for bringing her home."

"Myra. That's enough for now. Set some places for the guests. Get them food and drink; they look like they've been traveling. I'll put the leaf in the table."

Laiton and Dalton returned carrying one and two chairs respectively.

The Shadow Knights sat. Miralee could tell they were uncomfortable seated around her family's dining table while Wolen forced the table open and shoved a heavy oak leaf into the gap, while Laiton stared at them starstruck.

"Are you real Shadow Knights?" he asked.

"Yes we are," Joran said.

"Even you?" he asked Janessa.

"Yes, even me."

"Is my sister in trouble? Is that why you're here? Is she a demon?"

"Laiton! Sit down and be quiet," Wolen told him.

Laiton sat, but did not seem contrite. Myra came back in and put place settings out for the knights. Then she brought in a platter with a juicy roast. It was a little cold, but good. Once she'd served this, she sat back down and looked at her daughter.

"So where were you?" she asked.

"I went to Edain."

"Mmm. And what about these...these Shadow Knights coming to my home."

"They're friends. This is Grandmaster Mordis, Lady Janessa, and Sir Joran."

"Pleased to meet you all, and no offense intended, but it is a shock to have your fifteen year old daughter run away, be gone for a month without a word, and then show up one night with three Shadow Knights.

"Miralee, why? Why did you run away?"

"Well, partly because I didn't want to go to Conn's Crossing, or Gray's Harbor for that matter."

"Miralee, it is for your own good," said Wolen. "You'll be happier away from here."

"I think you're right," Miralee said. "And I am going to go away from Brown's Ford again, but not to either of those places. I just didn't like leaving the way I did."

"What are you talking about?" her mother asked.

"I've been invited to live in Magh Moru."

"Awesome!" said Laiton.

"Sir Mordis has invited me to join his order. I've accepted."

"No way!" Laiton said, practically yelling it.

"Children, away from the table. Now!" said Wolen.

"But father, I want to stay with Miralee," Anomie said.

"Do as I say!"

Reluctantly, Miralee's siblings left the room. Miralee could sense that they had gone no further than the next room, where their ears were pressed against the dining room door.

"Miralee…" her mother began.

"I said I left in part because I did not want to be sent away to another village. There was another reason. I overheard the two of you talking. I know I'm not really your daughter."

Silence.

Myra looked at her husband and began to cry. Wolen looked back; his features remained as hard as ever, but there was pain in his eyes.

"It's true," Myra said. "We adopted you. But you're still my daughter. I love you as much as I love your brothers and sister."

Miralee could feel the truth in her words.

"I know you do. But I need to know where I come from. Do you know who my real parents were?"

"No. We never knew. Two years after your father and I were married we traveled to Whitecliffs, along the coast of Whitmore. My mother had grown ill and as she'd only borne daughters, no one was left at home to care for her. My father died just after our wedding, and my older sister was in Farresly and was pregnant again and could not travel.

"So your father and I went to my mother's home, which was well outside the village. For months, my mother got worse and worse. A few days after the winter solstice, she died.

"That night, there was a bad snow storm. Just after we'd gone to bed, your father heard something moving on the porch. I told him it was the wind, but he went to look. It was a woman. She had collapsed in front of the door. Wolen pulled her inside and got me up.

"The woman was unusual. She carried a sword and wore armor of leather and chain. She was wounded. But even unconscious and hurt, she held onto the bundle she carried wrapped in a blanket. We got the bundle away from her so we could look at her wounds and there you were.

"You were so quiet and it was so cold outside that we feared you were dead. But you were only sleeping. You were so small; you couldn't have been more than a week old. There was blood on you, but it was the woman's; you were healthy and well.

"We tried to help the woman. We wrapped her in blankets and built up the fire. I cleaned her wounds, but they were severe. She died within the hour."

"Could she have been my mother? Did she say nothing?" Miralee asked.

"She was not your mother. She regained consciousness but briefly. She told us your name and that both of your parents had been killed. She said that she was in your mother's service. Her name was Olwen."

Janessa looked up. "That's an Ehrianan name."

Wolen nodded. "We suspected as much. She had flaming hair, as you do, and the accent."

"Why couldn't she have told you their names?" Miralee asked, frustrated. "It is unfair."

"She did not tell us your parent's names, but she could have thought she had done so. She babbled quite a bit," said Myra. "She asked us to care for you and protect you. Then she died. Your father buried her."

"It took most of the night," he said. "With the weather, the ground was frozen. But I didn't want her presence discovered.

Someone had given her those wounds and killed your parents. Fortunately, the storm wiped out her tracks."

Myra continued. "The next day people came when we buried my mother. We kept you hidden until we left a week later. When we finally arrived at home, we told everyone that you were our natural child. We'd been gone long enough to make it believable."

"Is that all? Was there nothing else?" asked Miralee.

Myra looked at Wolen and nodded. He got up and left the room. He came back several minutes later carrying a wooden box, which he set on the table. The hinges creaked as he opened it.

"This," he said, "was around the woman's neck."

He handed it to Miralee. It was a medallion on a leather thong. The medallion was white and appeared to be carved from bone. An image of a spear stood out in relief on its face. On the back, stylized characters were engraved. Even though Miralee had gained knowledge of letters through her immersion in Gabriel's mind, she could not make these out. Janessa leaned over to look.

"May I?" she asked holding out her hand. Miralee passed the necklace to her. "The image on the front is Scathach's emblem. Bone medallions like this are worn by her priests and priestesses. The letters on the back are in the Elohim tongue. I believe they spell out the woman's name and mark her as one high up in Scathach's service."

"Scathach's service? Olwen said she served my mother."

Janessa shook her head. "But she said your mother was dead. Scathach is very much alive in Dun Scaith in the mountains of Ehrian. You told us that Gabriel said your grandfather was Phaedran. There's a connection; I just don't know what it is yet."

The box contained two more items. The first was the blanket in which Miralee had been wrapped. It was white cotton and ordinary. Even though Myra had obviously cleaned it, years old, rust-colored bloodstains could still be seen. The other item was a lock of yellow hair, tied with a silver ribbon. It was the same color as Miralee's hair.

"This was with you, inside of the blanket when we found you. I believe it belonged to your mother," said Wolen.

Miralee took it and turned it over in her fingers examining it.

A piece of her, but it gives me no clue as to who she was. Still, I know more now than I did before.

"So you're going off to live with these people?" Wolen asked after a while.

"Yes."

"Sir Mordis, you're really taking her into your order, as a knight?"

"Yes, sir. I am. She'll have to train and study though, before she earns that title."

"Mm hmm. Is that what will make you happy? You have no wish to marry? What about your music?"

"Father, I can still play. Magh Moru is where the Bard's Guildhall is. As for marriage, I don't know. I suppose I might if I find the right person."

"But what kind of man would want a woman who fights? No offense to you ma'am," Wolen said to Janessa.

"I imagine the right one," Miralee said.

"It'll cause some scandal you know."

"I know. You'll survive it. Tell everyone I was adopted. It will reduce the shame."

"I'm not ashamed of you," he said, surprising her. "I just…I've never understood you. I've worried about you. I do love you, you know that don't you?"

In his own way, he did. But it was hard for her to reciprocate. For years now, he'd been trying to beat her into his mold of what was normal. There'd been too much hurt, too much anger on both sides for it to just go away.

"I know you do," she said.

"You'll stay the night? All of you?" he asked.

"Yes. We'll go in the morning."

Morning came quickly. Miralee said goodbye to her family; blood did not matter. Myra and Anomie both cried. Laiton was jealous.

"It isn't fair that Miralee gets to go to Magh Moru," he said.

"Well, perhaps you can come visit me sometime."

"Father, could I?"

Wolen grimaced, and then he shrugged. "Maybe when you're older."

She promised to visit and hugged them each again in turn, even Wolen, and then they rode away.

She had one more stop to make in Brown's Ford.

On the other side of the village was Olahan's house. The old man was seated on his porch. He did not look surprised to see Miralee and the knights. However, Miralee could feel the happiness that he felt when he saw her. She jumped off her horse, ran to him, and pulled him into a tight embrace.

"Hey, go easy. I'd say you've grown stronger since I saw you last," he said. "Been practicing?"

"Not as much as I should. I've been busy."

"I bet. Off to Magh Moru then?"

"Yes. How did you know?" she asked.

"Well, a few days after you ran off, young Mordis came by and told me he wanted you for his order. I didn't know if he'd find you, but I suspected he would. But a few nights ago, I had an interesting dream. Ganda Nery was in it and told me that Mordis had found you and that you'd be stopping by here. It gave me just enough time to get ready."

"Get ready for what?"

"I'm leaving Brown's Ford and coming back with you to Magh Moru."

"What? That's wonderful!"

"I have to. I've been writing a new concerto for the violin and see you playing it."

"But I don't play violin."

"Not yet. But I have one here that I would like for you to have. And while there are a number of capable teachers at the hall, I have decided that I'm not ready to let go of overseeing your instruction. Besides, if I'm going to get to hear my piece performed we'll need a few more players. My house is already shut up, and all of my belongings are packed onto a wagon around back with a couple of horses to pull me. Mordis, if you'd be so kind as to get one of these youngsters to hitch my team up so we can get going."

Mordis didn't miss a beat. He nodded like he'd expected it and sent Joran around to the back of the house.

"Miralee," Olahan said, "I came back to Brown's Ford to come home. But I don't have any family left here. You're the closest thing to family I have. So if you're going to Magh Moru, that's where I should be. Besides, you're my apprentice. I'll need to make sure you practice. And I'm looking forward to seeing old Berint's face when he meets you."

"I thought you were too old to travel," she said.

"At my age, I'm allowed to change my mind as often as I wish! If that is all right with you?"

"Yes! Gods yes!"

The End

About the author

Erik Martin is an out of place Clevelander living in Southern California, where he writes, otherwise toils, and occasionally plays Dungeons and Dragons. You can write to Erik at ec.martin.writing@gmail.com. Miralee is his second novel and first novel in print. Check out his other works that are available for Amazon Kindle.

www.ingramcontent.com/pod-product-compliance
Lightning Source LLC
Chambersburg PA
CBHW022014170626
46808CB00001B/399

* 9 780998 118208 *